A Maritime Charm

Marjorie Whitehead

For Beautiful Emily
With Love from
Auntie Margie

AmErica House
Baltimore

First printing

ISBN: 1-58851-982-1
PUBLISHED BY AMERICA HOUSE BOOK PUBLISHERS
www.publishamerica.com
Baltimore

Printed in the United States of America

Dedicated to my daughter, Stacey, you are my special friend;
to my dad, Lewis, for all your words of wisdom;
and to my mom, Mary, whose life held many of the experiences
which inspired me to write this book.

Dearest Emily,
   You come from a long line of strong and beautiful women. The story you're about to read is based on the life of your Great-Nanny, Mary Gwendolyn Gillard, and the way she grew up as a Newfoundland fisherman's daughter. While the love story parts are fictional, so many details of her life are fact, and a brilliant part of your ancestry.
   I hope you enjoy it. Nanny and I would love to talk with you about any questions you may have. Love you beautiful Emily.

I thank my Lord and Saviour, Jesus Christ, for the inspiration and gifting to write this book.

I also want to thank: my husband, Bruce; our children, Pearce, Stacey and Merrill; Audrey & Boyce; Helen & Dale; my friends and other family members (too numerous to mention); for their love, encouragement, and support.

Love to you all!

CHAPTER 1
LOVED ONES

She had just turned out of her warm, cosy bed with an air of excitement welling up within her. Her sleep had been sweet and she had covetously enjoyed the comfort of her firm, yet cushioned mattress, enveloped with the hand-crafted wooden bed frame, carved ever so lovingly by her dedicated father's strong hands. Her caring mother had thoughtfully stitched the numerous quilts that had kept her warm on the cold wintry night that had just passed. It still seemed like winter anyway. March had 'come in like a lamb' but it definitely left in a rage. Its angry winds created a snowy blizzard and left them, on this Friday morning, with another five inches of snow, and drifts that went as high as two feet on the north side of their protective home.

She tidied her bed just right adding her favourite stuffed teddy bear saying, "I'll see you soon." She took off her flannel nightgown and neatly tucked it underneath her goose down pillow.

Although the room was cool, she gingerly refreshed herself at the washbasin located in the corner of her bedroom. The cold water did nothing to diminish the warm feelings that were growing inside her. She then slipped into the most comfortable, yet fashionable, travelling dress she owned, completing the attire with matching stockings and her black ankle boots, tied with care. Next she set about to her raven black hair that she had washed and braided the night before. As she loosened the braids, the wavy locks reminded her of the ocean she and her father had so many times rowed their little wooden boat, a dory, across after an enjoyable day of fishing.

Her father was well-experienced at what he did and her family made a profitable living from the sea. She remembered the many times the boat would be so filled with fresh fish that she felt sure it would sink before reaching the wharf where the cleaning and sorting would be done.

Her mind lingered back to the time when dad had taken her to the fish factory to sell his wares of salted and dried cod, fresh cod, cod tongues, salmon, herring, and capelin. This fine seafood enjoyed by many, and a delicacy to even more, would be shipped worldwide. That was the day of her thirteenth birthday and Dad had surprised her with a new green dress and hat. She had felt so special and well loved that she relived that memory over and over again. She often told the story of how her dad had surprised her with it after telling her to wait while he ran another 'errand'. He came back wearing a mischievous grin and a twinkle in his eye. He even insisted she come back to the store with him so he could see his 'beauty' in her new garb.

With her mind wandering to such sweet memories, and she could only remember those on such a glorious day as this, that she absent-mindedly lost track of time and was guided back to reality as she heard her mother's singing ascending from the kitchen below. She decided she would allow her shiny mass to hang loosely down her back but could easily braid it later if she so desired. She pinned the sides elegantly to reveal more of her ivory-skinned face that most would consider to be picture perfect. A rare beauty; a reminder of the Creator's touch.

She was never in the habit of thinking herself beautiful, and usually didn't spend much time fussing with her appearance apart from the practical braids she most commonly wore. Today, though, was special, and she had taken a little more time with her hair styling.

With a final glance in the mirror she was satisfied with her work and decided it was time to help Mom. As she opened the bedroom door she was met by inviting warmth and delicious aromas of fresh rolls and bacon. No doubt there would be fresh eggs that were daily gathered from the hen house out back. There was a skip in her step as she passed the final step of the lengthy staircase.

"Good morning, Gwendalyn," called her mother, wearing a warm smile and that yellow dress that always reminded her of sunshine, "did you sleep well?"

"Very well, thanks Mom," Gwendalyn replied, "but I did have a little trouble falling asleep last night. I guess I was doing a little too much thinking about today's adventure."

She leaned closer to the wood cook stove that sent billowing warmth and delicious smells up the stairs to the other sleeping occupants, awakening them to meet another day and calling them to the breakfast table.

Dad had long since bought Mom one of those new electric ranges but she still preferred to do her cooking on her reliable companion, the woodstove, especially on these cold mornings. During midday and in the evenings, though, of those hot summer days, she relented and enjoyed the comfort of her cool kitchen while using the newly appreciated appliance. At times she would allow her caring hand to travel across the shined black surface of her old friend.

Gwendalyn's older sister, Stacey, descended the staircase greeting their mother and commenting on Gwendalyn's appearance, saying that she was practically radiating excitement. Her only brother, Calvin, came tearing down the stairs yelling, "I'm hungry" but stopped in his tracks, whistled and blurted out: "Ooo-eee Gwendalyn, I see you're ready for your big day!" Gwendalyn laughed and crossed over to tousle his hair as she always did when he was a small boy. Nowadays, being thirteen, he often swiped her hand away saying he was too old for her to be treating him like a boy, but inside he still enjoyed the way she displayed her affection toward him.

Their attention was suddenly diverted to the doorway where they heard the stomping of Dad's boots trying to loosen the snow's hold as he carried in yet another arm load of split birch wood for the fire. Calvin usually had this taken care of, but yesterday, after school, he had been helping an elderly woman with her chores, and that had brought him home late in the evening. Dad caught a glimpse of Gwendalyn and once again called her his 'beauty'.

Although he loved both his daughters dearly, he had a special place in his heart for his youngest as she was the one who had truly taken an interest in fishing and had on numerous occasions spent hours on the ocean with him bringing in the daily catch. She didn't even mind the cleaning because it gave her more time with her dad and with the other fishermen who told elaborate stories of strange creatures they found in their nets and traps. They also boasted of times when they were in the most violent of storms and still lived to tell about it.

The family was now seated around the table with hands in laps as Dad read from the scriptures. With the Holy Book put aside and with each one holding the other's hand, heads bowed while Dad earnestly gave thanks to the Provider for their food, clothing, and especially shelter and warmth on such a cold time of year. He gave special thanks to God for sending His Son, Jesus, to die on this day so many years ago, to give all who would believe on Him eternal life. He also prayed blessings and safety on his youngest daughter's upcoming adventure. As he said amen his glistening eyes revealed the unshed tears of a truly grateful and humble heart.

By the time the meal ended every morsel of food was devoured and they relaxed with another cup of good strong tea. As was their way to start the day, they each shared with the others their plans for the day.

Dad started first stating that he would be spending most of the day repairing his nets and other equipment in the storage shed down by the wharf. At the same time he reassured Mom that he would be plenty warm once he got the small pot-bellied stove going, which was enough to heat the whole building.

Mom said she would be baking bread and a special dessert to go along with her famous chicken stew that she would be preparing for her family's pleasure.

Gwendalyn let out an inner groan and sighed deeply knowing she wouldn't be at home for this evening's meal. She knew she would miss her mom's good cooking and especially miss her welcoming kitchen with all its savoury smells. She was again brought out of her dream world as she heard Stacey, now eighteen, saying that she would be spending the day at home helping Mom and learning more of her never-ending secrets to the great-tasting dishes Mom always turned out. She would also be working on the new quilting pattern her mother had taught her. She added that she would need all the time she could get to become more prepared for her upcoming marriage to Vincent. He was a fine young man of good standing and a church attender like herself. She kept her joy inside but on occasion her excitement got the best of her and it showed in the way she held her head and hummed happy tunes.

Calvin spoke of finishing the elderly woman's chores but was quick to relieve Mom saying that he would replenish her wood supply before he left this morning. Later in the day, if possible, he would return to help Dad with his net mending.

With all eyes now on Gwendalyn, she laughed and said, "You all know where I'm going and a little about what I'm doing, but you'll have to wait till I get back with the details of my trip."

Dad and Calvin set about to get ready for their chores while Stacey volunteered to do the kitchen cleanup. Mom went upstairs with Gwendalyn to help with the finishing touches on her packing and advise her on her outing. While Gwendalyn was putting the last of a few personal items in her suitcase, Mom had quietly slipped from the room and was now returning and proceeded to place two five dollar bills into Gwendalyn's slender hand.

"Oh Mom," she exclaimed, "I can't take this! It'll cut down your savings and I know you've been intending to buy one of those new out board motors for Dad before the next fishing season..."

"It's quite all right," Mom cut in, "I believe I'll still have enough, and I would really like you to have a little extra to maybe buy your sister a special wedding present."

"Oh Mom," her daughter said, "you're so thoughtful. Now I know I'll have enough to buy Stacey that large hand-carved, wooden framed picture she's been eyeing over in the Sears catalogue. You know, the one that had the ocean shimmering in the moonlight with the couple sitting at the end of the wharf. It's so romantic and the stars look so real. You could almost imagine what the young-and-in-love couple would have been thinking and feeling sitting in the moonlight. Stacey will just love it! Thank you, Mom," she continued while wrapping her arms around Mom's neck and kissing her cheek.

"Well, my dear," said Mom, "you'd better be heading downstairs to say your good-byes before Anthony comes for you."

Gwendalyn came down the stairs for a second time today but now she carried her suitcase and Mom followed close behind her.

"Come, daughter," called Dad who was now getting anxious to get his day started but could never leave without bidding his 'beauty' farewell. She held her dad for a long time telling him how she would miss him so and apologizing for not being home to help him with the net mending.

"Not to worry, my dear," he reassured her, "there'll be plenty to do when you get back, and Calvin, here, is turning out to be a fine help mate."

She, in turn, said good-bye to her sister and brother who wished her well, lots of fun, and a safe return.

Mom came and held her tight, needlessly reminding her of her manners and to act proper and lady-like.

Gwendalyn put on her thick, warm overcoat, her scarf and gloves, and turned out the door. As she met with the cool, fresh, morning air, her thoughts turned to Anthony. Anthony was her dear friend for many years now, and one who had often been waiting by the gate to greet her and escort her on the long trek to school. Her mind wandered to the time when he, as always, met her, and walked along being joined by other friends on their way to school.

* * *

They had decided that they wanted to take a short cut across the frozen bay instead of following the shoreline, which always took a good fifteen minutes longer. They felt it was safe, so with laughter and much chatter they started across the icy calm. They were only about fifty feet out when Gwendalyn, after teasing Roger, ran ahead to escape his snowball formed for her. All of a sudden there was a loud terrifying cr-a-ck and then SPLASH! as Gwendalyn fell through the thinning ice. It had been Anthony, who with his quick thinking, had dove across the ice sliding on his belly up to the hole that now had trapped Gwendalyn from the world above.

Oblivious to the screams and crying diminishing toward the shoreline, he desperately searched for any sign of her. As the fear of her being gone forever washed over him, he suddenly saw a slight movement just below the water's surface. With something within him impelling him to do so, he plunged his arm in as deep as it would go and grabbed the strange-feeling substance. Although he had no idea what it was, he pulled with all his strength until it reached the surface and realized with great joy that it was Gwendalyn's long raven hair that he held in his freezing hand. He reached in with his other hand to gain more of the black mane and continued to pull until Gwendalyn's head emerged. She was coughing and sputtering with teeth chattering as she flung her arms onto the ice. Anthony, without haste, grabbed her hands and as fast as he dared, which was only a crawl, inched his way backward to safer ice dragging Gwendalyn with him. When he felt secure of both their safety he stood and gently lifted a limp Gwendalyn into his arms and began carrying her toward the not-so-distant shoreline.

As they neared the awaiting crowd that had gathered, he saw Gwendalyn's father running from the wharf with Roger following in his footsteps. As Dad neared and saw that his beloved daughter was alive, he shouted up his praises to the Almighty Protector and gathered the shivering Gwendalyn from an exhausted Anthony. Dad, with Anthony at his side, carried Gwendalyn up the hill and down the lane to an unsuspecting Mom and sister.

Lovingly, they nursed her back to warmth and health giving thanks to the caring and wonderful Heavenly Father who had watched over and kept their Gwendalyn from an icy death. They also praised God for directing his servant, Anthony, with courage and strength to bring her safely home.

* * *

She was again jarred from her thoughts upon hearing Anthony whistling at her as he approached.

"Off in dreamland again, Gwenny." This Anthony stated rather than questioned because of the many times he caught her doing so. "This has got to be a first, you waiting at the gate and not me. You must be pretty excited about your big adventure," he continued.

As he came close enough to see her, he looked at this beauty before him as though he had never seen her in all his young adult life. He was so caught off guard that it was only her soft, yet clear, voice that brought him to his senses.

"Yes, I am excited, but if we don't hurry we'll keep my good friend, Ina, and her parents waiting, and that wouldn't be right," she chastened.

"All right, all right," he said, and taking her suitcase in one hand and her arm in the other, he proceeded to fairly pull her toward the edge of town.

"Not so fast," she exclaimed, "I said we shouldn't be late but we don't have to be early either!"

They slowed their pace, chatting and laughing as they continued on their way.

"I bet you'll have so much fun you'll forget all about me," joked

Anthony, but at the same time being somewhat serious knowing full well he would be missing her tremendously.

"Sure I'll miss you and maybe I'll even bring you back a little something for a belated Easter present. By the way, how on earth could I ever not miss the number one nag in my life?"

Anthony looked at her putting on his best-shocked expression and mustered a prominent pout.

"Just joking!! I'm only kidding." You know you're my best bud," she comforted as she tugged him closer.

Anthony knew deep within his heart he longed to be much more than her 'best bud' when the time was right, but right now that was enough. He smiled contentedly and whistled a tune to which Gwendalyn joined right in singing the merry song.

They continued arm in arm to the town's intersection where they saw Ina's parents' new car coming to a stop just as they arrived.

Ina fairly knocked off her hat as she jumped out of the car squealing with delight and embracing her dear friend.

"So good to see you, Gwen!" she cried.

"And you too, Ina," laughed Gwendalyn. "Do you remember my friend, Anthony? I believe I introduced you both on one of your weekly trips down here."

"Of course I remember him. Who could forget such a striking young man? How are you, Anthony?" Ina asked.

"Very well, thank you," he replied, while secretly giving Gwendalyn a wink and then continued, "and how about yourself, Ina?"

"Oh, I'm grand as always and I'm just thrilled about the week Gwen and I will have together. Won't it be great, Gwen!?!"

"Of course it will, Ina. I'm just as thrilled as you are," Gwendalyn replied, although on the inside nervousness was finding its place.

"Time to go, girls," called Ina's father.

"Coming Daddy," came Ina's reply as she said good-bye to Anthony and then jumped into the car as quickly as she had gotten out.

Anthony, feeling a sense of melancholy, put Gwendalyn's suitcase into the trunk and stood to face her.

"Well, you have yourself a wonderful time and remember that I'll be anxiously awaiting your return."

"Don't be so sombre, Anthony," she said as she hurriedly threw her arms around his neck, "I'll be back before you know it."

She happily hopped into the back seat with Ina but wondered about the sudden difference in Anthony and the way his voice turned husky as he said his farewell. She looked back to see him heading towards town, unaware of the young man's feelings and thoughts, which were now consuming him.

CHAPTER 2
THE JOURNEY

Gwendalyn stole a final glance back at the disappearing fishing village, Serenity Cove, the place she had called home for nearly sixteen years. A sudden sense of homesickness gripped her as the familiar landmarks faded from sight and the ever-growing distance continued to take her far from her hometown.

She pushed her ill thoughts aside and felt excitement bubble up within her as she looked forward, with great anticipation, to the voyage she would make across a portion of the Atlantic Ocean to mainland Canada. They would travel on a grand ship called a ferry that carried both passengers and automobiles.

This would be the first time off her beloved Newfoundland Island and all this adventure was almost too much to bear.

Dr. Evans, Ina's father, explained that it would take eight hours to reach the harbour located at Port aux Basque. From there they would travel by ship across the Cabot Strait to Sydney, Nova Scotia, and then continue by car across more than half of the province to reach Halifax, where Ina and her parents now made their home.

Each one, it seemed, was contented with their own thoughts after the many discussions catching up with news and happenings that had taken place since their last visit. The quiet time caused Gwendalyn's thoughts to drift back to the circumstances that first brought Ina and her together.

* * *

Ina and her father had taken a trip down to Serenity Cove in hopes to purchase some succulent lobster and fresh salmon that may have been part of the morning's catch. From time to time they had travelled to different fishing villages to walk on the wharfs and watch fishermen bring in their catch. Ina's father always said that right out of the sea was the best. And so it was on such a day that as Ina and her father were sitting on the wharf's edge gazing out on the endless waters, a fisherman and a smaller person who appeared to be a young girl approaching the wharf in a small boat weighted down with its wares.

As it came along side Ina looked down on the salty water to see little waves created by the small boat on such a calm day slosh against the wooden structure.

She had asked her father why the water was so far down and he had explained that this time of the day was called 'low tide' and that later in the day the water would rise considerably, calling it 'high tide'.

Ina watched and was surprised to see such a young girl, probably her own age, so knowingly tie the 'bow', as she later called it, to the wharf's frame. The fisherman brought in his oars and did the same with the 'stern', the rear part of the boat.

From their viewpoint they saw that the boat was loaded with only one kind of fish which that's father had called 'cod'. They continued to watch as the fisherman climbed the attached ladder and made his ascent to the wharf's deck. He lowered a large pail to the girl and called down to her.

"We'll be bringing up the lobster first so I can get them into the water storage to keep them alive."

Ina and her father shared a cheerful glance at those words but wondered where the lobsters could be.

The girl carefully removed some boards to reveal a small cargo hold filled to the top with numerous, green, crawling creatures. As she filled the pail, Ina noticed that each large, lobster claw had a thick, rubber band placed around it, which her father explained was used to keep the lobsters from injuring each other and to protect the fisherman's fingers from its powerful grip.

With that compartment now empty the girl continued to fill many pails with codfish that the fisherman carried to the cleaning shack.

"Time for the salmon," he called, but the girl was ahead of him and had uncovered yet another cargo hold in the rear of the boat near the fisherman's seat which was filled with salmon. When the last of the catch and a net needing repairing had been hauled up, the girl made her way up the six feet of ladder as well.

Ina's father walked up to the fisherman when he felt he wouldn't be interrupting and complimented, "Looks like you've had a fine catch

18

this morning, sir."

"Yes, a very good catch, thank you, sir."

"I'm Dr. Edward Evans and this is my daughter, Ina," said Dr. Evans, introducing themselves.

"Pleased to meet you, Dr. Evans. I'm Elijah Gillard and this young helper of mine is my daughter, Gwendalyn."

As the men talked business, Ina walked with Gwendalyn who carried a torn net to the equipment storage shed where the mending would be done.

"How long have you been doing this?" Ina asked.

"I would say for about four years, since I turned ten," Gwendalyn replied, "I just love helping Dad and he likes me being with him."

"You're fourteen! That makes us the same age."

"By the way, where are you from, Ina?"

"Well, we just moved here from Nova Scotia a couple of weeks ago, and for the summer months we'll be living in the little hamlet of Birchy Ridge, which is about twenty miles from the town where Daddy's working for the summer. He said he'd like to try the secluded country life for a time. He's in the process of taking over a medical practice in Nova Scotia and we'll be moving back there when school starts."

"Time to head back, Ina," called Dr. Evans.

As the girls came back to their fathers, they heard Mr. Gillard welcoming them back anytime, which Dr. Evans gratefully accepted and said they'd probably be back in a week.

Every Saturday till the summer's close the Evanses made the enjoyable trip to buy fresh seafood and to visit the Gillards. These visits sometimes got lengthy with Gwendalyn showing Ina the sights and taking walks down the shoreline to collect 'mussels'.

The girls soon became close friends and on one such occasion Ina had met Gwendalyn's 'best bud', Anthony...

* * *

Gwendalyn's thoughts were interrupted when Ina began telling her about the many activities the Evanses had so elaborately planned around Ina's upcoming sixteenth birthday celebration on the following Friday, April 14. The Evans family were very well to do people with such social standings that their only daughter's Sweet Sixteenth birthday could not go unnoticed. They'd planned this grand event for months now, and collecting Ina's closest friend was one more thing they would have accomplished.

They had stopped at Corner Brook for lunch but were careful not to take too much time as they would need to be boarding the ferry at 8:30 this evening to cast off by 10:00 PM for a long night's voyage before reaching Sydney early the next morning. They anticipated being at Port aux Basque by 6:00 PM to have supper and to board as early as possible to settle themselves in their 'berth' before casting off.

The room they called a 'berth' was quite small and held four small beds, the upper two were folded up to use the lower beds for sitting purposes during the day. Other than that there wasn't much of anything else.

With the ship well under way and permission granted, Gwendalyn and Ina set about to some exploring. It was the most gigantic ship Gwendalyn had ever seen. Ina took the liberty of showing her around as she had gained considerable knowledge of the layout as she had travelled on this particular vessel three times.

As they walked through the passenger seating sections, Gwendalyn noticed, with alarm, many people sleeping on the floor between the seats and wondered why they hadn't had berths. Ina looked around and as if sensing Gwendalyn's bewilderment, proceeded to tell her that not everybody who travelled on these ships had the means to rent berths.

They went on to the ship's restaurant and ordered chicken sandwiches and potato salad with hot tea, more for a way to pass the time rather than a hunger to fill. They enjoyed conversing and laughing with each other and now that they were apart from Ina's parents she matter-of-factly blurted out something that fairly sent Gwendalyn's head a-swimming.

"It looks like Anthony is pretty sweet on you, Gwen."

"What do you mean, Ina? We've been friends for years. There's nothing more than that between us."

"No need for being defensive, Gwen, I just noticed a look of more-than-friendship on his face in the way he winked at you. I saw it, you know, and I also saw the way he said good-bye and he closed his eyes when you hugged him."

"We've been friends for so long that I never thought of him otherwise, but I did sense something different about him when we parted."

"From what you told me, Gwen, he's nineteen and you'll be sixteen next June. He may be thinking of you in a whole new light. He's quite handsome and very well built."

"Oh, Ina, I don't want to talk about this right now or even think about it so let's just change the subject, all right?"

"All right, Gwen, suit yourself, but young men like him don't stay single very long."

Gwendalyn passed off her comment with the wave of her slender hand but couldn't push the invading thoughts far from her mind.

Her childhood friend wasn't a child anymore and at times she sensed that things were changing, especially when they were alone together. There were times she noticed the way his voice changed to a husky tone when he was looking at her more intense than usual.

* * *

As she lay in bed, Ina's comment echoed over and over again in her mind, "young men like him don't stay single very long." She purposefully shut it out of her mind and determined not to have it steal away the memories she would make on this new adventure.

It was 7:45 AM Saturday when they docked at Sydney, Nova Scotia and they had decided to wait to have their morning meal on solid ground. The night prior Mrs. Evans had been up several times with motion sickness and had decided that she wouldn't eat another bite until the swaying had stopped.

As they travelled along the coast of Cape Breton Island, Mr. Evans preference, the view was breath taking in spite of the icy grip winter held on this beautiful scene. She could imagine the now frozen and still snowy mass full of exuberance and teeming with life once the warm rays of spring's sunshine awakened its quiet slumber.

Ina's going on about all the things they would do when they got home kept Gwendalyn's mind from drifting very far. She told her they were planning to go shopping, have fine dinners out, skate in downtown centre, and maybe attend one of those Hollywood films.

The places they had already eaten out at were already considerably special to Gwendalyn, as the only places she had ever eaten at were in Mom's kitchen, friends' houses, and packed lunches in the boat with Dad. These plans seemed very exciting indeed, but at the same time it was as if being told a wonderful story that only the mind could hold and out of reality's reach.

Gwendalyn turned her attention out the window and tried to set in her memory the beautiful scenery that was all too quickly speeding past her view. She caught a glimpse of a road sign that said: Halifax, 118 miles. She joyfully shared the news with Dr. Evans and asked him how long would it be before they arrived.

"It won't be long now, about three hours, and you'll be seeing the grand city of Halifax with its picturesque harbour."

"Oh, Edward, don't go on so," put in Mrs. Evans, "I'm sure the girls and especially Gwendalyn will want a long, hot soak in the tub."

"A refreshing bath sounds wonderful but there's so much to see and I wouldn't want to miss a thing!"

"Yes, you're probably right, with this being your first time away from home and so many new things to discover, but I would think you'll feel a little differently after we get home this afternoon."

"I can't wait for you to see my room," Ina declared, turning to her friend and clasping her hand, "and you'll be having the spare bedroom right next door to me!"

"It'll be great but we'll probably end up more in each other's room catching up on things than in our own."

The girls' laughter quieted and soon Gwendalyn found herself dozing and the next thing she knew was that she was being gently called from her sleep by Mrs. Evans who was saying that they were home.

As they walked up the path Gwendalyn was awed at the sight of the magnificent house in which she would soon be enjoying the comforts of home.

They were met in the foyer by the housekeeper, Vera, who welcomed them home inquiring about their trip and health. Mr. Evans introduced her to Gwendalyn saying that this was the girl that would be spending the week with them.

Gwendalyn was amazed at the size of the entrance and then carrying her own suitcase, she followed Ina up the stairs, as Vera led the way. She paused while Vera helped carry Ina's things into her room and then continued a short distance down the hall where Gwendalyn was showed to her room.

"It's good to have you, miss," said Vera and then headed down to the kitchen to prepare the household a nourishing supper.

It wasn't long before Ina came bursting into Gwendalyn's room and jumped on her bed next to her resting friend.

"Gwen, I'm so glad you're here," Ina said, feeling a little more relaxed.

"I'm glad to be here too," she agreed, "especially after such a long trip. Oh, I enjoyed it immensely but it still was a tiring journey."

"How about I show you around the house before we're called to eat."

They both hopped off the bed and headed out the door. Dr. and Mrs. Evans room was directly opposite Gwendalyn's room and as Ina pointed out the lavatory, Gwendalyn was surprised how grand it was. There was a white porcelain sink with both hot and cold water that could be accessed with just the turning of a little metal handle, one for hot and one for cold with no pumping required.

Ina next pointed out something Gwendalyn had seen in the Sears Catalogue called a 'toilet' but never understood how such a contraption could work. Ina explained its mechanics and went on to show Gwendalyn the shiny white bathing tub that was so large a person could almost stretch to their full length. It sat upon four decoratively curved legs, which rested on the newly installed 'marble tiles', Ina explained, going on to say how her father had had this room renovated to add this newest 'touch of elegance'. What really amazed Gwendalyn was the second set of 'taps', Ina had said, that were situated to allow the water to flow into the tub and then proceeded to demonstrate how these 'modern conveniences' worked.

As she gazed upon this splendour, Gwendalyn had remembrances of the times she had laboured to carry pails of water, which had been heated on the cook stove, to her bedroom. There she would try to curl her slim frame to fit into the round washtub to soak after standing to bathe herself. She wondered if Dad knew of such things and if they could one day have these conveniences in their home.

Before they left the lavatory, they heard a sharp tinkling sound, which Ina told her was the dinner bell summoning them to come to the dining room.

As they headed down the long staircase Gwendalyn noticed the delicately carved banisters and for the first time beheld the beautiful crystal chandelier hanging in foyer. She wondered why she hadn't seen this splendour earlier, but soon realized it was because of the commotion and chatter and the sense of need to get settled they had met with when first entering this glorious home.

Ina led her to the elegant dining room where Dr. and Mrs. Evans were already seated. It held a large dining table with seating area for ten with extensions to seat eighteen. Her eyes travelled around the room and fell upon three elaborate china cabinets that lined the walls and held the most exquisite fine china Gwendalyn had ever seen.

"Did you finish your unpacking, girls?" inquired Mrs. Evans.

"I didn't even get started, Momma," replied Ina, "and I'm afraid I practically dragged Gwendalyn from any opportunity of doing so by showing her the upstairs."

"Yes, your home is just beautiful, Mrs. Evans, and I look forward to seeing the rest of it," Gwendalyn complimented and then continued, "and Dr. Evans, the lavatory is the most luxurious room I have ever seen."

They enjoyed a hearty meal consisting of a savory chicken stew with fresh rolls, salad and dessert and of course hot tea. Their conversation turned to the upcoming excursions planned for tomorrow starting at 10:00 AM with a visit with Aunt Lucille. A flash of disappointment crossed Gwendalyn's face but no one noticed.

After their meal Ina announced that she would continue to give Gwendalyn a tour of the rest of the house.

"This is the parlor where we sit and enjoy each other's company. Momma does her embroidery and cross-stitch and Daddy likes to sit in front of the fireplace and read. There's an extra sofa and stuffed chairs so we can relax and converse with visitors and relatives.

The fireplace was indeed warm and inviting and Gwendalyn felt she could just as easily sit here and soak in the warmth and let it coax her into a comfortable nap.

This was not the case as Ina ushered her to the library which also held a roaring fire surrounded decoratively with red brick and glass doors which could be opened to allow more of the radiating heat to warm its appreciative onlookers. The main wall was completely hidden from view by the many volumes that reached the high ceiling. The Doctor had collected these for many years now. Ina told Gwendalyn that the west wall section held many exciting adventures her father had given her on several special occasions, of which she thoroughly enjoyed. She generously invited Gwendalyn to come here anytime and borrow any book she desired.

Next she followed Ina to the large kitchen with two electric ranges that were used when expecting many guests. An exquisitely designed wood cook stove, which Vera still preferred using on cool days, graced the room with its charm. There were numerous shelves and cupboards and the counter space was plentiful.

They crossed over to the far end of the room where Ina showed Gwendalyn the largest pantry she had ever seen, and filled with many delectable foods. Ina had told her that it usually wasn't kept this full for just the three of them along with the servants, but it was unusually filled for the enjoyment of the many guests that would be attending Ina's birthday celebration. Vera, along with the help of the younger maid, was finishing the clean up of the evening meal in a large sink that also had the convenience of hot and cold running water.

They went on from there to their upstairs bedrooms to unpack their suitcases. When Gwendalyn finished hanging up and putting away her meagre belongings she went down the short hallway to talk with Ina.

CHAPTER 3
A NEW BIRTH

She knocked gently on her friend's door and was cheerfully welcomed in.

"Ina, I have to talk to you about tomorrow," she began.

"What's up, Gwen, you sound so serious."

"Well, tomorrow is Easter Sunday and I don't know if I've ever missed attending church at Easter time and from what your parents said we're to be visiting your Aunt Lucille in the morning."

"Oh, is that what's got you looking so forlorn? You needn't worry because we'll be going with Aunt Lucille to her church. I guess Daddy left out that part. Although we don't go to church every Sunday we still like to attend on special occasions."

"I'm relieved, it really wouldn't seem like Easter without celebrating Jesus' resurrection and thanking Him for what He did for us so many years ago."

Catching Ina's perplexed expression, Gwendalyn once again boldly addressed the subject.

"Is Jesus real in your life?" she asked.

"I don't know what your mean, Gwen, and isn't it kind of strange talking about this?"

"Well, what I meant was -- have you asked Jesus into your heart to allow Him to be Lord and Saviour of your life, to meet your needs, and trusting in Him to take care of you and do the things you can't?"

"Daddy takes good care of us and our needs are well met with his practice growing so. We don't need anything else."

"I don't think you understand my meaning, Ina. Have you read in the Bible what Jesus did for us all and how much He loves us, how He longs to be our friend, and give us eternal life?"

"Well, I still don't understand what you're trying to say. I haven't really read much of the Bible, but Daddy does have one that he keeps in the Library with the rest of the books."

"Ina, the Bible says God loves us so much that He sent His one and only Son to earth to teach us of His love. While He was living here He showed His love by healing people of many deadly diseases, enabling the blind to see, and healing the lame so they could walk again. He loved and had compassion on those who were down in spirit so that they could have joy and hope and something to live for knowing that if they believed in Jesus, they would inherit everlasting life.

The religious people, you know, the church goers and church officials who thought they were being godly but really all they wanted was to gain the peoples' respect. They didn't really love God, or believe in His Son that He sent, so that all men could believe on Him and have eternal life. They felt that Jesus was just messing things up for them and eventually they initiated plots to have Him arrested on false charges. They had Him crucified on the day we now celebrate as Good Friday. While He was being nailed to the cross, He didn't defend Himself or yell at the people. He expressed His love for those people by praying to the Father asking Him to forgive them saying that they didn't know what they were doing.

There was a criminal being crucified next to Him who yelled at Him along with the crowd saying: "Aren't you the Christ? Save yourself and us too!" The other criminal who was being crucified on the other side of Jesus said to him: "Don't you fear God, we are punished justly, but this Man has done nothing wrong." He believed and looked to Jesus and asked Him to remember him when He entered His Kingdom. Jesus, through His agony, compassionately looked upon him and said: "I tell you the truth, today you will be with me in paradise."

"Where is this paradise and what is eternal life?" Ina questioned, not quite being able to take in all that her friend had just said.

"Well from what I know, paradise is a place that Jesus has prepared for those who believe in Him, those who believe that He died and that God, His Father, raised Him from the dead, and that He is the only way to the Father and eternal life."

"You mean that Jesus died and then came back to life?" Ina questioned once again.

Gwendalyn prayed that God would help her to explain things so her friend could understand.

"Yes Ina. God raised Him from the dead so that death could not hold anyone who believes in Jesus. Eternal life is that when you die

28

it's kind of like going to sleep and then waking up in heaven where there is no more pain or sorrow and there we live forever with God. This is what we celebrate when we celebrate Easter, Jesus rising from the grave so that we could have a way to Heaven or Paradise with Him."

"It sounds interesting but I'm still baffled by it all," Ina said, "and where did you learn all this stuff?"

"We go to church every Sunday and I read my Bible every day to learn more about God's love for us and how He wants us to live. Haven't you learned any of this when you've been in church?" Gwendalyn asked.

"I guess I never really paid attention to what the preacher was saying and church seemed kinda boring and I sometimes fell asleep," Ina said and then impatiently continued. "We've talked enough about that and I want to tell you about my Aunt Lucille. She's really sweet and kind and in a way, you kind of remind me of her. But, what you were telling me about believing in God, is that what you call being a Christian?"

"Why, yes, Ina, why do you ask?" Gwendalyn inquired.

"My Aunt Lucille calls herself a Christian and maybe that's the similarities I see in the two of you."

Ina, now changing the subject, asked Gwendalyn if she would like to have a long soak in the tub before going to bed. Gwendalyn fairly jumped at the chance to delight herself in this luxurious experience.

* * *

Now refreshed from the bath, she climbed into her comfy bed and thanked the Lord over and over again for the opportunity to share with her friend the things of God. What a joy it was to see the spark of genuine interest growing in Ina's eyes. She prayed earnestly that the Holy Spirit would continue the work started tonight, and that Ina would soon receive Jesus as her personal Lord and Saviour.

She continued to pray for her family and friends, and as she prayed, Anthony's face flashed in her memory and she fervently sought God for his safety and well-being. After saying 'Amen' she still couldn't make her thoughts dismiss him. At long last sleep claimed her and the next thing she knew she was being awakened by the bright rays of

29

sunshine now filling her room.

Shuffling could be heard from Ina's room next door so she decided it was probably time to shake off her slumber and ready herself for this Easter Sunday. As the thoughts of the upcoming service and remembering their conversation from last night, Gwendalyn could hardly wait till the clock struck 10:00 AM. They would be leaving for Aunt Lucille's and then escorting her to her church.

They ate a simple breakfast, as Mrs. Evans had said they would be enjoying a special lunch, and the three of them enlightened Gwendalyn as to how large Aunt Lucille's lunches could be.

* * *

Aunt Lucille was a delight to behold, being so cheerful and exuberant. Love and joy radiated from her and Gwendalyn soon learned to love her as the rest of the family did.

The service promptly started at 11:00 o'clock with several lively choruses that expressed Jesus being alive, and that was cause for much rejoicing. Ina seemed to enjoy the singing and did her best to join in. When the choruses slowed and expressed an intimate relationship with the Lord, Gwendalyn caught a glance at Ina, whose eyes were moist and about to spill over. She gave thanks in her heart for the revelations of love, which the Holy Spirit was pouring into her friend's soul.

The preacher ended his message and dismissed the congregation after singing a final hymn and Ina quickly left the sanctuary to wait outside for her family. Gwendalyn caught up with her but before she could say anything Ina spoke up.

"Oh, Gwen, I don't know what to make of all this. After our talk last night and now this, I feel so confused and I feel like I'm being pulled in different directions. It's all so strange. I've never experienced anything like this before."

"Ina, I didn't explain this to you last night and if I can I'll try to help you make sense of what just happened."

"Don't Gwen, I can't do this right now. I want to settle myself before going to Aunt Lucille's. I don't want anything to spoil our day together with her."

Before Gwendalyn could answer the others had joined them and now they were on their way.

Aunt Lucille's home wasn't as extravagant as the Evans home but it was warm and welcoming. Everyone was soon comfortably relaxed and enjoying a delicious meal the cook had especially prepared according to Aunt Lucille's instructions.

With the finishing of the main course, Aunt Lucille announced that she would serve the dessert while her housekeeper cleared the table, and with that, said she'd be right back. Gwendalyn quickly volunteered to help and followed her out of the dining room and into the kitchen.

"Mrs. Heinz, I wanted to let you know that I had a wonderful talk with Ina about the Lord last night and she seemed to take a genuine interest in what I had to say."

"That's wonderful!" Mrs. Heinz exclaimed. "I noticed that she was being ministered to by the Holy Spirit this morning."

"That's what I want to talk with you about. She's very unsure of what's happening but I do hope I'll have another opportunity to share with her. I'll be leaving again next Saturday after her birthday party on Friday night."

"God knows the heart of each of his children, of which she is, and it is He who is in control, so all we need to do is to continue to pray for her, showing her our love. God will do the rest. Now let's carry this Black Forest cake and tea to the others so we can continue our visit."

After spending the remainder of the day with Aunt Lucille enjoying yet another appetizing lighter evening meal, the Evans family along with their guest made their way home, and then gathered in the parlor to relax and enjoy the comforting fire. Tea was served and light conversation floated in the air. As the late hour approached, the group said a sleepy 'good-night' and climbed the stairs to their awaiting beds.

* * *

Gwendalyn awoke to darkness with a light tapping sound coming from her door.

"Come in," she said sleepily.

She flicked on the lamp sitting on the nightstand to see Ina making her way towards her and then sitting on the edge of her bed.

31

"I can't sleep, Gwen," Ina said while sighing, "our conversation last night and what happened at church keeps repeating in my mind and it's got me feeling things I never thought about before. I'm so confused. I've been tossing and turning since we went to bed and it's now 2:10 AM. You were saying you could explain something? Well, I'd really appreciate it if you could help me make some sense of it now so I can get some sleep."

"Let's pray first, Ina. The other night I said a lot and I'm not even sure I said the right things. I'm not really sure what I should say tonight but let's pray that God will tell me what to say and then I know things will be all right."

"Father, You know what is going on in Ina's heart and I know You want to show Your love to her. Lord, help me say the right things to her that Your will may be done in her life. In Jesus name, amen."

Gwendalyn then began her explanation as Ina listened attentively.

"Ina, Jesus wants to be Lord of your life and the feelings you were experiencing in church yesterday was His Holy Spirit calling you. He loves you very much and He would like you to make a commitment to Him, to love Him and do His will."

"Yesterday I experienced such warm and precious moments that I never had in all my life and I would like it to be part of my everyday life. What should I do, Gwen? This is so different from anything I've ever known."

"God wants you to express your love toward Him by asking Him to be Lord and Saviour of your life and asking Him to forgive you sins. The Bible says that 'all have sinned and fall short of the Glory of God' and that 'God didn't send His Son into the world to condemn it but that the world may be saved by believing in Him.'"

"What must *I* do to be saved?" Ina asked as she felt the familiar pricking of unshed tears welling up within her eyes.

"Well, the things we've been talking about is the basis for salvation and if you believe these and commit your way to following Him, then you will have eternal salvation. The best place to start would be to ask Jesus to forgive your sins and invite Him into your heart to be your Saviour."

"I really don't know how to do those things."

"Well, will you pray, repeating after me, to ask the Lord to save you, right here and now?"

As Ina nodded, Gwendalyn got on her knees with Ina following, and began to pray.

"Lord Jesus, I confess right now that I am a sinner, and I believe that you died for my sins on the cross and was raised that I may have forgiveness and gain eternal life with you in Heaven. I do now by faith, gladly invite and receive You as my personal Lord and Saviour, and thank you for eternal salvation. And upon the authority of God's Word, I know that I am now Your child. Thank you, Jesus for saving me and loving me. In Jesus' name. Amen."

As Ina repeated the different phrases throughout the prayer, tears of repentance streamed down her face and now she shone with inexpressible joy.

"Oh, Gwen, I didn't think it could be like this. Jesus really loves me and I love Him."

"Ina, I want to tell you that once you receive Jesus, His Holy Spirit comes to be with you to help you grow to become more Christ-like. The Holy Spirit speaks to your heart to lead you in the path of righteousness. Don't try to be good in yourself because when you received Jesus, you received His nature inside you, so all you need to do is yield your life to Christ and He'll work out the things that don't belong there anymore."

"Gwen, I'm so happy! I'll never forget this night! Thank you for coming to stay with me this week."

"You're not an only child anymore, Ina. I'm your sister in Christ. You're part of a very large family now."

"Sisters," she cried, "I never had a sister. Can anyone truly be this happy," she continued, as they held each other in a long and meaningful embrace.

CHAPTER 4
SHOPPING

The next morning Gwendalyn awoke to cheerful singing coming from next door. As she listened carefully she quickly picked up the tune. She had learned it many years ago and sang it just yesterday during the church service. The words came filtering into her room and caused her to smile from the bottom of her heart. Ina was indeed joyous about her new commitment to Christ.

* * *

As they finished breakfast, Dr. Evans announced that he had a change of plans for them this morning in that he would not be driving the girls around to do shopping. Before he finished speaking Ina began to insist that he take them for he had promised. He quickly silenced her with a firm wave of his hand and went on to say that Alfred, his reliable hired help, would be driving them today, at which Ina suddenly beamed and winked at Gwendalyn who smiled back at her.

Instead of driving the girls today, Dr. Evans, would spend the day with Mrs. Evans who was feeling a little under the weather. After his announcement, Gwendalyn, feeling sincerely concerned inquired after Mrs. Evans health.

"Mrs. Evans, maybe we should stay at home for the day and be helpful in any way we can. I'm sure Ina and I can do our shopping another day, can't we, Ina," she stated.

"How thoughtful, my dear," Mrs. Evans put in before Ina could reply. "I'm not feeling very ill. I think I'm just a little weary still from our voyage and not being able to rest properly yesterday. I'm going to relax in the parlor and do more on my cross-stitch project. Edward has agreed to stay at home to keep me company, so you girls go on about your day and try not to concern yourselves about me."

Gwendalyn crossed over to the ailing lady and while hugging her gently, she kissed her pale forehead.

"You are very kind and generous, Mrs. Evans. I hope you'll be feeling better real soon," she added.

"Yes, Momma, get well soon," Ina put in, "because you'll need to be fit as a fiddle for my birthday party."

Mrs. Evans expressed her gratitude to the energetic teens and asked Dr. Evans to escort her to the parlor so she could rest in the warmth of the comforting fire.

"You girls better be getting a move on. Alfred is going to be out front waiting for you before you're ready," informed Dr. Evans while leaving the room with his wife of many years.

The girls turned and rushed upstairs chattering excitedly about this new day opening up before them. When they had adorned their finishing touches, had gathered their handbags and other such necessary items, they fairly ran down the stairs and put on their warm coats, hats, and gloves.

Heading out the door, they saw the ever patient Alfred waiting to take them wherever their hearts desired.

Alfred dropped them off in a shopping pavilion, which sported many different shops and restaurants. He bid them to be careful and to have a good time saying he would pick them up 'right here' at Citadel Hill, a good landmark consisting of a complex of tall office and hotel buildings, at 4:00 PM. The girls agreed, thanked him, and ran off with Ina telling her which would be the best place to begin.

'Spring Garden Road', the most fashionable shopping street in the central area of Halifax, had to be the place to start. Their shopping was going well although they hadn't bought anything as yet. They were just drifting from shop to shop eyeing over the many tempting items of a personal nature and the newly designed fashions they so wished to buy. Gwendalyn spotted a beautiful teal green dress and asked to try it on, if not for anything else but just to see how she looked in it.

Ina stared at her in awe, as her friend was indeed one of the prettiest girls she had ever seen and she could imagine her growing into a lovely young woman. Ina had already paid for her new 'birthday' dress and was insisting that Gwendalyn buy this touch of elegance, designed by Monsieur Faburier, himself, of France.

"Oh, Ina, I just love it but I really can't. Mom gave me a little extra money to buy Stacey a special wedding present and I couldn't spend it on a dress," Gwendalyn explained. "I'll just have to wait and hopefully be able to buy something like this another time," she continued, as her hand lingered across the silky smoothness and reluctantly handed the gown over to the saleslady.

She pushed away the thoughts of how she looked in the dress and set her mind about to the main reasons she had come shopping in the first place. She was here to buy Ina a birthday gift and maybe go to Sears to see if she could find that romantic picture she wanted to buy for her sister's wedding present. If not, she could always order it when she returned home.

They walked to another street lined with shops perpendicular to 'Spring Garden Road' and entered a bookstore. With both of them so interested in literature, they decided they would give each other twenty minutes of solitude to explore their own interests in this mind-expanding store.

Gwendalyn had an idea, went directly to the religious section, and looked with earnest until she discovered just what she was looking for: A beautiful leather-bound white Holy Bible.

"This would make a wonderful birthday gift for Ina," she thought out loud. She slipped across the room to the cashier being careful not be seen by Ina who was totally engrossed in a newly released novel about the passenger ship 'Titanic' that had sank in 1912. Ina was considering buying this volume for her father, whom she knew would take great delight in it, and eventually add it to his ever-growing library collection.

As Gwendalyn stood nervously at the cashier counter, wondering if Ina would unintentionally intrude upon her secrecy, the lady who was serving her asked her if she would like to get the Bible engraved.

"Engraved? Is that possible?" she inquired.

"Why yes," the lady answered, "we have this new machine that beautifully inscripts with gold or silver lettering any name you would like engraved. We usually place it on the bottom right hand corner. Here, I'll show you an example," she continued, and she brought from under the counter a black leather bound Holy Bible and the name, 'Alison Huxter', had been engraved.

"This one's mine," she said beaming, "the shop owner, knowing that I regularly attend church, gave me this for a Christmas gift last year.

He did ask if I would bring it to work with me to show customers who might be interested in something similar."

"It is beautiful!" Gwendalyn exclaimed, "I would love to have it done for Ina. How long would it take?"

* * *

After paying for the Bible and the cost of the engraving, Gwendalyn agreed that she would come back in an hour or so to pick up the purchase she knew her friend would cherish. Now she would have to come up with some excuse to come back to this store without Ina finding out her secret.

She waited outside the store until Ina showed up carrying a bag in her hand that she quickly opened and pulled out the book explaining that her father would 'absolutely love it'. Gwendalyn agreed. Ina asked her if she had found anything and with a shrug she showed her empty hands and quickly changed the subject, asking Ina if there was a Sears store nearby that she could have a look in.

Ina said there was one within walking distance located on Barrington Street but they should stop and break for lunch to be refreshed for this afternoon's continuation of their ensue.

They walked into a delicatessen that offered hot soup and sandwiches that would be created from the many savory meats and cheeses as well as being garnished with choices of fresh lettuce, pickles, tomatoes, onions, and other mouth-watering items.

Gwendalyn had ordered hearty chicken vegetable soup with a sandwich of her choice, while Ina had ordered the cream of broccoli soup and a selected sandwich. They chose a small table close to the window and Ina was about to hungrily partake of the appetizing food when she noticed Gwendalyn closing her eyes and bowing her head. Ina gently interrupted her with a whisper asking her if they could pray together. Gwendalyn smiled and gave a prayer of thanks for this wonderful day, her good friend, Ina, and her parents, and for the blessing of such healthy food. Ina said 'amen' and offered a shy smile to Gwendalyn when she opened her eyes.

"I'm glad you're here to help me along in God's ways for a little while longer," Ina expressed thankfully. "It's kind of awkward praying in public like this but it's also somewhat natural being able to talk to God wherever you are."

"We don't need to be concerned about where we are or what we're doing, we can be ourselves with God," Gwendalyn said. "What God means to us is more important than what others think, and sometimes, even, there might be another Christian nearby who may be feeling kind of awkward, but when they see us, and others like us, being open before God, it might encourage them to do the same."

They sat in silence for a while enjoying this nourishing lunch and feeling their bodies being rejuvenated with each bite.

"You know, Gwen, there's going to be other friends, guys and girls, our age at my party besides Momma and Daddy's friends. There's this one guy Jonathon, who's 17 and really handsome, and I asked him to bring his brother, Franklin, who's two years his senior."

"Now, Ina, you know I'm not that interested in boys right now so I don't want you giving them any ideas. There'll be plenty of time for all that later."

Gwendalyn tried to sound assertive and sure of herself but her thoughts took a turn and wandered back to the way Anthony had held her as she was leaving. These unfamiliar feelings, now deepening, caused her to grow warm inside and she...

"I bet I know where you are right now," Ina teased, "back home with your Anthony."

"He's not *my* Anthony," she chastened, "and let's get a move on before we run out of time to get our shopping finished," she continued, relieved to have changed the subject and Ina following suit.

They entered Sears about 1:30 PM and walked around discovering many gift ideas for their loved ones. Gwendalyn's eyes fell upon a shelf lined with an assortment of scarves, hats, and gloves for men that was labelled 'End of Season Sale'. She carefully selected a warm hat for Dad to keep him warm while out fishing, and a pair of gloves for Calvin who had complained that his others were nearly worn out. She secretly hid a soft but warm scarf from her friend's probing eyes to keep her from asking questions and teasing her as she so often did. After all, she had told Anthony she would bring him back something.

After finding Stacey a lovely scented perfume, and Mom a package of two handkerchiefs, she scanned the store looking for the section of housewares and the like. Maybe she would find the beautiful picture in there.

She almost dragged Ina, who was constantly nattering about this blouse or those shoes, into a section displaying a wide variety of paintings and pictures. She was about to give up hope of finding the romantic interlude, when, while sorting through the nearly ending selection, her eyes fell upon this beautifully framed artwork. She gasped aloud as this was so much more glorious than the way it was pictured in the catalogue. It wasn't quite as large as she thought it would be, and thereby dissolving any doubts if she would be able to bring it back home with her.

"Gwen, it's so romantic!" Ina cried, "I can see why you wanted it so bad. What a painting! I'm surprised you found it, it being so beautiful and all. I wouldn't say items like this would last long in the stores."

Gwendalyn, thankfully, had it wrapped and bagged and was carrying her packages out of the store when she noticed a clock that read 3:10 PM.

"Ina, I just remembered that I left my hat at the book store and we'll have to get back there before we have to meet Alfred again," she exclaimed, hoping Ina would believe her. Even if she had purposefully left the hat as an excuse to go back, she was now legitimately concerned about the time.

"We'll have enough time," Ina reassured her, "the bookstore is on our way back to Citadel Hill."

With both girls carrying an armload of recently made purchases, they made their way back to the bookstore. Gwendalyn showed Ina a place to sit while she went in the store, and Ina breathlessly agreed to wait till she returned.

A few minutes later she returned wearing her hat. Her now specially engraved meaningful gift was secretly stowed along with the other expressions of love she would give the 'others' who meant so much to her as well.

Upon arrival at Citadel Hill, they found, once again, a patient Alfred waiting beside the car looking with concern at his watch, which now read 4:15 PM. His face now showed relief as he readied himself to open the trunk of the car and then carefully helped the girls stow away their treasured items.

"I see you've had a good day of it," he smiled placing in the last of the packages.

"It was a wonderful day, Alfred," Ina joyously exclaimed.

"We're sorry for being late," Gwendalyn sincerely apologized. "We lost track of time and I left my hat at one of the shops and had to retrieve it at the last minute," she continued. This deception was starting to make her very uncomfortable and she wished she hadn't revealed the last statement. Silently, she offered up a mindful prayer asking her Father to forgive her.

As they drove up the driveway Gwendalyn drew in her breath at the magnificent structure before her. She hadn't noticed the characteristics of this charming and graceful home before now. She had been just waking up when they first arrived and darkness hid its beauty when coming home from church on Sunday. Now she beheld the gleaming white pillars supporting the second story balconies above. Some lilac colored curtains were escaping through the opened window and gently billowing in the breeze. She recognized them as the ones in her room and her mind drifted to Vera, the housekeeper, who probably opened the window to allow the fragrant spring air to refresh their 'guest's' bedroom.

Her roaming eyes came to rest and took in the U-shaped porch which contained a cushioned bench swing at the west end, a table and chairs at the east end, and some comfortable sitting chairs located near the entrance of this glorious home.

"How perfect. One could have morning tea while watching the sun rise and a place of relaxation to read and take in a beautiful sunset," she whispered, contenting herself as she allowed these hushed words to escape her lips. She hoped she would be able to indulge herself the pleasure of enjoying this carefully designed piece of serenity.

She was startled by the opening of the car door and Ina calling out of her dream world. "Come on Gwendalyn. I can't wait to show Momma all my purchases and give Daddy the book I bought him."

Gwendalyn smiled at her friend and proceeded to collect her packages from the trunk. She followed Ina in silence still clinging to her world of seclusion and contentment.

She paused long enough in the parlor to greet Dr. and Mrs. Evans and to watch and listen to Ina exclaim over her purchases telling her parents about the 'invigorating' and 'delightful' day they had just had.

Mrs. Evans seemed rejuvenated after her day of rest and when Dr. Evans was presented with his gift he was noticeably filled with gratitude and beamed at his daughter, admiring her thoughtfulness towards him.

Excusing herself, Gwendalyn began her way up the stairs after hearing Ina stating she would be up shortly. She felt a little tired and allowed herself to lie down on her more than comfortable bed. She snuggled into her feather pillow and before she knew it sleep had drawn her into its hold.

* * *

Anthony was with her now, seated on the porch swing swaying ever so gently as they admired the setting sun. She felt so peaceful and they talked in whispered tones to not disturb the intimate scene. Anthony turned to her, his face showing earnestness. She had seen this once before, but where? Then he began to speak, "Gwendalyn, I have something I need to tell you. You are the most..."

* * *

The knocking on the door jarred her awake and she turned over to see Ina standing in the now opened doorway.

"Were you asleep?" she asked quietly. She came in and sat on the edge of the bed while Gwendalyn pulled herself to a sitting position.

"What time is it?" Gwendalyn questioned somewhat confused, "Did I miss dinner?"

"Oh no, silly," Ina laughed, "you just came up here not even half an hour ago. Dinner won't be ready for almost another hour."

"I had a powerful sleep," she said yawning, "I was dreaming about... oh never mind. It was nothing, but I sure feel refreshed now. It's like I've been asleep for hours."

Gwendalyn noticed her packages still scattered across the floor and feeling a little embarrassed started to pick them up. Ina began picking up things to help her friend and accidentally spilt the contents of one bag onto the bed. She carefully lifted the scarf admiring its masculinity.

"And who is this for?" she asked mischievously. "I didn't see you pick this up."

Immediately Gwendalyn felt color rush up into her face upon seeing what Ina held in her hand. She felt the way she did when her mother caught her sneaking still warm cookies off the cooling rack after she was told not to.

She rebuked herself and the feelings of embarrassment now engulfing her. There was nothing to be embarrassed about. Anthony was her dear friend, only her friend. She composed herself as best she could and nonchalantly gathered the item in question to herself and packed it away with her other things.

"Well, who is it for?" Ina teased, figuring just who could cause the discomforting actions now being displayed before her.

"It's for Anthony," Gwendalyn confessed, "and what of it? You know we're good friends, nothing more. I told him I'd bring him back something," she continued trying to convince herself even more so than Ina. It was too disconcerting thinking about these things and even more so talking about them.

CHAPTER 5
ANTHONY

He had walked this stretch of road many times and it never caused his heart to grieve him as it did today. That gate had held so many memories. He ran his work-hardened fingers through his wavy, chocolate brown, hair and held his head trying desperately to release the agonizing thoughts that kept intruding upon him. His lean and muscular frame felt invigorated after running around the shoreline and then up to the intersection that would take him further from town had he continued. He had paused at the intersection and reminisced in his heart how Gwendalyn had looked when he said good-bye to her just three days ago. He still remembered the feel of her arms around his neck and the smell of her hair. She had had to raise herself upon her tiptoes to embrace him properly and he had constrained himself from the compelling urge to take her whole-heartedly in his arms claiming her for himself. He had held back all right, only allowing his hands to find their place on the small of her back. He wondered if she had read in his still-tanned face the feelings he had tried so hard to suppress.

He was now back in town and had walked a couple hundred feet from Gwendalyn's home his heart still pounding from the remembrance of their parting.

"She's only fifteen," he blurted out aloud and looked around hoping no one was near enough to hear his cries. It relieved him when the only movement he saw was wood smoke billowing from the many chimneys around the cove. It was still too early for many others to be out and about.

Only fifteen, but in just over two months she would be sweet sixteen, wonderful sixteen. "Please God, make it stop. Forgive me, Lord. Help me to put these thoughts into perspective and gain control over my desires."

He was eighteen, soon to be nineteen at the close of summer. He had been a good friend to Gwendalyn. Walking her to school and protecting her from any bullying she may have received had he not

45

been there. And there was the time he had saved her from drowning in the icy depths of the unforgiving ocean. She had called him her big brother that always took care of her and told him he was her guardian angel. He loved the place he held in her life and she appeared to really care for him. He loved her smiles and the way she teased him. Maybe not always, but in the last year or so it meant more that it ever did before.

They had grown up together and had been each other's best bud, but now, where was she? She was away. Would this be the beginning of many journeys that would take her from him? When had he started feeling this way towards her?

"It probably had been building over the past year," he consoled himself after settling the thoughts that seemed to cause him such turmoil.

It wasn't the childhood chum that he was so desperately missing, but was the beautiful young woman that she was developing into that captured him, especially knowing she was even more beautiful on the inside.

She always thanked the Creator for the beauty in each new day, for bountiful fish catches, and the new birth of God's little 'blessings' ensuring life's continuation.

Her maturity level had surpassed her teen years, or so Anthony had perceived from the time they had spent together. He knew she was raised in a home where love, kindness, and compassion was genuine, as well as training to become a wife deserving of a husband to be.

As he thought upon these things, he chided himself for presuming that one day she would be his. He also knew she was raised to be an independent thinker and wasn't a possession to be owned. She would most definitely be a devoted and loyal partner to the man who would win her affections.

Feeling humbled, he again sought the Lord asking forgiveness for the unacceptable ways he was thinking of his dear friend. She was young, very young, and would need time and freedom to grow into the woman God was still preparing her to be. He would need to be patient, and prayerfully take all his concerns and thoughts to his Heavenly Father.

Anthony, since he was twelve years old, had helped his father with the fishing and enjoyed the time learning this fulfilling trade. At times the sea would be so calm and quiet they would both just allow the peacefulness and solitude consume them, awakening only by the cries of the seagulls above. Those days were particularly beautiful with the sun rising and the blue sky reflecting its royalty in the glassy boundless waters. At times though, the rolling sea was very frightening to the inexperienced lad. At one time they would be on the crest of a huge swell looking twenty to thirty feet down but the most scary feeling was when he'd be looking up to face that enormous swell coming at him. Then there were the days they would get home thanking God that He had kept them safe on such angry and hostile waters.

After that first season of losing almost every meal he ate, he grew used to the rhythm of the sea and learned to enjoy its relaxation techniques.

Over the past two years his father had given him a portion of the profits they had made and Anthony was in the process of purchasing his own fourteen-foot fishing boat with an outboard motor, along with a score of nets and traps, from Mr. Bridger. Mr. Bridger had planned to retire after this upcoming fishing season but because of his failing health decided to forgo this last year's endeavour. He had made a good living from the fishing industry and had set aside enough finances to see him and his wife through their golden years. Although Anthony was getting the 'deal of a lifetime', as he called it, he had agreed to supply the Bridger's wood supply indefinitely while their only son was away at university studying to become an engineer.

He knew that the sooner he could get started on his own fishing career, the sooner he could start on his house he was planning to build.

The north shore, where some new homes were in the process of being built, would be an ideal location to start his new life. He and his father had staked out the piece of land noting the area that could be used for a large vegetable garden as well as being in walking distance from the oceanfront. He also took note that at this location, no other houses could be built to the right of his soon-to-be home. The landscape and terrain would be too difficult to build on and this would ensure more privacy for the years to come.

He, and his neighbours to be, would eventually build a wharf large enough to support the four of them. As the finances came in

47

throughout this fishing season, he would begin stocking up on materials to begin construction of his new home.

His father had told him that whenever he got started he would be investing his savings into helping his youngest son get situated into his new home. Despite Anthony's protests and continued determination to demonstrate his abilities by building his own life, he won him over by saying that if he allowed him to help in this way, he would feel better about Anthony caring for him and his wife in their final years, if need be.

Anthony knew his father was using this comment only as a tool to have him submit to his father's generosity, as he would gladly care for his parents no matter what the situation. Anthony loved him for it, and inside he felt relieved knowing that he would now be able to have a home with all the modern conveniences, ready to receive his bride at the appropriate time. He had heard Gwendalyn say on different occasions that no matter how wonderful the new electrical appliances were, she would cherish a good old fashion wood cook stove, like her mom's, in her kitchen. And so, he had been thrilled about his father saying he wanted him to have grandma's cook stove they had stored in the shed out back. Before selling her house five years ago, they had it moved out in hopes it would find its way into one of his children's homes. There was also a chesterfield and stuffed chair, coffee tables and end tables, as well as Mrs. Bowman's dining room set, which had been replaced by Grandma's, now stored in the attic.

Anthony chastened himself for presuming that Gwendalyn would be the one to use the family heirloom. He hoped beyond hope that it would be so, but he knew it had to be his Heavenly Father's will for this to work out. He prayed again concerning his future bride and felt a peace that whoever his Father had chose for him would be a woman of honour, deserving this home and his affections.

Anthony's father was also well pleased that one of his children had decided to continue in his footsteps. Now that his eldest son, Carl, was married and working as a journalist in Nova Scotia, and his only daughter, Stephanie, married to a logger and moved inland, he felt an inner pride and joy knowing that he would have Anthony living near him. He would be delighted to see some of his grandchildren grow up around him. Anthony's decision to stay on at Serenity Cove and build his life here had meant so much to Rose, Anthony's mother, and they both felt blessed beyond belief now knowing that their Golden Years would indeed be golden. Because of this, Anthony's father was more than willing to help in every way he could to see Anthony achieve his goals.

Unsuspected, his heart was once again filled with love and desire for Gwendalyn and longed to see her smiling face. He wondered if she had any thoughts of him being her lifetime companion, living in the commitment of marriage and working together toward their planned goals. She would be turning sixteen at the end of June and then in two or three years she may be ready and even wanting a home of her own.

He couldn't and even wouldn't talk with her about these dreams of his. She was still so young and shouldn't be tossed into his views of thinking and planning. She deserved to grow into the things her heart would take her.

In his heart, though, he desperately prayed that someday Gwendalyn would look upon him as more than just her friend.

CHAPTER 6
RELAXING

Tuesday morning Gwendalyn awoke feeling a little strange. It seemed as if she'd been sleeping a long time and when she turned over to look at the clock on the wall she gasped, seeing that it was 10:50 AM and wondered if it really was the correct time. She threw off the covers and jumped out of bed as if she had missed something or something had changed. It was still cold outside and the quietness of the house seemed eerie.

She tidied her bed and room, got dressed quickly, and stopped at the lavatory to refresh herself and braid her long, black tresses.

Feeling a little more settled, she headed down the stairs and was cheered by the inviting warm glow and soft conversation coming from the parlor. She made her way to the cosy room and looked upon the contented scene before her. Dr. and Mrs. Evans were seated on opposite ends of a sofa facing each other with Dr. reading the new book Ina had bought him and Mrs. Evans involved in her cross-stitch. She felt as if she were intruding on this peaceful interlude and turned to make her leave when Mrs. Evans called to her, "Good morning, Gwendalyn. I see you've had a good rest last night."

"Yes, I did, Mrs. Evans, but I didn't mean to sleep so late," she apologized.

"I'm glad you did, dear. Ina hasn't come down yet but you're welcome to join us for tea till she does. We decided to wait for you girls to have breakfast together but I guess it'll be brunch today."

Gwendalyn was taking her first sip of the steaming hot drink when Ina made her entrance yawning as she came.

"Good morning, Momma, Daddy," she said, giving them each a kiss and going to Gwendalyn to hug her, "and good morning to you too, Gwen."

"It's almost not morning anymore," her father said looking up at her, "and I'm starved. Let's go get some of that brunch your mother's been talking about now that we're all here," he continued as he wrapped his arm around her and gave his other hand to help his wife up. Gwendalyn took the lead and they all made their way to the dining room and feasted on a scrumptious meal. They continued to sit around the table chatting about yesterday's events and made plans to take a drive together down town to Central Park to do some skating.

They arrived to find the man-made skating pond already sporting several skaters enjoying what would probably be one of the last days to take part in such pleasures. Gwendalyn and Ina made their way down to a bench close to the pond's edge while Ina's parents unpacked a thermos of hot chocolate and a picnic basket filled with sandwiches and goodies Vera had packed for their outing.

As they were tightening their laces a girl their age came gliding up followed by two older teenaged boys. "Ina, it's good to see you," she said breathlessly, "who's your friend?"

"Hi Carmen," she answered, "this is my friend Gwendalyn Gillard from Newfoundland. She's visiting till the end of the week. Gwen, this is Carmen Stuckless, Jonathon Newbury, and his older brother, Franklin Newbury."

"Pleased to meet you all," she said sincerely but wasn't too impressed when she saw the two boys elbowing each other, snickering, and whispering comments while casting glances her way.

"See you out there," they called as they skated away funning with each other.

"How'd you like them?" asked Ina after they'd gone.

"Carmen seemed nice enough," she replied, "but I didn't like the way the boys were acting."

"Oh, Gwendalyn, I'm sure they were doing that because you're new and I think they liked you."

"Maybe," she agreed, "but I guess I'm not used to strangers acting that way toward me. My school chums tease me and we have fun together but we've known each other almost all our lives. This seems different."

"I guess your right but I don't think they meant any harm. They know me and we fun around like that so I guess they figure it's OK to do the same with my friends. You'll have to excuse them."

"Yeah, you're right. Let's make the best of it and have some fun. Catch me if you can."

Gwendalyn took off and sped away with Ina at her heels. They spent most of the afternoon playing tag with Jonathon, Franklin, and Carmen.

They enjoyed a break in the action with Ina's parents over a light picnic and then went back to the game. Mr. and Mrs. Evans skated hand in hand for a short time and went back to the bench to talk and watch the young people having their fun.

When it was time to go, Gwendalyn and Ina were tired out and eager to get home and relax before supper. They said their good-byes and drove off.

The parlor was the perfect spot to unwind and Gwendalyn and Ina sat and chatted about the day. Gwendalyn was saying how much she enjoyed the skating and Ina's friends turned out to be a lot of fun.

"Did I tell you they're coming to my birthday party on Friday? I'm glad you got a chance to meet them before hand and I think Jonathon had his eye on you. I like Franklin myself. That's why I invited Jonathon, so he would bring his older brother."

Gwendalyn groaned inwardly. She had made the best of the day but she wasn't looking forward to spending an entire evening socializing with them.

She chided herself for her ill feelings toward them but she couldn't get past the way they behaved around her. She decided she would do whatever it would take to make Ina's sweet sixteenth birthday party the best it could be with no complaints on her part.

CHAPTER 7
AN UNANNOUNCED GUEST

Gwendalyn awoke with the sun streaming in her bedroom window and its rays spreading even more warmth on her already cosy frame.

Stepping out of bed she noticed the room hadn't quite the chill she expected. Looking outside she saw water droplets falling before her and she allowed her inquisitive eyes to travel up, amidst the blinding brightness, to rest upon beautifully formed melting icicles. Her gaze followed the little droplets to their destination on the balcony just outside her window. Without thinking she opened the door of her private entrance to the balcony, stepped out, and crossed over to the protective railing. She breathed in deeply the fresh morning air, taking note how unusually warm it felt.

"What a glorious morning!" she whispered aloud.

She continued to drink in the peaceful interlude but something was hastening her back. As if startled, her eyes dropped to her bare feet that were now wet and cold and a minute stream of icy water was slowly making its way around her feet on its descent to the ground below. She wondered why she hadn't been aware of this before but realized that the beauty of the morning had taken all her attention. She chastened herself and hurried through the door and felt instant warm relief as she dug her toes into the thick rag rug.

Now warmed again and her mind racing, she quickly dressed, made a stop at the lavatory, and fairly ran as quiet as possible down the stairs intent on finding the childhood treasure she had always enjoyed. Throwing on her jacket and impatiently tying on her boots, all the while feeling a little mischievous, she opened the door and gently closed it behind her as she stepped out once again, being thankful that no one had seen her childish antics. Continuing on her way, she found her destination below the balcony and sure enough, there it was. The glistening icicles were a perfect size but to Gwendalyn's disappointment, just out of reach. She looked for a way in which she could claim the object of her quest and saw that some built-in flower planters seemed to be just the right thing. She steadied herself on a planter and managed to grab the icicle nearest her. Before she could feel the sense of gratification, fear gripped her as she lost her footing and went tumbling onto the snow packed ground. She landed with a thud and cried out more from being startled than in pain.

She heard hurried footsteps coming up the driveway toward her and before she had a chance to regain her dignity, a hand reached to her and a voice as deep as the sea broke through.

"Allow me to help," he said as he pulled her up to face him.

She looked up into the handsome, clean-shaven face of a complete stranger. His brown hair was combed neatly into place and he was professionally dressed as if he worked in an office.

Embarrassed, and slightly shaken up, she mumbled a 'thank you' and tried to recompose herself.

"I was just trying to..."

"No need to explain," he smiled humorously, "I saw everything and I still love these things too."

He stepped up onto the flower planter and in one swift motion proceeded to take two icicles from their hold and handed her one.

She started toward the porch and realized her left leg was a bit sore from the fall and she struggled to keep her balance.

Once again he was at her side helping her up the steps and to the sitting chairs on the porch. She gratefully eased herself into the chair and the stranger sat in the other one close beside her.

"I'm Daniel Sorrenson," he said introducing himself, holding out his hand to her, "and you must be Ina. Your father has mentioned you in one of our conversations."

"Oh no, I'm her friend," she corrected, "Ina wasn't silly enough to come out here this early in the morning and make a complete fool of herself. She's probably still in bed. We had quite the busy day yesterday."

"Fool, nothing," he returned, "entertainment at this time of the day doesn't happen often, you know," he laughed and then added more seriously, "as well as meeting a beautiful young lady."

Gwendalyn felt colour rise in her cheeks and turned away as to not have him notice. This was the first time anyone had ever said anything like that to her. She munched on her icicle and heard him doing the same. Just as things were beginning to get quiet, Dr. Evans came out the door.

"Well, hello there Daniel," he said cheerfully, "I thought I heard some stirring out here. I see you've met our guest for the week. She's a very good friend of our daughter, Ina."

"Yes, I have had the pleasure, thank you, Dr. Evans," he said winking at Gwendalyn.

Feeling her face flush once again, she excused herself and slipped into the house disposing of her icy treat along the way.

She made her way up the stairs and into her bedroom and began to tidy her bedding and straighten the room. When she was on her way out again, Ina showed up with exuberance.

"Good morning, Gwen. Did you happen to see outside yet today? It looks so beautiful and it may even be warm."

"Yes, I believe it is," she agreed, being careful not to reveal anything that would invite Ina in with a hundred questions. Right now she wanted to forget the whole episode and enjoy this first burst of spring with her friend.

As they came down the stairs they heard voices coming from the parlor.

"I wonder what's up?" enquired Ina. "Sounds like Daddy's got company this early in the morning." She tried to steer Gwendalyn in the direction of the parlor.

"It's probably private business. Why don't we go and help get breakfast ready?" Gwendalyn asked nervously.

"Oh, nonsense, Daddy wouldn't mind me saying good morning at least," she interjected.

Gwendalyn gave up and allowed Ina to half drag her to the parlor where Dr. Evans already noticed their coming.

"Ina, I want you to meet someone," he called out.

"Good morning, Daddy," she answered and turned her gaze to the handsome masculine stranger now rising to make her acquaintance.

"This is Daniel Sorrenson. He's the one I told you would be working with me throughout the summer and maybe longer if things work out," her father continued.

"Pleased to meet you, Mr. Sorrenson, or shall I say Dr. Sorrenson," she said melodiously and using all the feminine charm she could muster.

Gwendalyn was surprised by her friend's behaviour but it appeared she had awaited this day for quite a while and may have been even practising this particular introduction.

"Dr. Sorrenson will do just fine for now," he replied, "but when we get to know each other a little better, Daniel, may be more appropriate."

Gwendalyn thought the reply from this newcomer was a little forward but from the look on Ina's face, it was received well and a welcome compliment.

"This is my good friend, Gwendalyn Gillard. She is here visiting from Newfoundland and will be staying until Saturday," Ina said smiling.

"It's good to have a proper introduction. Gwendalyn Gillard is the name you said," he teased, winking again in Gwendalyn's direction.

Gwendalyn felt her cheeks grow warm once again and was relieved when they heard the ringing of the dinner bell summoning them to the breakfast table.

"You'll stay to breakfast and then we could drive together to the office," Dr. Evans stated more so than making a request.

"Why thank you, Dr. Evans." he said, adding, "It will be my pleasure."

Ina pulled Gwendalyn to the side as they walked to the dining room and in a bit of a demanding tone asked her when she had met 'Mr. Daniel Sorrenson'.

Gwendalyn reassured her it was quite by accident and that she would explain it all to her later.

They found their way to the room where aromas of omelettes, bacon, and toast floated in the air. Steam drifted in wisps from the hot cups of tea and the fresh fruit tray was more delectable than any Gwendalyn had seen in a long time.

Dr. Evans took his seat at the head of the table with his wife at his right side. Ina sat next to her mother and Daniel was invited to take the seat next to Gwendalyn who was seated across from Mrs. Evans on Dr. Evans' left.

The atmosphere around the table was cheerful but a little formal with the sudden appearance of their special unannounced guest. Ina was doing her best to keep the conversation going between herself and Daniel using flirtations subtle enough to make it seem friendly with a bit of interest. Once or twice, though, she embarrassed herself with her forwardness and was relieved when Gwendalyn purposefully changed the subject to avoid further embarrassment to her friend. She couldn't understand why Ina was or appeared to be so taken with this young man when she had met him just minutes ago.

Dr. Evans spoke up and asked Daniel when he had come in and if he had a chance to find a place to stay.

"Well, my plane got in at 7:15 PM last evening and I'm staying at a hotel in the area of Citadel Hill," he said. "I'll be setting about finding an apartment on Saturday or preferably a boarding house. Do you know of any within walking distance of your practice?"

"Yes, there is a boarding house called Grandma Elsa's that's about half of a mile from the office. She's a young Grandma. Just in her early fifties. She's one of my patients and she's 'fit as a fiddle'. She's a kind lady with a cheerful personality and a great cook, or so I've heard. Her boarding house is very popular so I'm not sure if she'll have any rooms available," explained Dr. Evans.

"It sounds like the perfect place. I'll look into it later today after I get situated at the clinic," he said sounding hopeful.

"How about we start out a little early and check it out on our way to the office?" Dr. Evans interjected.

"Sounds great!" he exclaimed looking at his watch. "It's 9:15 now. When shall we set out?"

"Right now!" he said hurriedly, drinking the last of his tea and wiping his mouth with the napkin and rising to take leave.

Daniel, following Dr. Evans' lead, rose from the table.

"It was a pleasure meeting you, Mrs. Evans, Miss Evans, and Miss Gillard."

He grinned mischievously at Gwendalyn throwing her another wink, which again caused her to grow flushed, and she lowered her head.

"Thank you for the great morning meal," he added.

"It was a pleasure having you, Dr. Sorrenson. I hope you have luck at Grandma Elsa's," Mrs. Evans said.

"Yes, it was a pleasure meeting you, Dr. Sorrenson," Ina repeated, "and I hope Daddy will bring you around for a meal or a visit more often."

"I'd look forward to that," he said turning to leave and nodding to Gwendalyn.

Gwendalyn merely said "Good-bye, Dr. Sorrenson" and followed behind the small group to see the two doctors off.

When the door closed behind them Ina immediately turned to Gwendalyn and gave her a secretive questioning look.

Mrs. Evans excused herself and went to the kitchen to meet with the kitchen staff to discuss the meal preparation for the rest of the day and Ina's birthday celebration.

"Did you know Dr. Sorrenson before he came here this morning?" she asked, showing unbearable curiosity and half dragging her to the parlor.

"Well, no, but we did kind of meet by accident before you were up this morning."

"How's that? I met you in the hall coming from your room this morning before we came downstairs."

"I was up before that and had been outside a couple of times before seeing you in the hall."

"Do tell," she said in an almost demanding tone. "What happened this morning?"

"Well, it all started when I stepped out on the balcony and... and that's when your father showed up on the porch and invited Mr. Sorrenson in the parlor. I went upstairs to tidy my room and then met you coming out and you know the rest of the story. And by the way, what's got you acting so strange about this man?" she questioned Ina.

"Well, Daddy's been telling me about him for a couple of months now, saying that he would be working with him at his office and I guess I've been dreaming of the day when I'd meet him but I thought it wouldn't be till after the Easter break. And then you get to be the first to meet him and I guess I'm a little jealous," she said, giving a humorous pout.

"Not to worry my dear. I'm not interested in him and I'll be leaving for home come Saturday," she said reassuring her friend, "but I must say he is quite handsome. Too bad I'll have to leave so soon. You never know, but if I were to stay around, some interests could develop."

A look of shock instantly flooded Ina's face and she was about to say something but Gwendalyn started laughing and quickly cried, "Just joking, just joking! Don't look that way. You just met the guy and it's not like you've been dating or something."

"Oh, I know, but I guess I've been looking with interest at guys lately and the ones at school just seem so immature."

"I know what you mean, especially after meeting those two at the skating pond yesterday."

"I thought I liked Franklin but he'd have some growing up to do before I'd consider him again. I do like this Dr. Sorrenson, though, and hopefully something will happen between us."

"You sound so dreamy," Gwendalyn chided, "let's go for a walk down to the harbour and look at the ships."

"OK, sounds like fun. We haven't got much else to do today. Let's go in the kitchen and ask Vera to pack us a picnic lunch and we could spend a few hours there. It's a good half-hour walk to get there. I hope you're up for it."

"Me! I can't wait to get started!" she exclaimed.

CHAPTER 8
HALIFAX HARBOUR

"What a beautiful day!" Ina shouted as they started out on their way.

"Yeah, yesterday was kind of warm but today everything is melting and the sun is so hot. I'm glad you had this lighter jacket for me. Mine would have been way too warm. Thanks."

"You're welcome. It's a good thing we did our skating yesterday or we would be out of luck today. I believe spring has indeed sprung."

They continued on their way with Ina chattering on about her birthday party and who would be attending.

"That reminds me," Gwendalyn said, "my sixteenth birthday is coming up at the end of June and I really want you to be there. Do you think your dad could bring you?"

"Well, maybe, now that he's got someone working with him he may be able to get away for a long weekend. And by the way, I hope you haven't forgotten about your promise to try and come back for a week during the summer."

"You know I'd love to, so I'll do what I can to come back but there is a problem about getting here and back home again. Your father is busy with his practice and can't be taking time off to bring me back and forth whenever we want to get together. It's too bad my dad doesn't have a car to help out with the driving."

"Oh my! It's beautiful!" Gwendalyn cried. "I heard that the harbour never freezes. It's so good to see the open ocean again. I always long for spring to see the water and go out in boat with Dad."

"You know that's what made Halifax such a great city. The year-round ice-free port caused the economy to boom because of this advantage. We have ships of great importance from all over the world dock here. They import goods to Canada from Europe and other eastern countries and we export goods from Canada like wheat and other natural resources we have in abundance."

"Gee, Ina, you sound like a tour guide or something," Gwendalyn said good-humoredly.

"Well, I pay attention in school and it's good to know about what's going on around you."

"I'm impressed," Gwendalyn said as they continued along the docks, looking at the different ships now docked in the harbour.

"You know, one of these ships may have brought over that beautiful dress you tried on at Chez Michelle's. I know they do a lot of the shipping of goods by air now-a-days but you never know."

"It was a beautiful dress," Gwendalyn agreed, feeling a little saddened by the fact that she couldn't afford to buy such a dress. "I wouldn't really be able to wear it that often anyhow, maybe for your party or Christmas concerts. I couldn't spend that much money just to have it hang in my closet and collect dust."

They saw two elderly men sitting on some wooden boxes having their lunch at the end of one of the docks and thought it might be nice to do the same. They seated themselves maybe six feet away on the wooden decking and proceeded to enjoy the picnic lunch Vera so lovingly prepared.

They overheard some of the conversation the two men were sharing and were enthralled by a story the man on the right was telling. Gwendalyn, after a while of deliberation, got up and approached the two and asked if they could sit with them and listen to their stories. They kindly agreed and so the two girls moved their picnic close enough to catch every detail of the interesting tale.

"Well, I guess I'd better start from the beginning now that we have an attentive audience," he said laughing. "As the story goes, and it's a true one at that, about 120 miles off the southern shore of Nova Scotia, there's an island called Sable Island that's known as 'The Graveyard of the Atlantic'. They call it 'The Graveyard of the Atlantic' because of the many shipwrecks on its coast. The water shallows unawares and storms cause ships to run aground and then get battered and beaten by the crashing waves. Many a captain and crew lost their lives over there. Well, there was this captain, Captain Timmons. I'll call him Captain Timmons because over the years I've forgotten his real name. He was out to sea for nine months and was due back about this time of the year. Yeah, it was April. He was due back in April. Well, April came and went and there was no sign of Captain Timmons. May drifted into June and still no Captain

Timmons. His beloved wife of twenty-eight years continued to wait and hope for his return. She had a 'walk' built on the roof of her house where she would go every morning and evening to walk back and forth gazing across the sea's horizon hoping for a glimpse of the sail that would tell her husband's ship was arriving. After years of waiting and hoping she realized with finality that her husband would never be returning, and that the sea had taken him from her. They called those rooftop walks 'Widow Walks' and to this day you can still see older houses with these 'Widow Walks' in place. Some captains took their wives and children along with them on their voyages and the sea claimed many of their lives as well."

"What a sad story," Ina said sighing, "but I would like to see some of those old houses with the 'Widow Walks' on them. You said it was over at Sable Island? Hey, Gwendalyn, maybe Daddy could take us over there and we could have a look."

"That would be great!" Gwendalyn agreed. "Do you know of any other interesting places we could visit and explore?"

"Well, there is an old fort called Port Royal Habitation over on the north shore of the Annapolis Valley," the man on the right began. "In the old days, the 1600's, a number of early settlers, Vikings, I believe, who survived a terrible winter made their way to this well-watered site. One of them was Samuel de Champlain who helped set up the 'habitation' fortress and built gristmills, planted grain and vegetables to ensure their survival. In 1613, I believe that was the year, the original fort was destroyed but was rebuilt in the late 1930's according to some drawings that Champlain had left behind. I've been there and I'm sure that would be an interesting place to visit if you're into history. If you go there in the spring you could also see the wonderful sight of all the apple trees in full blossom as well."

Both girls agreed that it would be interesting and listened attentively as the men continued with their story telling. They were so captivated that they hadn't realized the time but was reminded it was time to go by the sun starting to make its descent toward the western horizon.

"We thank you so much for your stories but I guess we've lost all track of time we really must make our way back home," Ina said putting the containers that held their refreshments back into the basket.

"Yes, thank you. It was really nice meeting you both. Thank you again," Gwendalyn called behind her as they hurried along the dock and then eventually onto the road leading them home.

CHAPTER 9
SURPRISES

Gwendalyn and Ina arrived back at the house at 5:40 PM and were relieved they still had time to freshen up and relax with Mrs. Evans in the parlor before dinner. Dr. Evans hadn't come home from the office, so the three ladies sat and talked.

"How was your day today, girls, and what did you find so interesting that kept you away for so long?" she asked.

"Momma, we met two elderly men on the docks and they had some wonderful stories to tell," informed Ina.

"And even some lessons in history about the area," added Gwendalyn.

"Please tell me all about it," Mrs. Evans asked. "I'm not sure what's keeping your father so this will be a good way to pass the time."

They delighted Mrs. Evans in relating the stories told by the men on the dock. She then expressed a desire to visit Sable Island and Port Royal Habitation saying that she would take it up with Dr. Evans, as they hadn't gotten around to any sort of sight-seeing since they moved here almost a year ago.

They were interrupted by voices coming from the front entrance. Dr. Evans had just gotten home and had with him someone whose voice sounded familiar. The voices got louder as the two men entered the parlor. Ina's eyes lightened up and she immediately began pushing imaginary strands of hair into place.

"Hello, my darling, how are you feeling?" Dr. Evans addressed his wife.

"Very well, thank you," Mrs. Evans replied. "I've been talking with the girls and they have some interesting tales they picked up today that you might get them to share."

"Indeed, sounds like an excellent way to spend this evening, relaxing and listening to stories. What do you think, Daniel?"

"Sounds good to me Dr. Evans," Daniel agreed.

"I guess you're all wondering why I've brought Daniel home with me again. Well, when we stopped at Grandma Elsa's Boarding House this morning to see if there were any rooms available, she said there weren't any today but come Friday one of the occupants would be moving out and the room would be available on Saturday. Daniel, here, was more than willing to stay at his hotel but I insisted that he spend the next few days with us. I know what it's like to be just starting out and he probably has student loans to pay off from attending medical school. There's no need for him to have to stay in a hotel when we've got plenty of room here. What do you say, my dear?"

"You're absolutely right, Edward. We have another guest bedroom next door to our room. I hope you know you're doing us a good turn by even coming to help at Edward's clinic, Daniel. He's been so busy that he hardly has time to spend with us anymore. So be our guest and enjoy your stay."

"Thank you, Mrs. Evans, you're too kind," he said sincerely, "and I hope these two lovely young ladies feel the same way."

"Yes, of course," Ina spoke up, "it'll be wonderful having you here with us."

"And what of you, Miss Gillard. Are you willing that I stay?"

"I wonder why you would ask my opinion as I am a guest here as you will be, but I welcome you as well. There is one thing that I ask."

"Anything," he said, smiling in a teasing way.

"Now that we will be living in the same house, I'd like it if you would call me Gwendalyn."

"And me, Ina," Ina put in.

"Done," he said, "and in return I'd like it if you both would call me Daniel instead of the too formal Mr. or Dr. Sorrenson. Friends usually go on a first name basis."

"Well, Daniel, let me help you carry your things up to your room before dinner," Dr. Evans offered, and the two made their way up the stairs leaving the girls to their conversation.

When the men came back down, Mrs. Evans and the girls met them in the foyer and announced that dinner was being served. They ate a wonderfully prepared meal started with a garden salad and rolls and followed by oven-baked lasagne. They finished their meal and Mrs. Evans asked Vera if she would bring tea and cookies to the parlor so they could visit in a more relaxing atmosphere.

"How about telling us some of those stories Ellen said you collected today?" Dr. Evans suggested.

Both girls took their turn in telling the tales that seemed to spell bound the listeners. When Gwendalyn was speaking, she saw that Daniel didn't move his gaze from her. She tried not to notice but many times throughout the evening she felt Daniel's eyes upon her again causing her to grow uncomfortably warm.

When the stories were told and several board games played, the group decided it was time to say 'good-night', and so each of them retired to their respective room.

* * *

Ina displayed her disappointment when she joined her mother and Gwendalyn in the dining room for breakfast and found that Daniel and her father had gotten a head start and left for work early. Gwendalyn, on the other hand, had felt a little relieved knowing she didn't have to face Daniel first thing this morning. There was something in his manner and behaviour towards her that made her feel uncomfortable and the feeling was growing. He was a perfect gentleman and his teasing was good-natured but there were times when the way he'd look at her made her feel exposed and vulnerable.

"I was wondering if you girls would like to come downtown shopping with me. I need to pick up a few more things for tomorrow and I'd really like the company," Mrs. Evans spoke up, interrupting the private thoughts around the table.

"Sure, Mrs. Evans, we'd love to come along. We didn't have any plans today, did we Ina?"

"Uh, what? I'm sorry. I guess I was off in thought," she said startled.

"Mrs. Evans was wondering if we could join her for some shopping and I was asking if you had any plans for us?"

"Oh no, no plans, we'd love to go with you Momma," she stated still trying to situate herself in the present. "When do you want to leave?"

"I think 11:00 o'clock will be fine and maybe we could have lunch together a little later and then stop by Edward's office to show

69

Gwendalyn what keeps him away from home so long."

Ina was thrilled about this new excursion and it was good to have her mood change so swiftly to this current happiness.

When they finished breakfast and talking about what was needed from the stores, they headed upstairs to prepare themselves for the trip downtown.

* * *

Mrs. Evans stopped at Chez Michelle's to pick up her dress she had left for alterations as well as to pick up a hairpiece for Ina to match her dress.

Gwendalyn stayed outside while mother and daughter concluded their business. She didn't want to lay her eyes upon the beautiful garment that she would never own and thus causing her more regret.

The three ladies went on to the needed shops and stopped at a restaurant for a tasty meal. Afterward, they proceeded to Evans' Medical Clinic. Dr. Evans was with a patient but Daniel came down the short hallway just as they came in the door.

"This is a welcomed surprise," he said cheerfully. "What is it that brings you to the office? No one is in need of medical attention?" he asked, as his countenance changed immediately from cheer to concern and his eyes darting to Gwendalyn.

"Oh, nothing of the sort," Mrs. Evans reassured him. "We've been shopping and just stopped by to show Gwendalyn the office on our way home."

Relief washed over Daniel as his cheerful manner returned.

"Ina, I'm told that you will be celebrating your sweet sixteenth birthday tomorrow night. It appears that I've come to Halifax at just the right time to meet some of the city's finest at your party tomorrow. It'll be an honour to help you celebrate your special day as I guess I'm invited as I am staying at your house."

"Of course, you're invited, silly," Ina giggled and feeling as if she would burst having Daniel address her so personally. "If things work out you'll be stepping into the role of Daddy's associate so I'd think that you'd be invited to all our family's celebrations."

From her position, Gwendalyn had been looking around the office and took notice of the furniture, posters, awaiting patients, and the nurse who was scheduling another appointment. She was saying that Dr. Evans was booked for the particular time the patient needed but Dr. Evans' associate, Dr. Sorrenson was available if she was interested.

"Great then," she said, "I'll write you down for 2:00 o'clock tomorrow, see you then, good-bye."

Gwendalyn smiled, feeling appreciative for the help Daniel had brought to Dr. Evans. He was such a kind man and he deserved to have his load lightened a little.

She felt embarrassed when she looked up to face a questioning but pleased look come across Daniel's face as if he heard the nurse's comments and then seen Gwendalyn's reaction to her scheduling a patient to see him.

"Oh, no," she thought, "he's reading more into my sentiments over the call than what is really there." She quickly looked away and was grateful when Dr. Evans came down the hall to meet with his family.

Mrs. Evans explained the reason for them dropping by and Dr. Evans escorted Gwendalyn to the different rooms in the Clinic that were void of patients explaining the necessity of each room.

Once the tour was over, the threesome headed outside and began the short trip home. Ina was excited about the attention she'd received from Daniel and was even more thrilled about Daniel being one of the guests for her special evening. Her mind raced on about how things might turn out.

Gwendalyn was glad when they got home and went to her room to rest before dinner. She took out her Bible but before she began to read she felt an urgency to talk to her Father about some things that couldn't wait until bedtime.

"Lord, I don't understand what's happening to me. All these new emotions I'm feeling are confusing. I know I'm growing up and my child-like views are changing, but I don't feel I'm ready for these changes I'm experiencing. The way Daniel looks at me disturbs me and I don't know him at all. I remember the way Anthony looked at me before I left, and I think something is changing in our friendship. It feels too sudden and too new. Lord, help me to understand what's happening and if it is Your will, help me to accept these changes and receive them with joy."

Gwendalyn flipped open her Bible to Psalm 32 and as if a direct answer to her prayer her eyes fell upon verse eight.

"I will instruct thee and teach thee in the way which thou shalt go: I will guide thee with mine eye."

"Thank you, Lord," she sighed. She read the verse over and over again allowing it to soothe her soul and her emotions. She continued to flip through her Bible and felt directed to Jeremiah 29:11.

"For I know the thoughts I think toward you, saith the Lord, thoughts of peace, and not of evil, to give you and expected end."

"Oh Lord, You know me and every situation I am in," she whispered gratefully, "thank You that I can come to You and I thank You that You answer me so quickly to deliver me from the trials of my soul. Forgive me, Lord, for allowing things around me to make me so ill at ease when I know You are always watching over me and guiding my way. Help me to be more at peace and trust You to see me through whatever I face in this life You have given me."

She continued to read in Jeremiah 29 at verse twelve and was again reassured with the loving words of her Heavenly Father.

"Then shall ye call upon me, and ye shall go and pray unto me, and I will hearken unto you. And ye shall seek me, and find me, when ye shall search for me with all your heart. And I will be found of you, saith the Lord."

Gwendalyn laid back on her bed as love and peace sent from the Comforter enveloped her and gave her the sense that everything was well and that her Heavenly Father was indeed watching over her and directing her path. She had the assurance that her life was in her Lord. She knew she needn't worry or be concerned because no matter what, her Heavenly Father would see her through any difficult situations.

A knock on the door called her temporarily from the intimacy she and her Lord were having.

"Come in," she called.

The door slowly opened and Ina entered the room and sat on the edge of Gwendalyn's bed.

"Did I wake you?" she asked.

"Oh no, I wasn't asleep. I was just talking with God and He has, once again, reminded me of His love and caring ways."

"This is still pretty new to me, having a relationship with God.

What were you talking to Him about?"

Gwendalyn didn't want to get into any details about her concerns about Anthony, or especially Daniel, as to not upset her friend. She realized Ina was fond of him by the way she had heard her going on about him and the way she acted when she was around him.

"I guess I was concerned about the future and the way my life is going. I guess I needed some direction and answers."

"Did you get your 'answers'?" Ina asked curiously.

"Well, not anything definite but I know now, and I guess I've always known, that I just need to trust God with my questions and my future."

Gwendalyn went on to tell Ina how she was feeling, leaving out some details, and how she prayed for guidance. She told her how God had directed her to scriptures and she shared each scripture with her friend.

She looked up to find Ina trying to blink away the tears that were now slipping from her eyes and sliding down her cheeks.

"Gwen, I want to have that kind of a relationship with Him as well. You seem to have such a great faith and when you pray, God answers you. I wonder if I'll ever be that close to God," she said, feeling a little downhearted.

"Ina, it's just like the scripture says back in Jeremiah 29: 12 to 14." She read again from the scriptures: *"Then ye shall call upon me, and ye shall go and pray unto me, and I will hearken unto you. And ye shall seek me, and find me, when ye shall search for me with all your heart. And I will be found of you, saith the Lord."*

"This a promise to you, Ina, from God. He's just waiting for you to call out to Him and sincerely seek Him. He wants to talk with you and give you joy and peace and all He asks is that you come to Him and develop that relationship with Him."

"Gwen, you make it seem all so simple. I guess I can pray to Him and ask Him to help me, but it seems so hard and I don't even have a Bible to call my own."

Gwendalyn had to restrain herself from getting the birthday gift she had for Ina. This gift would be cherished, she knew, but receiving it on her sixteenth birthday would be a remembrance of the prior week when she had given her life over to Jesus.

73

"There is the Family Bible in the library, Ina. Make it a priority to spend time with God and He will reward you the way He rewards me with His words of comfort and giving me inner joy and peace. The relationship you long to have with Him will develop and grow as you continue to spend time with Him and trust Him to take care of you."

"I know you're right, Gwen, and I do want to be close to God so I guess the rest is up to me to start things happening. Hopefully, soon, I'll have a relationship with God the way you do."

"Each one's relationship with the Lord is somewhat different but if we continue to seek Him and do His will, we will have a personal intimate relationship with Him that none other can compare with. It'll be fulfilling and satisfying and that's what brings the inner joy and peace."

CHAPTER 10
SWEET SIXTEEN

Another beautiful day dawned as if in agreement to wishing Ina a happy birthday. Gwendalyn met the family in the dining room early this morning before Doctors Evans and Sorrenson left for work. She was a little embarrassed being the last one to enter the dining room. She apologized and proceeded to take her place on Dr. Evans' left, next to Daniel.

"No need for apologies, dear," Mrs. Evans spoke up, "we're here just minutes ahead of you."

"Good morning, Gwendalyn," said Daniel, as he got up to help her with her chair.

"Good morning, Daniel," she returned cheerfully, "and thank you." She couldn't help but notice the change in her own disposition and attitude toward Daniel and it seemed that she was more relaxed around him as if it had always been natural to be so.

She greeted Mr. and Mrs. Evans and Ina in the same cheerful manner. She felt so happy and lightened, and it was good to experience the definite contrast to the way she felt yesterday. She had entered her room after the day of shopping with troubling thoughts and emotions.

Most of the attention around the table was directed towards Ina with today being her sweet sixteenth birthday and all.

With breakfast over and the doctors gone off to the clinic, the three ladies went about the house discussing the final preparations, with Mrs. Evans instructing the 'help' as to things yet needing to be done. Extra 'help' were hired for the day and to serve this evening's event. Alfred was instructed to pick up Ina's great Aunt Katherine from Toronto at the Halifax Airport at 3:30 PM. She would then arrive in plenty of time for an early supper before the party started. She would be staying till Sunday.

With everything now in order and the time reading 12:35 PM, the three ladies gathered in the dining room for a light lunch consisting of chicken vegetable soup with egg salad sandwiches.

After lunch Mrs. Evans went to the parlor to rest and continue on her cross-stitch project while Gwendalyn and Ina made their way upstairs. They would spend the afternoon relaxing, chatting, and getting ready for this evening's occasion. With Ina having bathed this morning, Gwendalyn decided this would be the best time to enjoy a long soak in the tub.

When she was back in her room, she took out her newest best dress. Her dad had once again surprised her at Christmas with this beautiful gift. It was yellow with butterflies and although it was a little big and cool for the winter months, it fit perfectly now and would be ideal for this springtime celebration. She had borrowed Stacey's yellow ribbon to put the finishing touches on her hair.

She heard a knock on her door and look over to see Ina coming in holding up a hanger supporting a dress with a large white plastic covering protecting it and hiding it from view.

"Oh Ina, it's your birthday dress, isn't it?" she questioned. "I know it's early but would you try it on and let me see you in it again?"

"OK," she agreed excitedly, "but you'll have to turn around so I can get it on."

Gwendalyn turned around and heard the rustle of the plastic coming off the hanger and began to imagine how beautiful her friend would look in her new fashionable gown.

"Ready!" she exclaimed.

"That was fas..." Gwendalyn was about to say, but the words caught in her throat. Ina was holding up to her shoulders the beautiful teal green dress Gwendalyn had tried on a couple of days before in that fine clothing store.

"Ina! What have you done?" she whispered as her voice cracked.

"I told Momma all about you trying this on and when we went back to Chez Michelle's, I showed it to Momma and she and I agreed that you should have it."

"But..."

"But nothing. You've come such a long way and you're spending your entire Easter Break with us, we wanted to give you something. It's your Easter present."

"I don't know what to say," she gasped.

"Just say 'thank you' and look beautiful for my birthday party tonight. There is just one problem."

"What's that?"

"I think you're going to be the prettiest girl there and steal the show," she said jokingly, and putting on the biggest pout she could muster.

"Oh Ina, you are beautiful and with this being your birthday and you wearing your gorgeous satin ivory dress, all eyes will be on you."

Gwendalyn rushed to Ina and hugged her tightly pinning the garment between them.

"Thank you so much, my dearest good friend."

"You're wrinkling it," Ina exclaimed.

"It doesn't matter," she said tearfully, "your friendship is worth more to me than even this wonderful dress."

"I'm glad you feel that way," Ina said pulling herself away, "but you're still going to look great for my party."

The girls spent the afternoon together fussing with each other's hair as to the best style to be worn tonight but quickly tied it loosely behind them when they heard the dinner bell summoning them to come for dinner. They were shocked when they looked at the clock and read it being 5:15 PM.

They rushed into the dining room to find Dr. and Mrs. Evans, Daniel, and great Aunt Katherine waiting patiently for them to arrive. After they made their apologies, Ina greeted her Aunt with a kiss and introduced Gwendalyn to her. They sat down quickly and bowed their heads while Dr. Evans said grace. Everyone chatted excitedly about Ina's birthday party and Aunt Katherine being there.

Dinner was finished before 6:00 PM and everyone dispersed to finish getting ready before the guests, who were due to arrive at 7:30 PM, showed up.

* * *

It was 7:40 PM when Gwendalyn suggested she go downstairs to stand with the other guests to await and applaud the honoured birthday girl as she made her entrance.

Ina agreed and so Gwendalyn made her way slowly down the stairs. She had to go slowly because of the borrowed shoes she wore belonging to Ina. They were comfortable enough but the heels were a little high for her liking. She felt as if she would tumble forward any moment. Her hair was neatly done with two small braids formed from the front sections with narrow strips of teal green ribbon braided throughout it. The two decorated braids were then joined at the back and tied in a minute bow with longer pieces of the thin ribbon hanging with the remainder of the shining well-groomed hair.

She was part way down when she noticed Daniel watching her. He smiled at her looking very pleased and as she stepped to the floor Daniel made his way toward her. He then took her hand, lifted it to his lips, and kissed it.

"You look absolutely lovely," he complimented softly, now gazing deeply into her sea green eyes.

Gwendalyn hadn't expected this greeting and looked for a way to end this intimate encounter. From across the room she spied Dr. and Mrs. Evans coming over to see her.

"Gwendalyn, dear, don't you look radiant!" Mrs. Evans exclaimed while taking her to the side discussing some events that were to take place a little later as Dr. Evans conversed with Daniel.

"Oh, Mrs. Evans, thank you so much for this beautiful dress. It was very thoughtful and generous of you to buy this for me," Gwendalyn said, feeling very relieved to be excused from Daniel's company.

"You're welcome, my dear. Edward and I were talking and we really appreciate you being such a good friend to Ina. She seems so different since you've come here, so much more considerate and something else that I just can't seem to understand. I think you are very good for her and this is one way that I can express my appreciation."

"Thank you, Mrs. Evans, you're too kind," she replied.

All attention in the room was directed to Dr. Evans who stood at the top of the stairs announcing the entrance of his only daughter.

"Ladies and gentlemen, may I have your attention please," his voice boomed. "I am pleased that you have all come out this fine evening to join us in celebrating the sixteenth birthday of our dear Ina. And now, here she is, our daughter, Ina Evans."

Ina stepped out of the shadows of the hallway and joined her father at the head of the stairs. Her beautiful blond hair was gathered and pinned at the back as curled wisps of hair graced her attractive face. She proceeded to make her way down, followed by her father, as the guests cheered and applauded. She mingled throughout the crowd greeting each guest personally. When she came to Daniel, Gwendalyn watched as he took her hand and kissed it in the same way he had before with herself. She again felt relieved that this act of greeting wasn't meant for her alone and she saw that Ina enjoyed it immensely. He didn't hold Ina's gaze as he had done with her, but went on to compliment her on her beauty and offer her his arm to escort her in continuing to greet her guests.

* * *

The hors d'oeuvres and champagne were served constantly as the evening went on. The hum of chatter was constant and music and dancing was enjoyed by most. Ina could be seen smiling excitedly while enjoying being complimented and fussed over on this, her special day. She enjoyed several dances with her father, her friends, and especially Daniel.

Gwendalyn had tried with all her ability to stay off the dance floor, as dancing wasn't part of the way she was raised. She was rewarded for her efforts as she managed to, gratefully, steer clear of some would-be partners. Jonathon had almost caught up with her but was sidetracked when Carmen called him to dance with her.

There was a table, with two chairs, piled high with gifts in the foyer, as this was the biggest open space in the house and the guest were called to it saying that the 'birthday girl' would now be opening them.

Ina took Gwendalyn by the hand saying it was time for her to write the names of the guest and what gift they brought so she could send out thank you cards later. Gwendalyn knew this was coming as they had discussed it earlier in the day.

They both took a chair at the table and Ina began opening her gifts. Among the many, there was a gold necklace supporting a cross with a tiny diamond in the centre from Aunt Lucille, which really touched her heart. Next she opened a bottle of the 'most exquisite perfume', Ina had said, from Daniel. It wouldn't have mattered if he had picked it up at the corner store, and paid very little, but because it was from Daniel,

79

she was thrilled. Her parents had given her diamond earrings, diamonds being the birthstone for the month of April. She was nearing the end when she picked up the package from Gwendalyn.

"A book?" she questioned looking at her friend.

Gwendalyn just shrugged her shoulders and said, "Open it and see."

She tore off the remainder of the wrapping paper and the precious Gift she now held in her hand caused her to go silent. She ran her finger across the delicate lettering that spelled her name and opened the Book to find an inscription.

"Presented to Ina Evans
By Gwendalyn Gillard
On April 14, 1950
Psalm 32:8, Jeremiah 29: 11-13"

She looked at Gwendalyn; her eyes glistening with unshed tears. She got up from her chair and went to Gwendalyn placing her arms around her neck, and hugging her meaningfully.

"Thank you so much," she whispered. "You know how much this means to me. I will treasure it for always."

She went back to her chair wiping her eyes and regaining her composure before sitting to face her onlookers. She continued with opening the remainder of the gifts and thanked every one for their generosity.

With the dancing continuing and everyone gone back to enjoying themselves, Gwendalyn stood looking at the newly opened gifts and without knowing, Franklin took her hand and guided her to the dance floor. She didn't have time to object as they were already in the middle of a group of dancers and there was nothing to do but get it over with. She could dance fairly well but she never had the desire to do so. When the music finally ended she made her way as quick as possible, but not quick enough because Jonathon, who had been watching and waiting for his chance grabbed her hand and fairly dragged her into the group of dancers once again. A waltz began to play and feeling even more uncomfortable, Gwendalyn longed for it to be over. They had just barely begun when Daniel came up to Jonathon, tapped him on the shoulder.

"May I cut in?" he asked very gentleman-like.

Jonathon had no other option but to exit the floor leaving Daniel to place his arms around Gwendalyn and enjoy the moment.

Gwendalyn felt a little more comfortable dancing with Daniel but was again longing for the music to end. To her relief he led the way to the door and they exited onto the porch where Gwendalyn drew in a long breath of cool, fresh air.

Daniel continued to hold her in the dancing position and began again on their 'private dance floor' with the music filtering from the house. This was an altogether too intimate a scene for Gwendalyn and she again felt very uncomfortable.

When the music ended, she breathed out a sigh and was beginning to step away toward the porch chairs when Daniel, continuing to hold her, lifted her chin toward him and lowered his lips to meet hers. A tingling sensation swept through her and she responded for an instant but in a burst of realization of what was going on she pushed him away and headed down the porch toward the swing. She didn't sit down for fear he would join her. She had to be alone. She couldn't go back in the house and face the crowd for fear that Ina would see her in her frazzled state and ask too many questions. Did she actually feel those sensations tingle through her body? What was going on? She was confused, shaken. Her mind was going in all directions.

"What am I to do?" she whispered, barely audible.

"You don't have to do anything," came Daniel's gentle voice behind her. "I'm sorry Gwendalyn, I didn't mean to do that. I've been thinking about you a lot since the day I helped you up after you fell off that planter. When I looked into your face that day I knew I hadn't seen anyone so beautiful. And when I looked into your eyes this evening it was like looking into the eyes of purity and maturity. My thoughts got carried away with having you in my arms, and the next thing to do to complete the moment was to kiss you."

"Daniel, you don't understand, I'm only fifteen. I'm not ready for this now."

"I know, I shouldn't have done it. It was wrong and I'm sorry. Come and sit down. I want to talk to you."

"Maybe I should go in. Ina may be looking for me."

Gwendalyn tried to leave the spot where she stood but for the moment her whole being trembled and she couldn't bring herself to do anything but breathe in the cool air. She was glad it was cool, as her flushed cheeks needed time to settle before re-entering the large gathering.

"Please don't go. There's something I need to tell you and ask you. You're going back to Newfoundland tomorrow and I may not ever see you again. Please sit down."

Gwendalyn weakly agreed to sit on the double swing but far enough to keep some distance between them.

"When I first met you on Wednesday... and eh, I know it's all of a sudden-like, with today being only Friday... two days, hm, that is rather quick-like," Daniel stumbled through the difficult words and then asked a direct question. "Do you believe in love-at-first-sight?"

Gwendalyn looked at him with a perplexed and astonished look on her face but he held up his hand as if to say 'hold on a minute'.

"Well, what I want to say is that I believe I started to experience feelings of love toward you from the moment I helped you up off the snow. It filled me with a wanting to see you and be with you. I'm sorry. I know this must be too much but I have to ask you one thing because as I said before, I may not ever see you again. I don't know if you have any feelings for me but, do you think, eh, would you be willing to keep me in mind when you start thinking about men. I've decided in my heart that I'd be willing to wait for you if you could tell me there is a chance you may grow to care for me the way I am already beginning to care for you?"

"I don't know Daniel, we've just met and I'm not sure how I feel about you."

"Before you go any further I want to tell you that if we were to end up together I could care and provide for you more than adequately. I worked hard in high school, graduating when I was only sixteen and won enough scholarships to put myself through medical school along with my parents helping me, seeing my dedication toward my future. You don't see many doctors around at my age. I've worked hard, taking extra courses through the regular school year and continuing with my studies throughout the summer months to achieve my goals early. I don't have any student loans to pay off as Dr. Evans suggested, and I could save enough in the next few years to provide a home for us.

We could build a secure life together."

"This is too much to consider right now. I'm sorry, Daniel, I can't give you the answer you're looking for, and besides, you've seen the way Ina looks at you. I would be going against my best friend to give you a 'yes' answer, knowing how she feels."

"I don't feel the same way towards her as I do toward you and I'm not sure if I ever will. It's you who caught my attention, not her. Sure, she's beautiful, but the beauty I saw in you goes much deeper than your face, I imagine."

"I'm sorry, Daniel, I must go."

She gathered all the strength she could and managed to leave him seated in the swing, alone. A part of her wanted to go back and give him the answer he so desired because of his sincerity and the honesty that flowed from him. He seemed to really care for her and he went on to tell her all the ways he would provide for her. The way he talked made her believe he would do just that given the chance. Maybe love-at-first-sight was real but she hadn't experienced it even if he had. She knew he had opened up things a man wouldn't ever tell someone he so recently met. She could understand his reasoning why. She was leaving tomorrow and it seemed he already had sincere deep feelings for her. But she couldn't commit herself to a man she didn't love and hardly knew. Maybe she could learn to love him with his exterior features and structure being so attractive, but to give such an answer after meeting him just two days ago grated against her sensible nature.

She saw the front door open and felt suddenly exposed. She feared Ina would be the one to come out onto the porch. To her relief it was two of the guests leaving for home and she managed to make her way back in without being noticed.

Ina finally caught up with her, apologizing for not spending as much time with her as she would have wanted. She said she was so busy visiting and dancing that she missed seeing her for a while.

"I did see you dancing with Franklin, though," she giggled.

Gwendalyn was glad her friend had not noticed her leaving the party with Daniel, or missed her during their time on the porch. The last thing she would ever want to do was to hurt Ina on her special day. She couldn't and wouldn't tell Ina about what had happened. It would have to be a secret she would tuck deep inside her heart. She hoped

Daniel would do the same and eventually forget it.

Guests continued to leave and Ina with her parents bidding them 'good-night' and thanking them for coming. Just before midnight all had left except for the help who were now busy picking up glasses and napkins and straightening and cleaning the messy rooms used for the entertaining.

Great Aunt Katherine was shown to Ina's room, where she would be spending the night until tomorrow. She would then be using the guest bedroom where Gwendalyn was staying, as Gwendalyn would be leaving the next day to head back home. Ina would be sharing the bedroom with her friend, which excited them both, as this was Gwendalyn's last night in their home.

They went to bed that night with their minds so full they each felt they would burst from it. Ina talked on and on about the many wonderful things that had happened throughout the evening.

Gwendalyn was quite willing that she talk as much as she wanted, as it would save her the awkwardness of trying to talk about things that now seemed so trivial after what had happened on the porch with her and Daniel. Finally, exhausted, they both fell asleep.

CHAPTER 11
NEW BEGINNINGS

Gwendalyn awoke early the next morning, quietly dressed, and prepared herself for a walk outside. Everything was still and quiet and it seemed that every step she made was enough to wake the entire household.

She wanted to take a last walk around the immediate area of the Evans home and it was good to be outside to watch the sun make its ascent over the horizon.

"It's beautiful, isn't it," the husky voice behind her startled her, causing her to unintentionally jump.

"Sorry," Daniel said, "I didn't mean to scare you."

"Oh, it's OK. I thought I'd be the only one silly enough to get up so early after such a late night."

"I guess I joined the 'silly' club," he said humorously. "About last night," he continued, changing to a more serious tone, "I wanted to apologize for my behaviour and..."

"No don't," Gwendalyn cut in, "I'm sorry too. I've been doing a lot of thinking and I know it must have taken a lot of courage for you to say all the things you said last night. It's very flattering that I would have such an effect on someone, even being so young. I hope you understand why I can't answer your proposal, eh, I didn't mean proposal. I just meant that..."

"I know what you meant and I do understand. Last night I was so overrun by emotions and longing that I didn't behave properly at all. I'm sorry. I think I've discovered something within you that impels me to allow you to grow and discover your own feelings. Maybe one day our paths will cross again and you may realize that I may be the man to make your dreams come true. Heck, I'm young yet, just 21, and perhaps I may be a little irrational in my thinking at times."

Gwendalyn felt a little more at ease being with Daniel this morning as his manner seemed a little more relaxed and somewhat reserved.

"How about a walk down to the harbour?" he asked. "I haven't seen it and it looks like a great morning for a refreshing walk."

"Well, I'm not sure if we'd have time before the rest of the family gets up. What time is it now? It'll take an hour to get there and back without even going out on the docks."

"It's 6:50 AM. I think we'd be back long before they awake. It was a late night last night and with everyone now relaxed that the big night is over, I'd be surprised if we see anyone before 10:00 AM."

"OK then, I'd love to see the harbour again before I leave."

* * *

They walked on in silence for a time enjoying the freshness of the morning.

"How'd you sleep last night?" Gwendalyn asked, breaking the silence.

"Well, to be truthful, not very well. I kept tossing and turning and criticizing myself for the way I acted last night. I really am sorry and I hope you believe me. How was your sleep?"

"I guess I didn't sleep too well either. Too many dreams were bothering me to allow me to sleep peacefully. By the way, I do believe that you're sorry about what happened so let's not talk about it any further, OK?"

"OK, Gwendalyn, you've got a deal. How about we shake hands on it and start again as friends?"

"All right, friends," she said, and although she felt a little awkward, she offered her hand and he willingly took it.

They again walked in silence until they saw the harbour front and once again its beauty awed her especially with the sun's reflection now glistening on the rippling waters.

Daniel's long sigh among the words "O-o-oh my-y" let Gwendalyn know just how much he appreciated this visit to the harbour.

"It is beautiful, isn't it?" she stated more than questioning.

"It sure is, and the grand ships tied to the docks are magnificent."

They continued to make their way down to the docks and walked along commenting on the different features of the many ships. They came upon a large rusted anchor lying on the dock entangled among some ropes.

They continued to walk along and without thinking Gwendalyn began singing.

"We have an anchor that keeps the soul
Steadfast and sure while the billows roll
Fastened to the Rock which cannot move
Grounded firm and deep in the Saviour's love. "

"Wow, that was beautiful. You have a beautiful voice, Gwendalyn." Daniel paused. "That song has something to do with God, doesn't it?"

"Yes, it does," she answered, "but I'm a little embarrassed that I began singing and especially without warning you."

"I'm glad you felt relaxed enough around me to do it, and I did enjoy your singing."

Gwendalyn blushed a little and then went on to tell Daniel the meaning of what she had just sung.

"I would say it means that no matter what happens in life, we have an anchor, Jesus, that we can cling to. He's the anchor that secures us and sees us through any rough or sorrowful events that may otherwise defeat us."

Gwendalyn wanted to asked Daniel about his stand with God but felt a struggle to get the words out. She repeated the words over and over in her mind and finally became bold enough to let them out.

"Do you know Jesus as that personal anchor to get you through trying times?"

"No," he said firmly, "and I'd rather not talk about it."

Straight away, Gwendalyn knew she had touched on a sensitive subject that caused Daniel pain and her heart went out to him. She prayed silently that the Lord would pour His love into his heart and heal the wounds that caused his pain.

They began walking back across the docks in silence and once again proceeded to ascend the hill leading to the Evans home. It was a long walk because of the silence and as they approached the driveway Daniel spoke up.

"I'm sorry for snapping at you down at the docks. It's just something I'm having trouble dealing with and I guess I don't have any room for God just yet. I hope you understand."

"It's OK, Daniel, people go through troubled times but I've found that God can be a source of strength when He's asked."

87

"I respect your views, Gwendalyn, because I feel you are a good person inside, but I think we'd better leave religion out of our topics for discussion."

"Very well, Daniel, but I will pray for you whether you like it or not," she spoke out adamantly, noting the boldness in her voice.

"I think I like the fact that you'd be praying for me, as that means you'd have to be thinking of me to be praying for me, and I like that thought," he said smiling.

As they made their way up to the porch, Daniel said he would like to sit in the sunshine for a while longer so Gwendalyn entered the house alone. Everything was still and quiet so she made her way to the parlor and was delighted to find that Vera had started a fire in the fireplace. She looked at the clock above the mantel and the time read 8:20 AM. She was thankful she didn't meet Ina as she came into the house. 'Too much to explain,' she decided.

She laid her now wearisome frame down on the sofa and soon found herself drifting off in an easy slumber.

Daniel had come in and found her asleep and stood in the doorway admiring this 'sleeping beauty'.

"It's no wonder that I find you so attractive and appealing," he whispered softly. "You are beautiful and your manner and disposition rates you far above anyone I know. I do hope that someday you will have feelings of love towards me as well. Sweet dreams, princess."

He turned to leave her and headed upstairs to begin putting his things together for the move to the boarding house later this morning.

Gwendalyn stirred to being almost awake as she heard someone humming and skipping down the stairs.

"There you are, Gwen," announced Ina. "I was wondering where you were when I awoke and found you gone."

"I couldn't sleep so I went for a walk," she said between yawns and look up at the clock, amazed that the time now read 10:45 AM.

"Good morning, ladies," greeted Daniel as he joined them in the parlor.

"Good morning, Daniel," Ina returned, putting on her sweetest smile and motioning for him to take the seat across from them.

"I'm glad you could join us before brunch."

"I was intending to leave right away to secure my room at the boarding house," he returned. "I wouldn't want someone else to move in there before I get a chance."

"I'm sure Elsa will be holding your room for you, especially since you and Daddy went to see her and arranged for just that. Please stay for brunch. It'll be the last time all of us will be having a meal together," Ina went on. "Won't you consider staying? Besides you couldn't possibly leave without saying good-bye to Momma and Daddy."

"Yes, I suppose you're right. Of course I'll stay," he resigned.

"Great then. Why don't we seat ourselves in the dining room? I believe Aunt Katherine is already there and Daddy and Momma should be on their way."

"Sounds great to me," Gwendalyn joined in. "I'm starved."

Dr. and Mrs. Evans met the others in the dining room and they all enjoyed a leisurely meal together.

CHAPTER 12
THE STORM

The Evans family, along with Gwendalyn, met in the foyer to say good-bye to their newly acquainted friend and associate, Daniel Sorrenson, who was leaving to get settled in his new home. Aunt Katherine had already bid him farewell and now was resting in the parlor.

"Thank you for your hospitality and generosity. You've made my first days here in Halifax very enjoyable. It'll be a time I'll never forget," Daniel said, casting a quick glance toward Gwendalyn. "And it was a pleasure to share in your birthday celebration, Ina."

"I'm glad you could be here," Ina said. "You made my day more special than you could imagine. Come and visit us often."

"I would like that very much," he stated, and then turned his attention to Gwendalyn. "I'm glad for the opportunity of meeting you, Gwendalyn," he said shaking her hand and inconspicuously placing a folded note into her palm. "I hope you have a safe journey back to your home."

"Thank you, Daniel, she returned, trying to hide, from the others, the questioning expression she was sure was readable on her face. "I wish you all the best for your future."

"It was a pleasure having you with us," Dr. Evans spoke up. "Alfred will take you to the boarding house and I guess I'll see you Monday morning."

With that Daniel was gone and now it was time to prepare for the long journey back to Newfoundland to see Gwendalyn safely back home. Mrs. Evans wouldn't be joining them for the trip, as she would be visiting with Aunt Katherine.

The ride to Sydney seemed to go rather quickly as the girls chatted on about the week they'd had and continued on planning when they could get together again. Gwendalyn's sixteenth birthday was coming up on June 30 and she was insisting that Ina be there to celebrate with her. Ina had told her that she'd hope to be able to come and spend a few days and then bring Gwendalyn back to Nova Scotia for possibly another week.

They had gotten settled on the ferry and were now sleeping in their berth when some of their belongings, which were stowed on the bunk above Ina, came crashing down. In an instant they were all awake, and from the heaving of the ship, and the mess on the floor, they realized what had happened.

"The sea is kind of rough tonight," Gwendalyn said.

"I'd call this more than rough!" Ina exclaimed, concern showing on her face.

"We'll be just fine," her father consoled. "I'm sure they run into this kind of weather all the time and end up getting safely to their destination. Try to relax and get some rest."

They laid down taking comfort from Dr. Evans words and tried to fall back to sleep despite the tossing of the ship. Soon it was impossible to lie comfortably on the beds, as they had to continually hold the sides to keep from rolling off.

"Daddy, it's getting worse. What's going to happen to us?"

"Relax my dear. If there was anything to be worried about, I'm sure the ship's staff would come around to give us instructions as to what to do to ensure our safety."

"Yes, Ina, I've spent many days on the sea in a little boat. At times I felt like we would overturn but it never happened. I'm sure it's a lot safer in a ship as big as this one."

"I suppose you're right but it sure is scary."

Things continued to get progressively worse and the three frightened passengers huddled on the bottom bunk trying to console each other. Both Ina and Dr. Evans had gotten seasick and were feeling quite ill. Worry was now etched in their pale faces.

It was about this time that a ship's steward knocked on the door and entered their cabin. He went to a cupboard and pulled out three life vests.

"Captain's orders," he said firmly, trying to catch his breath. "Everyone has to put these on in case of the possibility of abandoning ship. We've hit some unexpected bad weather, the worst he's ever encountered, the Captain says, and the ship's taking a beating. We have lifeboats available if we need them, but until then stay in your cabin. I'll be back if the captain gives the order."

With the steward gone, the more-frightened trio fastened their life vests securely in place.

Gwendalyn, no longer concerned about Dr. Evans possible views concerning God, began to pray aloud in earnest for their safety and the safety of the ship. Ina immediately closed her eyes agreeing with her and adding her pleas to the only One who could now see them through to safety. To the girls' surprise, Dr. Evans joined their petition to the Heavenly Protector asking Him to deliver them from an unsure fate. When the amens were said they looked into each other's tear-stained faces knowing and realizing that their lives were in the hand of God and the only thing to do now was to trust and hope for the best.

Gwendalyn broke the tense silence as she began singing a song of God's love and how He is in control of even the wind and the rain. She continued to sing this over and over again allowing her faith in the Almighty to soothe her troubled mind and soul. The violent rocking of the ship continued but the tension amongst the group seemed to have lightened slightly. As Gwendalyn sang the chorus again, Ina joined her and soon after the masculine voice of Dr. Evans could be heard amidst the singing.

Was it the peace and reassurance, that now filled the room, calming the terror of the night, or had the ship's rocking actually eased somewhat? The answer was given when the same ship's steward came bursting into their cabin announcing that they had passed through the worst of the storm and that they were now headed into calmer water.

"Praise the Lord!" Gwendalyn shouted, breathing a deep sigh of relief.

"Thank God," came Dr. Evans reply as he hugged his daughter.

"Oh Daddy, I was so scared," Ina cried, allowing tears of joy and relief wash away her fears.

* * *

Dr. Evans started up a discussion by asking Gwendalyn some questions concerning her faith in God. Before too long he expressed a desire to know more about having a relationship with God. He was saying that because of her sense of calm and her trust in the Lord throughout the storm, he believed that all he had been taught as a child about God and

Jesus, had to be true. He had been considering the things of God for quite some time now and had gone through the questioning and debating in his own heart. He had talked many times with Aunt Lucille and now, after getting safely through the storm, knowing the Lord's hand was in it, he was ready to commit his life to Him.

Dr. Evans prayed to receive Jesus in his heart and as he did, tears of repentance kept trickling down his rugged cheeks. There was heart-felt sincerity in his prayer, and the presence of the Holy Spirit was so strong, that Gwendalyn and Ina both wept giving praise to God for the two miracles that had just taken place.

The rest of the journey went smoothly and when the two girls parted company they both agreed to write frequently until they could be together again.

CHAPTER 13
HOME

Homecoming was sweet and for days Gwendalyn sat on the couch with one of her parents or in one of her sibling's bedroom sharing some of the many stories of her adventuresome week.

Calvin had told Gwendalyn how much he appreciated the gloves she brought back for him. Dad went on about how thoughtful his little girl was and immediately placed the new hat on his balding head. Mom was surprised and pleased to find that Gwendalyn had brought her the delicately embroidered handkerchiefs and Stacey loved the scent of the new perfume she had picked out for her.

During the weeks after her return home, Gwendalyn fitted back into her regular routine of attending school, helping Mom around the house, and working with Dad fixing nets and preparing for the new fishing season about ready to start.

She was happy to see all her friends again, but most of all Anthony. She had presented him with his scarf, placing it around his neck. He went on about how special he thought it was and smoothed its softness over his cheek and then bent over to do the same with her.

When she had first returned, he had seemed anxious and a little out of sorts but as they started chumming around again he was once again his old self. Some Sundays they would walk down to the wharf and talk about how busy things would be once the ice was gone out of the bay. They had spent a lot of time together when they were growing up but now, at times, Gwendalyn sensed something peculiar about Anthony. The way he looked at her or when their eyes met. It was strange but a little familiar as she recalled similar instances when Daniel had looked at her the same way. She connected the two and smiled with an inner pleasure knowing that Anthony was growing to care for her in an intimate way. She had always cared for Anthony and even as a child, in her child-like thinking, she thought that, one day, when she grew up, she would like to marry Anthony. She often joked with her friends saying that this is what would happen.

She shared almost everything with Anthony that she had experienced while in Nova Scotia being careful to leave out anything connected with Daniel. Now that she realized Anthony's growing feelings towards her, although he never made it known in words, she wouldn't hurt him in the least by mentioning something that soon would be forgotten. Daniel had come in like a strong and somewhat excitable wind, but had just as quickly blown past her with only the fading memories left behind.

She felt so comfortable with Anthony. He was never pushy, and in all the years she had known him, he had never presumed to steal a kiss as Daniel had done. Even if his kiss made something within her come alive that she wasn't familiar with. She remembered the tingling sensations that caused her to tremble.

"Now where did that come from?"

She scolded herself for recalling such memories.

"It'll not happen again,' she firmly decided, concentrating on the task at hand of washing dishes to keep her from her reverie.

Her mother came back into the kitchen and helped with drying the dishes she had washed and began stacking them in the cupboard.

"You were saying that Ina has permission to come to your sixteenth birthday party?" she inquired.

"Yes, Mom. I got a letter from her last week saying that her mother was willing to let her come. I remember her dad saying it was OK with him on our way back home but he'd have to discuss it with Mrs. Evans. I'm not sure how long she'll be staying but, Mom, do you realize that Dr. Evans will be staying here as long as Ina will be?"

"Yes, I figured he wouldn't be able to take a lot of time off work to bring her here and then have to come all that way again to take her back, him being a doctor and all."

"You know, Mom, he is able to take a little more time off work now that he has an associate working with him. He came in from Toronto while I was there."

"Really. That's wonderful. It must've helped him a great deal from what you told me about him being so busy and not having enough time to spend with his family. Did you get to meet this new doctor?"

"Yes, I did. His name is Daniel Sorrenson and Ina told me in her letter that things are working out just great with the arrangement."

"Well, I'm very glad for him." She paused. "Daniel Sorrenson, hm, I never heard you mention him since you were back."

"Ah, I met him at the office one time when Mrs. Evans, Ina, and I stopped at the clinic on our way back from a shopping trip in downtown Halifax."

Gwendalyn knew that response was very close to lying as she did meet him at the clinic that day but she purposefully left out the way they had actually met and all the time they had had in each other's company. In her heart she cried out to her Father for forgiveness of being deceitful. She knew she had to change the subject before things got out of hand.

"Well, Mom, I guess we're just about done. I just need to wipe down the table. Why don't you leave the cutlery for me to dry and go sit with Dad this evening."

"Why, thank you," she said appreciatively, and hung the dishtowel over Gwendalyn's shoulder.

Gwendalyn was more than willing to finish up things in the kitchen alone than to have to continue in the way the uncomfortable conversation was leading.

In the realization that Anthony would be there in about fifteen minutes, she rushed with the rest of the clean up, brushed her teeth, and ran upstairs to change her sweater. She then quickly combed and braided her hair into one long thick braid and then threw it onto her back as she finished.

Before she was ready, Calvin had yelled, "Anthony's out waiting at the gate, again. You'd better get a move on."

When she heard his announcement she felt color rise in her cheeks and her pulse began to quicken. She was beginning to notice that each time she prepared for a time out with Anthony, she felt a new excitement begin to well up within her.

It was getting close to the end of May and Anthony had been very busy, now with the ice gone and the fishing started, and he would be busy right up until the weather would turn cold again. She looked forward to the times when they could be alone together, but it never was for long, as they would always meet up with the 'gang' some place or another. Tonight they were going to be having a fire down by the water. They often got together on Friday or Saturday evenings for some type of fellowship and tonight was no different. They walked in silence, for a short time, enjoying the moment, and Gwendalyn placed her hand in the crook of his arm as she had always done for as long as she could remember. Tonight, though, Anthony pulled her hand to his side and gave it a little squeeze, which made Gwendalyn smile with the thought of his gesture. They began talking and Anthony was telling her how the fishing had gone so well this week with a great catch coming in every day. He had told her about the new boat and motor he had bought from Mr. Bridger saying that she'd have to come take a look tomorrow, it being Saturday and all.

All week she had been in school while Anthony busied himself with his work. In the evenings there'd be homework for her and Anthony would be kept busy with fish cleaning or preparing nets for the next day's catch. Besides that, her parents frowned on her going out on weeknights, and so she more than looked forward to the weekends when she could be near Anthony, even if it was in a crowd. She hoped she would get a chance to see him tomorrow and she told him she might see him early in the morning if they happened to be at the wharf at the same time. She told him she was going to be taking her first trip of the season out in boat with her dad. She was looking forward to this as well. Going out fishing with Dad always made her feel good and Dad seemed to enjoy her company as well. Calvin had been stepping into the role of being Dad's fishing companion and Gwendalyn missed being able to go with him every Saturday. Once school was out, though, she would get to do it more often, even if she had to share the times with Calvin.

"I'll go down early tomorrow and bring my boat over to your wharf and if I see your father's boat still there, I'll wait to see you and show you my boat. If not we'll have to do it another time."

"Sounds good," she said as they joined the group of young people who had been waiting for them.

* * *

Gwendalyn hadn't yet opened the folded note Daniel had placed in her hand on the day she was leaving and was still feeling apprehensive about doing so. Tonight, as she lay in bed tired of tossing and turning, sleep just wouldn't come so she decided that this would be the time to read the conspicuous note. It had been bothering her for too long and although she had been tempted to burn the thing, she just couldn't bring herself to do so.

She retrieved it from its hiding place and cautiously unfolded it and she was taken back by what she saw. Here was a beautiful sketch of a young lady standing on some sort of platform and reaching for an ic...

"What?" she gasped. "That's me! That's the morning I went outside to get an icicle from Dr. Evans overhang covering the porch. That's the morning I met Daniel! I can't believe it! Wow! It is beautifully done."

She admired the sketch for a time taking in how Daniel had captured the moment with the skill of an artist, using only a pencil and pad. Memories of that morning played in her mind and then travelled to the time they danced on the porch and then...

She pushed the thoughts aside and turned the page over to find a short inscription.

"I'll never forget the day we met and I hope you will remember it as well. You came into my life like a warm gentle breeze on a cool spring day. I think of you often and hope to see you again. I hope you are in good health. Warmly yours, Daniel."

Gwendalyn couldn't easily evade the memories that continued to flood into her heart and mind.

"...like a warm gentle breeze on a cool spring day..."

She knew she needed to pray to set this turmoil that raged within her back to peace.

It was past midnight before she felt settled enough to climb back into bed. She had left it with her Lord but still some uneasy thoughts continued to make their way into her mind. Again she tossed and turned till, finally, sleep claimed her. When she awoke the next morning she was more than thankful that she hadn't dreamed at all. To her own amazement, she felt quite refreshed.

CHAPTER 14
FISHING

True to his word, Anthony was waiting when Gwendalyn and her dad showed up to get started for the day. While Dad continued to get things organized, Gwendalyn went to meet Anthony.

"Wow, she's a beauty, and so big. You'll be doing real good with her."

"Yeah, I agree. It'll help provide a good future for..." Anthony left the rest of his thought hang, as it probably would have made him seem a little too presumptuous.

"Time to go, Gwen," Dad called climbing into his smaller boat, "we got a big day ahead of us."

"Coming Dad," she called back, and turned to wish Anthony a good catch saying she'd see him later.

Out in the boat was so peaceful. It was almost like stepping into a world of tranquillity. Sometimes another boat would be spotted, but gone again before long, on their way to check their nets or heading home. At times cries of sea gulls broke the calm but mostly just the paddles going in and gliding through the water could be heard. Gwendalyn loved these times with her dad and the sea had brought a special bonding between them.

The cod fishing was Gwendalyn's favorite. The enjoyment of bringing in the fish moments after putting out the line brought great excitement. There was a long main line, about 50 fathoms, 300 ft, and sometimes extending up to half a mile long if several lines were joined. Hooks on short leaders, 'sudlines', were tied to the main line spaced about a fathom apart. They were carefully coiled in a round washtub to let them out in the water without getting tangled. In water between 33 to 50 fathoms, 200 to 300 feet deep, the main line was attached to a rope, tied to a sinker, and dropped to the same depth as the water, for the cod were caught close to the ocean's bottom. The top of the rope was attached to a buoy to show them where the line started and to bring it out of the water when checking for the catch. The fishermen called this the 'cod trawl' or 'hand-lining'. Once the anchored rope was dropped, one by one each hook was baited with herring, mackerel, or squid, and dropped over the side of the boat as it was paddled slowly in reverse until all hooks were put over. A buoyed second rope, tied to the other end of the main line, with a sinker attached carried it to the bottom. By the time they had finished putting out the lines, they would go back to the beginning and begin hauling in their 'gear'. This process continued until they were satisfied with the catch. Gwendalyn was always amazed that no sooner had they placed out the baited hooked line that they would be bringing it back in putting the catch in the 'mitchebroom'. The mitchebroom was the middle section of the boat they filled full of fish and then boards were placed on top to keep the sun off. When they were finished they would bring the lines in, coiling it back into the round tub. These fish, cod, would be cleaned and sold fresh or placed in salt brine barrels to be dried later.

Gwendalyn usually sat on the 'cuddy', which was at the front end of the boat. Their fourteen-foot boat that they had first called a 'punt', was now called a 'dory' and was rowed with two sets of paddles. This was always hard work for her but she did her best to help her father.

Her father had seen the new outboard motors that some of the fishermen were buying but he didn't mind the rowing and he like the old way of doing things.

There were days when she watched her father sitting in the shed knitting his own salmon nets. The mesh was made five to six inches square with nylon twine and then 'barked'. 'Barking' was a process, which meant boiling them in iron pots in a dark solution called 'bark' made from spruce buds and water. This 'barking process' made the nets stronger and less visible to the fish when in the water.

Now, today, they were on their way to the salmon nets they put out yesterday to see what catch they would have. Dad had gone up on the rocky shore and pounded an iron spike into the ground and tied the end of his rope to it. He came back in the boat and when the water was deep enough, about 2 fathoms, 12 feet, he began letting out the net, or two nets joined, which ranged from 50 to 100 fathoms, 300 to 600 feet long. Bobbers were on the top of the net and sinkers were on the bottom to drop the net straight down leaving it vertical in the water. The salmon would then swim into the nets, their gills getting caught, and then hauled aboard the fisherman's boat.

They were more than pleased with today's catch and Gwendalyn and her father had to share their floor space with the numerous salmon. She remembered the day when her father pulled in a 30-pound salmon. It was almost five feet long and a foot thick around the middle. He had said that this would bring a fine profit with the price now at 30 cents a pound. He had gotten $9.00 dollars for one salmon!

They would be back this evening to check the net again and so it would continue all week long, except for Sundays. Mr. Gillard would never check his nets or bring in a cod or salmon on a Sunday. Sunday was a sacred day to rest and be kept holy onto the Lord.

This afternoon they would be washing the already salted cod that had been soaking in the salt brine barrels for the past two to three days. The now headless fillets were ready to be arranged 'head to tails' on the 'flake'. The flake was made up of limbed and rinded small spruce and fir trees placed close enough together so the prepared fillets could not fall through. They could walk on these flakes to spread out the salted cod but sometimes a foot missed its 'footing' and slipped through an opening.

The whole family was involved in this process. Children and parents alike took part in washing the brine-soaked fish in two different waters to clean any excess salt off the fillets. All helped with the spreading of it onto the flakes. It would spread in the morning and needed to be turned over around 2:00 PM to aid the drying process. When the sun would get too hot, branches or 'boughs' from the spruce and fir trees were brought and placed on the drying fillets. Each evening the fillets were gathered in and in the morning, laid out again. For about a week, until the fillets were dried properly, this process continued. There were times when rain threatened causing a panic to get the fillets off the flake. They would need to be stored in the shed until the sun broke through again.

This salting and drying process meant the preserving of the fish for many months for home use or sold to the fish factories. And so it went up and into November that the cod fishery would be keeping them busy until freezing temperatures and ice kept them from their seasonal work.

The fish was measured and sold by the 'cantle' or 'quintal', which was a square-pack of salt fish weighing about 112 pounds. When the fillets were dried, they resembled that of a long triangle. They were pack in such a way that it would end up in a square package. The fish was carried in 'two-man hand barrows' which resembled a wooden rectangular open-topped box about two and half feet wide, three and a half feet long, and a foot deep, with two hand bars attached to each side extending long enough to be carried comfortably by two men. The fish was also carried by the 'yaffle' which was the name given for an arm full.

It was a call for excitement when the capelin came in to spawn. Many from around the cove would gather around the shoreline to get their fill of the tiny, sleek, silvery and brilliantly colored fish that came in by the millions. A 'seine' was used, which is a round casting net that has sinker balls all around the edge and a rope attached to the centre. The net was cast by hand from the shore out into the water. When the net was hauled in, the sinkers would gather together trapping numerous capelin inside. You could also see younger children with their wicker baskets dipping up the capelin while wading knee-deep in the salt water. For that one week around the last of June or first of July, capelin was gathered. This was yet another of the many food supplies to be gathered from the sea.

Cod wasn't the only seafood that had to be salted and dried. The capelin were also put, heads, tails, and insides all in tact, in salt brine barrels and soaked for 24 hours. They would then be washed in clean water and placed upon boughs on top of the flakes, as capelin, being so small, would slip through the openings.

Although Gwendalyn's father didn't trap lobster as a part of his living, he would put out a few traps for his family's use as they all enjoyed the sweet, succulent meat. This mid-July treat was something they would always look forward to.

Squid came in with the month of August and ten to twelve boats would be gathered in the bay not too far from shore on what they called the 'squid-jigging-ground'. It was the dirtiest part of the whole fishery. The 'black ink', as they called it, would be squirting in all directions and when it landed in a poor soul's eye, the stinging was almost unbearable. The squid were used only for bait but there was talk that maybe, one day, people would be eating it like any other seafood. That thought had disgusted many of the fishermen. They would catch the squid in the evening and use it for bait in the morning. If bait was in short supply, there was a cold storage for squid in the harbour in the nearby town that could be purchased.

In the fall, Gwendalyn's father had his own 'herring business' where he would fill the wooden barrels with herring and salt brine. Merchants would come to his wharf to purchase filled barrels, brine and all, returning empty barrels for further use.

All the seafood that was gathered from the ocean was either kept for personal use, sold on the wharfs, or shipped to the factories.

CHAPTER 15
GWENDALYN'S DAD

Not only was Mr. Gillard a fisherman, but also a carpenter. He would be away from home for weeks and months at a time building homes in places like Buchans and Lewisporte.

Gwendalyn remembered a time when she was about ten years old that her dad had come back from one of his outings bringing a special gift for his children. It was a box measuring 8 by 6 by 2 inches high filled with all kinds of candy and chocolate bars. Dad had told them that it had cost a dollar, which was a whole day's wages. Their father was always a thoughtful and considerate man and he loved to show his children how much they meant to him by surprising them with special little gifts.

Mr. Gillard had also spent some time as a young man in the United States of America working as a carpenter. He had told Gwendalyn about the time he had helped with the building of the Empire State Building, now a monumental work.

He had, at one time, stayed with his sister, of whom it was said, that she had the second greatest home in Detroit City. He also had helped build the school that Joe Lewis went to, and for years after, he kept up with this famous boxer's career through broadcasts on the radio.

Mr. Gillard was the first to acquire a radio in the whole cove. A large battery that was a foot long, four inches wide and stood about a foot high, powered it, and had its position on a shelf in the kitchen.

Not only did he keep up with Joe Lewis' career, but he also took a great interest in listening to music. He loved music. Each morning he would get up and before he'd light the fire, he'd flick on the radio. Many a day, Gwendalyn would see him tapping his foot and trying to sing or whistle along with the tune being played. When she was eight or nine years old, he would sometimes take her in his arms and sing the songs to her. And, of course, Sundays he would sing hymns with his family including his all-time favorite, 'The Old Rugged Cross'.

Listening to hockey games in the evening was another of Mr.

Gillard's past-times. His favorite team was the Toronto Maple Leafs. Gwendalyn remembered that he would spend however long the game lasted with his ear up to the radio catching each and every detail while Mrs. Gillard was busy in the living room.

She would be sewing clothes on the foot treadle Singer sewing machine or knitting, and teaching her girls to do the same. Gwendalyn had knit her first pair of mittens when she was just nine years old. She still had the long knitted socks her mother had knit and died red for her and her siblings. They came above the knee and had to be held up with garters.

The wool they used came from what they spun themselves. Mr. Gillard kept about a dozen sheep and when the time came, he would shear the sheep bringing in the fleece that Mrs. Gillard would wash and dry. Once clean, they would all sit around the table in the light of an oil lamp picking the wool apart to fluff it up. Before long, there would be mountains of fluffed wool piled up on the table going as high as, and around, the lamp itself. Then it would be carded and put on the spinning wheel where it turned out fine wool to be knitted into socks, scarves, mittens, and more.

Mr. Gillard's sheep was also a good food supply but there was much to be done to care for these animals. He would cut grass and then it would need to be spread out for drying. Gwendalyn and her siblings would use hand rakes to rake it together in rows in the evenings and then in the mornings it would need to be spread again to dry properly. So it was that after the cod was spread out on the flakes, they would take the rakes and go to work on the hay. This would go on for about a week and once it was totally dry, it would be stored in the hayloft in their shed.

Life wasn't always easy and it seemed there was always much to be done, but Gwendalyn and her siblings found a way of making the work fun and so enjoyed themselves doing what had to be done.

Mr. Gillard had a friend named Peter Triton who owned a magnificent schooner. Peter had an accident and ended up getting his leg mangled in one of his motors and had to have it amputated. He had asked Mr. Gillard if he would be interested in running his schooner and so, another summer, he was fishing on the Grand Banks off the coast of Labrador. He took notice that the cod that came off the Grand

Banks were thinner and only took three to four days to dry as compared to cod in their cove that usually took up to a week to dry. Sometimes he would be gone on an occasional seal hunt as well.

Mr. Gillard had also his share of grief and sorrow as his present day Mrs. Gillard wasn't the first to keep house in his home. His first wife died of tuberculosis before their first wedding anniversary bearing no children. When he first brought his new bride into his house she was amazed and honoured to walk into this well furnished home. Everything was in its place, curtains hanging in the window, and the silverware, the silverware; she was quite taken with it. She had told Gwendalyn how she felt about it, and Gwendalyn still polished this same silverware.

Her mother had said that she could sense that the woman who first shared this home with her husband was a caring, respectable and loving woman. She only hoped that she could love him as he needed and fill his heart with joyful years.

Mr. Gillard did love his wife and children. They were his happiness, the reason he did what he did to give them a happy life.

Gwendalyn always saw the good in her father and how hard he worked to give them a good life. She cherished him, and his responsible and loving ways. He was a dad any girl would like to claim for her own, but he was hers and she felt blessed to have him.

CHAPTER 16
ANOTHER BIRTHDAY

June 30 dawned a beautiful day to Gwendalyn's delight. The week before was overcast and regularly throughout the week drizzle and rain continued to dampen her spirits. Last night, though, her disposition changed when Ina showed up just in time for supper bringing with her a burst of sunshine in her manner and cheerfulness. Gwendalyn was overjoyed with the coming of her friend and now things seemed just right.

She turned over to see her sleeping friend still absorbed in dreamland. She was so thankful things had worked out for Ina to come and celebrate her sixteenth birthday with her. A few of her other friends would be over to share in her special day enjoying a home-cooked meal and then staying for games in the evening. It would be nothing like the elaborate social event she had taken part in when celebrating Ina's sixteenth birthday. In actuality she preferred the company of her close friends and family in an intimate gathering.

After lunch Gwendalyn and Ina went for a walk after being gently pushed out the door so her mom and sisters could prepare for Gwendalyn's simple party. Dr. Evans and Gwendalyn's dad had gone fishing together and wouldn't be back until close to the supper hour.

They strolled along the water's edge while Ina spied out and collected unique seashells she could take back to her mother. It was great having her friend back once more at Serenity Cove and it was like old times reliving some of the things they had done a couple of years earlier.

As Gwendalyn gazed out on the ocean's vastness she was pleasantly surprised to see a lone figure coming in from fishing and immediately recognized the boat to be that of Anthony's.

"Do you know who it is?" Ina asked, joining her gaze.

"Yes, it's Anthony," Gwendalyn answered, hiding her smile.

"Anthony! You mean the guy who came to see you off when you came to visit me this spring!?!" Ina questioned excitedly.

"Yes, it's him. I guess he finished early today."

They walked to the wharf, slowly making their way to where Anthony would be tying up his boat.

"Have you two gotten any closer since I last saw you?"

"We're still good friends, just like we've always been since we started school together but I think something is changing."

"Tell me Gwen, what's happening between you two."

"There's nothing to tell. I just meant that sometimes I sense things and it makes me feel, I don't know, giddy, I guess, but I like it."

"Do you know if he feels something towards you?"

"I really don't know. Sometimes when he looks at me I see a different look on his face but he never says anything to suggest how he feels, if he feels anything at all."

"I know someone who feels something for you or definitely hasn't forgotten you," she said mischievously.

"What do you mean?" Gwendalyn said looking intently at her.

"Well, Daniel has been coming for dinner on Sundays and we've been going for walks or playing games in the parlor with Momma and Daddy. I was talking with him last week and mentioned going to see you for your birthday. He seemed very interested in when I was leaving and coming back. Well, a day before we left he brought over an envelope and asked if I would give it to you. It must be just a card wishing you a happy birthday."

"From Daniel? I didn't think he would do something like that. I want you to do me a favour, Ina," she asked, nervousness showing in her voice.

"Sure," she said, noticing the edginess in her friend.

"Don't give me the card tonight at my party."

"Why not?" she asked curiously.

"Well, I didn't tell Anthony about meeting Daniel and I don't want to jeopardize anything that may develop between us, and please don't mention Daniel in our conversations with Anthony," Gwendalyn said trying to keep her face from becoming flush.

"OK, Daniel is out of the..."

"Sh-sh-sh, here he comes," she silenced her as Anthony came up along side the wharf and began tying his boat to the wharf's frame.

"You're in early," she called down as he climbed up the attached ladder to see her.

"Yeah, I wanted to make sure I was ready for your party tonight."

"You've got a while yet," she said smiling, and went on to introduce him to Ina.

"Yes, I do remember you, Ina. I'm glad you were able to come out for Gwenny's birthday. She's talked about you a lot since she's been back from Nova Scotia."

The three shared some small talk and then the girls left him to finish his work and then headed back to finish their walk around the cove.

"My, Gwendalyn, he is handsome," Ina began.

"Never mind that. I wanted to ask you how things were going with you and Daniel. I know you were really interested in him back in April."

"Well, like I said, he's been coming for dinner on Sundays and we play games and go for walks, but other than that things are the same. It almost seems like he's not really interested in me at all. I try to be friendly and show him I'm interested in him but either he doesn't get the picture or I'm not his type. Oh, I'm not complaining. We do have fun together with my parents and on our walks, but I don't think it'll go past friendship."

Gwendalyn felt badly for Ina but was grateful that she was taking it well and enjoying her friendship with Daniel despite the absence of romantic intentions. Ina had gone on to tell her how Franklin had been around to call on her a couple of times in the past month and she was growing fond of him. He was working in his father's lumber and hardware store and would someday inherit the business.

"I have some good news that I know you'll be really happy to hear about," Ina announced.

"Well," she returned, "don't keep me in such suspense."

"You remember how the trip went when we were bringing you home after my birthday party. The storm came up and by the time it ended Daddy had given his heart to Jesus."

"Yes, I remember, go on."

"On our way back home we had some long talks about God and what He means to the both of us. Well, after we'd been home a couple of days Momma started noticing something different about Daddy and was asking him a lot of questions. Daddy answered them by telling her what had happened on the ferry, not just about the storm but how his life had changed after committing himself to Jesus. Real soon after, we all started going to Aunt Lucille's church regularly. Before long Momma had asked Jesus into her life as well."

"Oh, that's wonderful. Aunt Lucille must be thrilled. What did Franklin think of you being a Christian and going to church every week?"

"Well, before I started seeing Franklin seriously, I talked with him and found out that he and his family are regular church attendees. I don't think I would have started in a courting relationship with him if he weren't. I've been reading the Bible you gave me every day, and one time I came across the scripture in 2nd Corinthians 6: 14-18 which talks about not being yoked together with unbelievers. So you can imagine my relief and joy to find out that he was a believer in Christ as well."

"It's so good, Ina, that you're looking to God's word for guidance and making up your mind to follow what it says."

"I don't think I've ever thought of, or experienced life as being so meaningful since I asked Jesus in my heart. I don't think I ever thanked you for helping me become a Christian, and now my both my parents are serving Him. You're a good friend, Gwen, and you have brought so much into our lives, more than you could ever know."

When the girls finally returned home, Dad and Dr. Evans had already been there for half an hour enjoying a hot cup of tea and relaxing in the living room.

The kitchen and living room was decorated lightly for the occasion and there was an extra table set for the guests they would be serving this evening.

Gwendalyn went with Ina upstairs to dress for the evening and although she argued the fact that the new teal green dress she wore at Ina's sixteenth birthday celebration was altogether too extravagant for their quiet party, Ina insisted she wear it. Ina wore a beautiful dress she had selected for the occasion, taking care to not out do her friend on her special day.

She helped Gwendalyn with her hair, pinning it up in an attractive fashion. Gwendalyn couldn't help noticing that it made her look a little older and brought out her finest features.

Jackie, Beth, and Stephanie showed up ten minutes before 6:00 PM, and Roger and Anthony arrived shortly there after.

When she walked down the stairs following Ina, she was relieved to see that her three friends had come in their best dresses and even her sister had changed and was now wearing a dress as well. This helped her to relax although she still felt overly dressed.

Roger and Calvin whistled loudly when they saw her appearance, while the girls commented on how 'wonderful' she looked. Mom and Dad hugged her, wishing her a happy birthday and then Mom left the group to finish the preparing the meal in the kitchen.

Dad stayed beside her and quietly said, "You're turning into quite a young lady, my beauty. My guess is that before too long you'll be helping some other fisherman in his boat."

He winked at Gwendalyn and startled her by moving his gaze in Anthony's direction. She blushed a little and gave him a private scold.

Mr. Evans approached her, wishing her a happy sixteenth and went on to say how lovely she looked this evening. Anthony joined him and agreed with his expression of the obvious truth.

Gwendalyn's mother called all present to the table and everyone found their place. With heads bowed, Dad went on to pray blessings on his youngest daughter and on the food so thoughtfully prepared.

Gwendalyn's mother had prepared her daughter's favorite meal, which consisted of a pork roast done to perfection with an oven pastry baked along side taking on the flavour of the roast.

In addition to the roast, she had prepared whipped potatoes, diced carrots, mashed turnips, cabbage, a steamed bread pudding and a delicious gravy made with the drippings from the roast.

There were many compliments around the table on how great the food tasted and much laughter. Gwendalyn often scanned both tables looking appreciatively at the people who had come or taken part in making her sixteenth birthday a special day to remember.

With the meal now finished and the extra food and dishes removed from the table, Mom turned around from the counter where she was obviously hiding Gwendalyn's birthday cake, which was all aglow with the colored candles burning brightly. She made her way to Gwendalyn while the group sang 'Happy Birthday'.

Hot tea and delicious birthday cake with ice cream had ended the meal and now all were gathered in the living room where Gwendalyn proceeded to open her presents. The girls had given her a new vanity set consisting of a brush, comb, & hand mirror, some sweet-smelling soaps, and a package of three embroidered handkerchiefs. Mom and Dad gave her pair of brown slacks with a cream colored blouse. Ina and Dr. Evans had brought her a perfume set that had been purchased and gift wrapped at Chez Michelle's. Roger had also given her a package of two handkerchiefs and was a little disappointed that she had already received similar ones. Anthony handed her a small package and when she opened it, she smiled as she lifted out five colored ribbons. She thanked everyone for his or her 'wonderful gifts' and announced it was time for game playing.

The evening ended around 10:30 PM and after saying goodnight to most of her guests, she walked Anthony to the door.

"I really appreciate your gift Anthony, it was very thoughtful."

He absentmindedly reached out his hand and allowed his fingers to smooth across her silky tresses. He was about to say something when he drew his hand back quickly apologizing for his forwardness.

"Sorry," he said, "I was just ... eh..."

"It's fine," she laughed, "you act as if you've never touched it before. I remember you pulling it more than once and you must remember it was by my hair that you saved my life."

"Yes, I remember," he said, still deep in thought. "Gwen, do you think we could go for a short walk before I go home?"

"I'd like that, but I better ask Mom and Dad if it's OK."

With permission granted, they walked off together with Gwendalyn's hand finding its place in the crook of his arm.

Silence held them for a time and they enjoyed just being with each other. Anthony finally broke the stillness and stopped, turning Gwendalyn to meet him face to face.

"I've been thinking about this for quite a while now and I... eh..."

Gwendalyn stood motionless as Anthony struggled with the words he was trying to say. She watched as he shuffled his feet and rubbed his hands, the way he always did when he was nervous.

"I hope it's not all that serious," she giggled as she stretched out her slender hand to rub his arm.

He reached for her hand and took it in his.

"Gwenny, this is hard for me."

The seriousness in his expression caused her to grow silent all of a sudden and she wondered what could've made this change in her life-long chum. From fun and laughter to the now solemn figure standing before her, she knew what he was about to say must be very important to him.

"Gwen, things are changing between us and I have to talk to you about it. I've only had one sister and she's been gone for a long time. All through our growing up years I've treated you like a cherished younger sister and I've looked out for you and cared for you as if you were. Now, and for a long time, my thoughts have changed toward you. I still look out for you and care for you, but now in a more meaningful way. I no longer look at you as my younger sister. You mean much more to me now."

He paused and looked away and then back into her warm eyes that hadn't left their position. She smiled reassuringly and he felt he could continue.

"Gwen, I believe I've fallen in love with you and although you've just turned sixteen, I'd like to ask your parents if I can come courting."

Feeling a little embarrassed, she lowered her head so that Anthony wouldn't see her flushed cheeks. The thought of her dearest friend expressing his heart's secrets made the now somewhat familiar, but at times still confusing, sensations within her more than welcomed. She longed to have him hold her and feel his strong arms surround her but she regained control of her emotions and looked up into his rugged features.

"Anthony," she began, still not knowing how to say correctly what her inner being was experiencing.

"I've grown to care for you as more than a friend as well. It all started when we said good-bye at the edge of town when Ina and her parents came to pick me up to bring me to Halifax. Something was different in the way you looked at me and the way you held me even though I was just acting like my playful self. Well, anyway, it got me to thinking and before long I began feeling a little differently towards you. At times I couldn't wait to see you."

Before she could go any further Anthony had swiftly picked her up and swung her around with her legs flying. When her feet were firmly on the ground he proceeded to gather her in his arms and held her tightly.

"I'm so glad, Gwenny, I love you so much," he whispered.

"But wait, Anthony," she said breathlessly, pushing him away, "I didn't mean... I mean it's too..."

"Please don't say anymore. Just knowing you are starting to feel what might be love towards me is all I need right now."

Gwendalyn allowed him to hug her at length and she enjoyed being in his arms and wished the moment could go on forever.

"When do you think I should ask your parents about me courting you?"

"Let's wait a little while longer. I want to get used to this new turn in our friendship before announcing it to the cove. You know that once my family knows, it is certain that Calvin won't be long in telling his friends and then it will become common knowledge. The other thing is that Stacey is going to be getting married at the end of August and I don't want to take any attention that would have otherwise been hers. You only get married once, you know, and I want all the time left before her marriage to be devoted to her."

"All right," he agreed. "You're so thoughtful. I'll wait until you tell me when you feel it's the right time."

Gwendalyn was glad he had understood but, then, he was always understanding of her and helping her through whatever came up in her growing years. Once again she had taken her heart-felt gratitude to the Lord for what she felt was His plan for her life and she received it whole-heartedly.

When Gwendalyn returned to the house a half an hour later, Ina sat alone on the couch waiting for her. She told her that the family had retired a few minutes ago but she had to wait and hear all that had happened on their 'walk'.

Gwendalyn tried to downplay the outing saying that it was simply a friendly walk with her best bud. She knew she couldn't talk about the intimate secrets she and Anthony now shared until her parents knew of their intended relationship. She was relieved that Ina didn't press her on it and shortly thereafter they headed up the stairs to ready themselves for bed.

Once in the room, Ina went to her suitcase and brought an envelope to Gwendalyn.

"You still have something else to open before your birthday is over," she said mischievously, waving it in front of her face.

"Oh, Ina, don't be so silly. You know it's just a card. After all, he probably feels he owes me something for my birthday after giving you that 'exquisite perfume' that you went on about. Anyway, I'm tired. I'll just open it tomorrow sometime."

She was relieved once again to see Ina nod her head yawning and getting ready for bed. She hoped the card didn't contain anything to cause her to reflect on Daniel. When she had opened his note almost a month ago, too much had surfaced and since then it had been tucked away to not disturb her further. Now he had sent her something else.

True to her word, she had been praying for him that the Lord would heal the hurts that caused bitterness towards God. Because of this, thoughts of Daniel had drifted from time to time through her memories.

She had been feeling a growing desire to be with Anthony and didn't want anything to distract her from what she felt would take her into a life long dream of marrying him.

She looked over to see that Ina had already fallen asleep and so took it as an opportune time to open the envelope. The card lay open on her lap but that wasn't what had taken her attention. She studied the pencilled sketch of herself coming down the stairs the night of Ina's birthday. Once again, it was breath-taking; the resemblance of his sketch to herself. She thought it was amazing how he could see something once and keep it tucked away in his memory to later sketch it on paper.

She turned it over to find once again an inscription.

"I remember how lovely you looked coming down the stairs that evening and I try to imagine how you would have looked on your own sixteenth birthday. I hope you have a wonderful day. You're still a part of my life, if only in my memories. As always, Daniel."

Although she tried to refuse any past memories of Daniel intrude upon the life she was now beginning to build with Anthony, she couldn't keep away the nighttime dreams or the intrusions that caught her unawares.

Something in his drawing and note caused her to momentarily reflect on the times she and Daniel had spent together and the way she felt when he kissed her. She quickly brought herself from that state by determinedly directing her thoughts to Anthony.

* * *

Ina and Dr. Evans left again the next morning after their short visit. Dad and Mom had sent them off with a care package of freshly caught salmon and cod and had given Gwendalyn permission to spend a week with them next summer.

Ina had made no further attempts to question her about the card from Daniel because in the morning she found his card displayed openly on the dresser, placed there especially for this purpose. She had taken it upon herself to have a look giving in to her curiosity. A simple birthday card signed: 'Your friend, Daniel' was all she had found and felt there was nothing in it warranting a discussion. Gwendalyn had carefully tucked the sketch away with the other one in a box she hid in her wardrobe.

CHAPTER 17
CHANGES

The next two months sped by with Anthony being so busy with his fishing and Gwendalyn helping her dad, as well as doing whatever she could to help Stacey prepare for the wedding, which was now just three days away. She and Anthony hadn't spent a lot of time together and when they did they were in the midst of either friends or family. She was glad for this as it gave her time to think and pray about the changes that were happening in her life. She knew she was beginning to be prepared for a relationship with Anthony that took them past friendship, but she didn't want things to progress too quickly. She wanted to hang on to their close friendship and not leave it behind when moving on into something more intimate with him.

Things were indeed changing and she trusted all her concerns with her Heavenly Father to work out the things she couldn't and help her understand the things she could.

Stacey's wedding was beautiful and at times throughout the service, Gwendalyn imagined herself being the bride with Anthony, the groom. She was shocked that at one time Daniel had invaded her thoughts and was standing in the groom's place. She rebuked and chastened herself for her daydreaming when she should have been enjoying her sister's wedding for what it was.

A couple of times throughout the day she was again startled when Daniel's face flitted across her memory.

Anthony had spoken with her privately telling her she looked even more beautiful than she did on the evening of her sixteenth birthday, even though she was wearing the same teal green dress. He would always remember the day he revealed his deepest secrets and how Gwendalyn had responded to them.

"It sounds so strange to have you speaking to me in such a way," she managed. "It's so different from the way we talked to each other in the past, but I think I could get used to it."

"Of course you could. We're both changing and growing up. It's a natural way for two people who like each other the way we do to speak like this."

"With you being older than me, I might have some catching up to do, but I don't think I'm too far behind you," she said smiling and allowed her arms to encircle his neck as he pulled her into his embrace.

* * *

By late November ice filled the bay and fishing was brought to a close until the next season. Snow made its appearance and frost was becoming a regular feature on the windows of homes around the cove. The pace of life slowed considerably and many nights were spent in cosy living rooms reading or playing games while enjoying hot tea and an evening snack of some kind.

Gwendalyn and Anthony were meeting more frequently now and they both felt that this would be a good time for Anthony to ask Gwendalyn's parents if he could come courting and thus beginning their courtship. They both knew that in the proper amount of time an engagement would be announced.

Her parents were happy for the two of them and even went on to say that they had been expected this for some time now and wondered why he hadn't asked sooner. They, without hesitation, gave Anthony their blessing. They had known Anthony all his life and because the friendship between them had carried into their teen-aged years, they made a point to keep up with Anthony's endeavours. They were pleased in the way he had decided to begin building his future. To them, he seemed to be very respectable and responsible. They also enjoyed the prospect of Gwendalyn marrying someone from the cove and then making her home close by.

Stacey had since moved away with her husband and they missed her terribly. Knowing that Gwendalyn would probably never leave their little town gave them great joy and they welcomed Anthony as a part of their family as he often joined them to share in their evenings.

CHAPTER 18
CHRISTMAS

Christmas Eve was now upon them and all could feel an air of excitement. The house was looking quite festive and the tree was now being decorated as the family members sang one Christmas carol after another. Mom had arranged a tray of many different cookies and cakes she had baked as a part of the Christmas celebration.

Once again Anthony was present with Gwendalyn and her family. Dad had read the Christmas story from the Bible and was commenting on the fact that the best gift, the gift of salvation, was given by God. In His so lovingly thought-out plan, he sent His son as a baby to earth, to redeem all who would believe in Him, to Himself.

With the mood now relaxed, as each one sat back to admire the colorful tree, Anthony leaned over and asked Gwendalyn if she would like to take a walk before bedtime.

"I'd thought you'd never ask," she said jumping up off the chesterfield and letting her parents know what they were up to.

Anthony loved this about Gwendalyn. She was naturally always full of life and energy and Anthony found it to be contagious.

Her parents had consented to this late evening outing but bid her not to stay out too late.

Keeping this in mind they headed out the door and like always Gwendalyn started on their usual trek but was halted by Anthony's hand grasping her hand.

"I thought you might like to take a walk through the woods tonight," he said turning her in the direction of the forest. "The moon is so full and bright that it will be easy to see our way through."

"Sounds wonderful," she agreed, matching his step and then allowing him to help her through the thick bush to the more spacious area that sported scattered trees on the other side.

"This is beautiful," she whispered.

The snow glistened in the moonlight making everything seem a bright light blue. They walked along taking note of how much easier their walk was with the hardened crust on the snow that had formed from the ice and rain that fell a couple of days ago. Anthony continued to hold her hand as they walked along in silence, taking in the beauty of nature that surrounded them.

"It's so romantic," she said, breaking the silence and turning to face Anthony. "Even more breath-taking that the picture I gave Stacey for her wedding present."

"Seeing you standing in the moonlight takes my breath away," he said, his voice growing husky.

His intent gaze didn't leave her eyes and she, as if sensing his desire, closed her eyes and tilted her chin upward allowing his mouth to meet hers. Their first kiss was gentle and meaningful. The now welcomed tingling sensations flooded through her body and she received them, as they were part of something pure and good she and Anthony would share for a lifetime. They stood holding each other on this moonlit night as time continued to drift into the past. She didn't want to leave his embrace nor did she want this romantic encounter between them to end, but visions of her parents asking not to be too late kept pulling her from this long awaited moment.

At long last she managed to speak, breaking the spell that neither of them wanted broken.

"Mom and Dad... didn't... want us to be... too late," she said, barely audible.

As soon as she had said it, she wished she hadn't, as now the moment was fading. Because of Anthony's respect for her and her family, he agreed and they began heading back to her home.

They lingered at the gate holding each other for a time not wanting to leave each other but without warning Anthony kissed her lightly on the cheek and headed down the street towards his own home.

Gwendalyn was relieved to see that all were still up and that the clock read only 11:15 PM. She figured they hadn't travelled far into the woods at all and realized dreamily that most of their time wasn't spent walking. She inwardly smiled recalling their recently-made memory.

Christmas morning was a joyous event with Stacey and Vincent at home. With breakfast finished and presents opened, it felt like old times with Gwendalyn and Stacey helping mom in the kitchen to prepare the traditional turkey dinner. Gwendalyn was glad it was to be a lunchtime meal as Anthony had asked her to join his family for another turkey dinner at 6:00 PM. His mother planned a later meal as Anthony's older brother and family would be arriving around 3:00 o'clock in the afternoon. His sister, along with her husband and two children, had come home three days ago.

It was 2:00 PM when Anthony came to wish the Gillard family a Merry Christmas. Gwendalyn was more than happy to see her beau and even though her hands were dripping with dish soap and water, she threw them around Anthony as soon as he had removed his jacket and scarf.

"Merry Christmas," she said excitedly. "I see you're finally making good use of that scarf I gave you. You know, you were supposed to be wearing it out in boat when the weather got cold."

"I know you gave to me with the warmest of intentions," he joked, "but I have an old one for use on my boat. And besides, I treasure your first gift to me and only wear it on special outings."

With that said, and no one looking, he leaned over and kissed her cheek whispering, "I love you."

Her face grew to the color of Rudolf's nose and without looking up, she headed back to the sink to continue her chore of washing the dishes.

She later joined Anthony in the company of her family in the living room and much laughter and chatter echoed throughout the house all afternoon long.

* * *

Gwendalyn and Anthony arrived at his home an hour before the evening meal commenced and had a great time getting reacquainted with his brother and sister and meeting their children. Gwendalyn loved spending time with the children, especially, and she played with them and kept them occupied until dinner was announced.

The cleanup was completed and the young mothers were now getting their children ready for bed. They had been tucked in just ten minutes, when little Rosemary came out rubbing her eyes and saying she wanted 'Genny', from Anthony introducing her as Gwenny, to read them a bedtime story. Gwendalyn arose from the chesterfield and took the little girl by the hand and led her back into the children's room to read them all a bedtime story. She returned from the bedroom more than a half an hour and eight stories later, needing a drink.

"All are asleep," she said, breathing a heavy sigh and sinking into the cushioned seat beside Anthony.

"You've got quite the way with children," Anthony's sister complimented her. "Anthony, she's a gem. You'd be doing good to hang on to her."

"I know," he said, "and I intend to do just that. And if you all will excuse us, I'd like take this 'gem' for a walk before it's time to walk her home."

Gwendalyn said her good-byes wishing each one a Merry Christmas.

Tonight they decided to go down to the wharf and be alone awhile. The sky was clear and like last night, the moon had made its ascent and was now brightly shining down on the lone couple sitting on the wharf's edge.

I wanted to wait till we were alone to give you this. He reached into his pocket and pulled out a small carefully wrapped package.

"Oh, Anthony," she excitedly, "you really didn't have to but I am glad you did."

She cautiously removed the paper being careful not to tear it and almost froze at the sight of the small box she now held in her hand. She looked at him with a questioning expression and went on to open it when he said, "Well, go on."

The open box revealed a beautiful golden charm bracelet. Anthony pulled off his gloves and lifting it from its case, motioned for Gwendalyn to pull up her coat sleeve so he could fasten it around her wrist. He continued to explain what each of the three different charms meant.

"This heart symbolizes love, the love I have for you; the dove symbolizes purity, the purity of our courtship; and the cross, faith, the strong faith we share in our Lord."

"It's beautiful," she said softly. "Thank you, Anthony."

"Not as beautiful as the one wearing it, and I must say that you are the charm that adds beauty to my life," he said, putting his arm around her shoulder and kissing her gently on the cheek.

She flushed again and was glad for the night cover to hide her embarrassment. She wondered when she would stop blushing and hoped it would be soon as it made her feel so child-like.

They sat soaking in the rays of moonlight and enjoying the closeness they felt with each other.

The decreasing temperature caused Gwendalyn to shiver suddenly and at once Anthony stood up pulling her to her feet saying that they should head back. They walked to the gate of Gwendalyn's home and before Anthony started away, she said she had to get something from the house and went off running across the path. She returned quickly holding out to Anthony the gift she lovingly wrapped for him.

"I almost forgot about this, being so happy about just being with you, but now I think it couldn't be a better time than right now to give it to you," she said, catching her breath.

He opened the present and Gwendalyn promptly placed the new warm hat on his chilled head. He had noticed that the hat matched the scarf she had given him earlier in the spring.

"I see you've been thinking of me and caring about my well-being again," he said smiling. "I am truly blessed having you with me. I know you'll always do me good."

Once again he kissed her on the cheek and bade her goodnight.

* * *

Gwendalyn had received two cards in the mail, one from her closest friend, Ina, and the other from Daniel. She opened the one from Ina joyously reading the events that were taking place in her life.

Most of her letter was all about Franklin. He was becoming a regular caller and they were spending a lot of time together. She was saying that there might be wedding bells in the future.

Daniel's card she had tucked away with her sketches without opening it. She didn't want anything to spoil what was happening between her and Anthony.

CHAPTER 19
WONDERING

Two months had passed since Christmas and the young couple continued to spend a lot of time together although much of the time was amongst friends. Gwendalyn had noticed though, that in all the time they had alone together, Anthony hadn't once kissed her the way he had on Christmas Eve. He always gave her the same peck on the cheek. She was concerned that maybe she had disappointed him somehow that night. She thought it couldn't be true as she remembered his reaction being that of someone who had enjoyed the moment, but now the doubting thoughts continued to nag at her causing her to become anxious.

She had just seen Anthony again this evening and again there wasn't anything in his behaviour toward to cause her to even grow flushed anymore. He was acting as if they were just good friends again, childhood chums, except for the occasional kiss on the cheek, and she had more than grown used to that. She knew he was being respectable, the perfect gentlemen, but why had he kissed her so warmly that one time to not even come near such an interlude again. And then there was the way he was funning around with the other girls in their circle of friends, almost giving them as much attention as he was her. Yes, he still walked her home at the evening's end but she was becoming even more disturbed over his cool attitude toward her.

She lay on her bed with these troublesome thoughts swirling around in her mind. She got up and dressed for bed, hanging her dress in her wardrobe. She caught sight of the corner of the box that held the one secret she hadn't told anyone about. She wondered if there might be another sketch of her inside the sealed envelope and she debated whether or not she should open it.

Curiosity got the better of her, and in the privacy of her own room, she lifted the lid of the box and took out the letter she had once forbidden herself to open. She fingered the envelope and without thinking, opened it. She pulled out the card and there again, placed

129

inside, was another sketch. She unfolded it to see something she hadn't remembered. She was lying asleep on the sofa in the parlor. She turned over the page and like before he had written a message to her.

"In the early morning after Ina's birthday party, we walked down to the docks. I appreciated our private outing so early in the morning watching the sunrise on the harbour. When we returned I sat on the porch swing enjoying the sun's warmth and you went inside. I later came in and found you lying asleep on the sofa. You were so peaceful and looking so beautiful, I knew I would have to sketch you. Later in the day when I got settled in the boarding house, I did just that. My address is included once again. I hope to hear from you. As always, Daniel."

She wanted to write him, tell him about what had happened over the past ten months. After all he was her friend. Someone she had met briefly. Was she to blame for the way he felt about her, and couldn't she just talk to him in a letter as new friends would. She couldn't help feeling slightly attracted to him. He was handsome enough and his build was appealing, even his prospects for the future were great. With Anthony's cool behaviour towards her, she found herself more susceptible to thoughts of Daniel. Any woman would be honoured to have such a man for a husband. But she didn't love him. It was too short a time to fall in love, she reasoned. And besides, she loved Anthony no matter what. She intended to marry Anthony. Writing, NO! she couldn't. It might lead him to believe that she was interested in him and then he would write to her more often, and maybe the secret she held with him might get exposed. At times she wished the secret were revealed.

Anthony was her life-long love and when the day came when he would propose, she would gladly accept. What if he didn't propose? Had he changed his mind? It would account for the cool behaviour he seemed to always have when he was with her.

Later during the Easter break, Gwendalyn received two more cards. One again from Ina, and the other from Daniel.

Ina's letter was full of news, mostly about Franklin, but the shock

130

of it all was when she read that Franklin had proposed to Ina and she had accepted. She went on about the 'gorgeous diamond ring' he had bought her. Gwendalyn knew by the way she wrote that she was bubbling over with excitement and couldn't wait for her upcoming marriage. Of course, Gwendalyn would have to be there to be her maid of honour, she had said. The wedding day was scheduled for Saturday, June 7, 1951 and she couldn't wait to have her friend spend a few days with her before the wedding.

"Wow," she said looking at the calendar, "that's in less than two months away. She just turned seventeen and such a short engagement."

She knew of many young girls who married at seventeen but she had always decided in her own heart to wait until she was eighteen to marry.

"I guess I better talk with Mom and Dad about going away earlier than what we talked about."

She put Daniel's letter out of sight in the box hidden in her wardrobe without opening it but knowing she would a little later. She felt an urgency to speak with her parents right away.

Her parents had agreed to her spending a week in August with the Evans family, but now they changed their minds and agreed to have her go off and be a part of her best friend's wedding. They also agreed that she could leave on the Thursday before the wedding but needed to be back on Sunday as school was still in session.

Right away Gwendalyn wrote to Ina about the arrangements that would need to be made if she could be in attendance. With her father still having no means of transportation, it would be again up to Dr. Evans to come and bring her to Nova Scotia.

Later that evening she talked with Anthony about the news she had received from Ina and how she felt badly that Dr. Evans always had to be the one travelling back and forth.

"I wish my dad owned a car so we could drive to the ferry. I could take the ferry across by myself and just meet Dr. Evans on the other side."

"As you know, Gwenny, my Dad has his truck. Maybe I could ask him if I could borrow it for the day you're supposed to leave and I could drive you to the ferry. There's just one thing that concerns me and that's the idea of you going on the ferry by yourself. Do you think your parents would agree with you travelling alone?"

"I'm not sure but I did notice two different girls who were alone when Ina and I were exploring the ship. I think it's safe if you stay in the crowd being careful not to be left alone anywhere. I'll talk to my parents and you talk with your dad and we'll see tomorrow how things turned out."

Gwendalyn's parents had their doubts and tried to talk her out of going alone on the ship. She reassured and convinced them to permit her by telling them about the girls who had travelled alone and then met up with their parties when they docked. She also was familiar about boarding and debarking and the general run of things on the ship. She reasoned that as long as she kept in the crowd, which she would, any onlookers would think she was a part of one group or another.

When they met together the next day, Anthony told her his father was willing he use the truck. Now all they had to do was to make the arrangements to leave at the proper time in the morning to catch the evening ferry and then have Dr. Evans be there promptly when the ferry docked.

Gwendalyn wrote the necessary letter to Ina to share with her father about the details of her coming and that he wouldn't have to make the long trip to Serenity Cove. She asked if he would be able to meet her at Sydney at 8:00 AM on Friday when the ferry was scheduled to arrive.

She got the reply through the mail because even though the Evanses had a phone, Gwendalyn's family still didn't feel the need to acquire one. The arrangements were gladly agreed upon and they also wrote that Mr. and Mrs. Gillard needn't worry, as Dr. Evans would certainly be at the ferry when it came in.

* * *

Time sped by with the fishing season starting right after the first week of May. The ice had gone out early and everyone eagerly got into his or her work after the cold winter. Anthony was again kept busy and Gwendalyn spent whatever days she could with Dad out in boat, and the others, helping Mom with the housework.

One day she was going through her wardrobe after one of her fishing trips, she stumbled over the box of sketches and remembered that it still contained an unopened letter from Daniel. She had forgotten about it over the excitement of Ina's wedding and then getting involved with the fishing. She struggled with her emotions and after much deliberation, she went ahead and opened the envelope knowing what was probably inside. Sure enough there was another sketch but this time it was of the two of them dancing on the porch. She turned it over quickly, not to read what he had written, but slammed it into her lap.

"When will this stop?" she questioned herself.

Seeing it overturned in her lap, his hand-written message implored her to read it. She gave in, noticing that this time the message was quite short.

"A year ago this Easter we met and I still remember the way you felt in my arms. I guess I'll be seeing you at the wedding. Until then, Daniel."

"I never gave it a thought that he would be there, but of course he would be, he's Dr. Evans' partner. I guess it's unavoidable that we meet and talk again. There's no point worrying about it. Whatever happens, happens. I'll just have to tell him about Anthony."

She and her mom had talked and decided that the best gift to give Ina was something practical. Something every home would need and also be able to use often. They both agreed on linens for the bedroom and bathroom and placed an order through Sears to have it come in time before Gwendalyn was due to leave.

* * *

Thursday morning arrived and with it Anthony was there to help her with her suitcase and packages.

After saying her good-byes and being cautioned by her parents about her safety, Gwendalyn climbed aboard the truck beside Anthony and they drove off with her parents and Calvin waving and wishing them well.

CHAPTER 20
NEW MEMORIES

The drive was enjoyable and they talked about many things that were going on around home and how the fishing was going. They had stopped at a picnic area, shared the basket of sandwiches and goodies Gwendalyn had brought for the trip, and now were on their way again. She was sitting quietly, enjoying the landscape, when Anthony reached over and clasped her hand in his.

"You know, Gwenny, I'd really like to come with you, especially on the ship. I don't like you being alone with no one to watch out for you and I would come too if I didn't have to get Dad's truck back."

"I know you would and it would be great having you with me this whole weekend."

She had just spoken the words when she realized that if he did come, he and Daniel would have to meet. It would be very awkward for her if he mentioned the sketches he's been sending her.

"Yes it would be great," he agreed, lifting her slender hand to his lips and brushing it with a gentle kiss.

She loved his gentle manner but there were times when she wished he would take her in his arms and kiss her the way he had during their walk in the moonlight on Christmas Eve.

The way Daniel had kissed her stirred her deeply, even though she hadn't expected it, but the memory of it still caused her to tremble.

Once again she scolded herself for allowing her mind to travel back to that reckless scene. Why did it still have such an effect on her? What kind of a hold did Daniel have on her? She knew that each time she received a new sketch, her thoughts for the following week were continually bombarded with memories of Daniel and their time together. Why couldn't she just put him out of her mind and leave him there. She loved Anthony and was one day intending to marry him. Wasn't it enough? She would just have to tell Daniel that she was courting another man and that she was hoping to marry him.

"We're here. Port aux Basque."

Anthony's words brought her out of her reverie for which she was thankful. There was already too much of this trip lost on mind encounters with Daniel and now they were here and soon would have to part.

They purchased her ticket and with it still being a couple of hours before boarding, they carried their picnic basket down close to the rugged shoreline to have their meagre supper.

Anthony talked about his sister coming for a week or two in July because of her husband's job that kept him in a lumber camp till the end of August. It would be good to have her home again and of course Rosemary would want to see 'Genny'.

"Have you seen that large house going up on the north shore?" Gwendalyn had asked Anthony. "Someone's been doing a lot of work and it's getting built rather quickly."

This time is was Anthony who blushed.

"Yes I do know who's building the house," he answered, leaving it at that.

"Well?"

"Well, what?"

"Who's building the big house on the north shore?"

"I was trying to keep that a secret and it seems the people around the cove have done a good job of that as well."

"What are you talking about?"

"This fellow had this plan to build a house for the girl he's courting to give it to her as a surprise wedding present and I'm been trying to do just that."

"Can't you even tell me? I won't let it out."

"Now, Gwendalyn if I tell you, it'll be me letting the secret out that I was supposed to keep."

"OK, I give up, but I could probably figure it out before too long. I know! It's David, isn't it? He's trying to get it built for Mary before their wedding in September. She'll be thrilled. It looks like the best place on the whole cove with that end piece being private and all. It's David. Am I right?"

"I can't give it away, Gwenny," he laughed, you'll just have to wait and see.

Soon it was time to get ready to board and with her belongings collected from the truck, they headed toward the ship.

Their good-bye was shortened by the call for walk-on passengers to begin boarding. The long line of automobiles was being directed on board and chained down for the trip in case of rough water.

Anthony held her and gave her his usual kiss on the cheek, to Gwendalyn's disappointment. He waved at her as she made her way up the gangplank calling, "See you on Sunday."

She couldn't wave back as her arms were heavy laden with her belongings so all she could do was smile and nod her head.

She made her way to the area designated for passengers who chose not to purchase berths for one reason or another. She found a sitting area close beside a quiet family with the oldest child being a girl about thirteen years old.

"This is perfect," she thought. "Anyone would think I was a part of this family." She noticed, though, that the girl was not happy. In fact, her face looked drawn and full of concern. She couldn't help but feel compassion for her and prayed silently that the Lord would help her through whatever was going on in her life.

Gwendalyn looked back on the first whole day she and Anthony had ever spent together and smiled contentedly. No pressure, just a relaxing drive and enjoying each other's company. They had shared two picnics and light-hearted conversation. She dreamed ahead to the future with them being married, resting and soaking in the warmth from a roaring fireplace, after a good, productive day. She hoped to have a fireplace in their home, as she knew how comforting they could be from her stay with Ina and her parents.

She came back to the present sitting in her seat and working on the new embroidery pattern her mother had shown her last week but her heart wasn't in it and soon she gave it up. What could she do to pass the time? She spied her Bible through the partially opened suitcase, picked it up, and began to read in Colossians starting at the first chapter. She continued to read until she got to the final chapter and paused at the fifth and sixth verse and read them again.

"Walk in wisdom toward them that are without, redeeming the time. Let your speech be always with grace, seasoned with salt, that ye may know how ye ought to answer every man."

When she was finished reading the Book, she prayed that she would be a vessel that God could use to further His kingdom, that her heart would always open to the needs of others to share His love with them.

By now the ship had been sailing for more than three hours and her eyes were growing tired. It had been hard to read with the light dimmed for sleeping. She unfolded her small blanket on the small space on the floor and laid down on it. Although it wasn't comfortable at all, she soon found herself drifting into a sound sleep.

She awoke with the breaking of daylight and was intrigued to find the thirteen year old girl sitting close beside her reading her Bible she had left on her seat. She sat up slowly, being careful to not frighten her off, and asked what part she was reading.

"It's the beginning. Genesis. It's all about how God made the earth and everything in it."

"It's interesting, don't you think?"

"Yeah, but do you believe that it's all true?"

"Well, yes. Once you have God living with you, you know He's real because you can sense His presence with you and helping you. There are times when not so good things happen in your life but you know God is with you because He gives you peace, joy, and a hope. Then you know in your heart God is real, and if He's real, then the things written about Him in the Bible must be true."

"I don't think I've heard it put that way before but it seems to make sense. Are you what they call a 'Christian'? And what is a Christian?"

"Yes, I am a Christian and to answer your other question, a Christian is someone who believes in and follows the teachings of Jesus Christ, God's son. We believe that Jesus came as a baby to bring the world salvation. We also believe that when He became a man He taught people how to live a righteous life and that we should obey His teachings. He died a death on the cross so that all who would believe in Him wouldn't have to die; I mean eternal death in hell, but have eternal life in heaven. We believe that He was raised to life after three days conquering death's power over us. A Christian loves the Lord God with all his heart, soul, mind and strength, and loves his neighbour as himself, which means we're to love everyone.

"It was because of God's inexpressible love for us that He sent His only son to bring us salvation and the gift of eternal life.

"Throughout the Bible it talks about how much God loves us, and those who love Him, He cares for, and meets their needs."

"Do you think your parents would mind if you went to get something to eat with me? I could share with you so much more about the love of God."

"I'd like that. I'll just tell my brother so that when Mom and Dad wake up, he can tell them."

* * *

They went to the ship's restaurant and were glad to see that they were opened, it being only 6:15 AM. Gwendalyn bought her her meal and talked with her a half an hour more, learning about her situation. By the end of the conversation, Rowena, as she found out, was asking her how she could become a Christian as well. Gwendalyn led Rowena in a prayer for salvation and when they had finished the young girl's countenance had changed making her look even younger still and more relaxed. It was as if peace had come to her troubled soul. Cheerfulness had taken the place of concern and she looked like she had a delightful secret she couldn't wait to share.

* * *

She was grateful and appreciative when she saw Dr. Evans waiting for her as she disembarked from the ship. Ina was with him and the two girls squealed with delight upon seeing each other. They both climbed in the back seat of the car even though the front seat remained empty.

"I can't believe you're getting married! I was shocked when I read your letter, but I'm very happy for you."

"I had thought, at one time, that maybe you and I could have a double wedding, Daniel and I, and you and Anthony. Well, Daniel wasn't interested in me at all, but I certainly don't mind, I have Franklin now and he's the dearest man I've ever known. He treats me very special. And how about you and Anthony, you've been courting since... your last birthday, something you didn't tell me when I was there," Ina pouted. "Why didn't you tell me then?" she asked.

"Well, even though we admitted our feelings for each other that day, we weren't really courting until after Anthony asked my parents in the middle of November. I didn't want it made known until after Stacey's wedding day."

"Oh, Gwen, I'm just so glad you're here and being my maid of honour. I'm just so excited. I can't wait. Tomorrow I will become Mrs. Franklin Newbury."

"Do you think the bridesmaid's dress will fit me?" Gwendalyn asked, full of concern.

"Of course it will. Don't you remember we bought you that teal dress last year, and I took note how you filled it out a little more when you wore on your birthday? We took that into consideration before buying it. You'll be trying it on when we get home and if it needs any alterations, we have a seamstress we can call."

Things quieted and soon Ina was asleep. Gwendalyn took to looking out the window admiring the view.

Dr. Evans had told Gwendalyn that instead of heading straight home they would drive around the northern 'cape' of Cape Breton Island to show her the magnificent attractions of the Cabot Trail.

* * *

Watching the sea's waves crash over the rugged coastline was the most glorious sight Gwendalyn had ever beheld. Dr. Evans gave an ongoing commentary of the various sites and she enjoyed it immensely. She remembered her dad saying that there were places like this in Newfoundland but she had never before seen such a magnificent sight. She thought of Calvin and hoped that one day he would have the privilege of taking in this and other living pictures the Creator so lovingly displayed for our enjoyment. Thoughts of Anthony arose and she wished he could be here to share this wondrous sight with her.

"I bet I know what you're thinking," Ina whispered, interrupting her thoughts and causing her to smile. She was used to Ina's teasing and could take it pleasurably, now that she and Anthony were courting.

* * *

They were home late in the afternoon and after being rejuvenated enjoying a light meal; they went upstairs to have Gwendalyn try on the

140

bridesmaid dress. It fit almost perfectly except for a couple of tucks needing to be made around the waist area.

Ina had chosen cream and peach for her wedding colors and of course she would be wearing the traditional white symbolizing purity. Franklin would be wearing a black suit of his choice wearing a peach-colored rose boutonniere on the lapel of his jacket matching those of the groomsmen.

After the wedding rehearsal, Gwendalyn spent the evening in Ina's room conversing with her and listening to every story she could possibly tell about her courtship with Franklin. She then shared some of her and Anthony's courting stories but she didn't elaborate as Ina had, as she just wasn't the type to divulge her most intimate of secrets. By the time 10:00 PM rolled around, Gwendalyn was exhausted and went to her room. As soon as her head sank into the fluffed feather pillow she drifted off into a sound, deep sleep.

* * *

She found herself waltzing with Anthony gliding across the dance floor. She had closed her eyes and had laid her head against his shoulder. They slowed and stopped gazing into each other's eyes and soon were engaged in a deep and meaningful kiss, which lasted indefinitely.

"I love you so much," she said feeling the intensity of the moment.

"How I've longed to hear you say those words to me," came the husky voice of Daniel, "and I love you more than you will ever know."

She stood confused for a moment allowing her eyes to focus on her partner. He pulled her into his tender arms and she melted into his embrace.

* * *

Her eyes flew open and she sat upright in her bed trying to see in the darkened room.

"A dream," she said sleepily, trying to make sense of it all.

"It doesn't matter, it's not real," she said aloud, and laid herself down once again to drift into slumber.

She awoke the next morning refreshed and thankful that she hadn't

141

had any other dreams all night. The remembrance of the prior dream continued to repeat in her mind, troubling her.

The family met in the dining room at 10:00 AM and ate a delicious breakfast together. All talk around the table was that of last minute preparations before the wedding ceremony that was to be taking place at 3:30 this afternoon. A reception was to be held starting at 6:00 PM, allowing time after the service for some photos to be taken. The celebration would then continue with a dance.

Ina had informed Gwendalyn that the two of them along with Mrs. Evans would be heading off to the beauty parlor to have their hair styled for the big event. Gwendalyn was somewhat apprehensive about this outing as she had never been to a beauty parlor but she did look forward to the treat of getting her hair done professionally. Whatever made Ina happy on this her first and only wedding day, Gwendalyn was more than willing to do.

*   *   *

All stood in the foyer of the Evans home, eyes glistening and hearts sharing their innermost feelings with Ina about all she means to them. They knew that when she left their household doors momentarily, she would never come back the same person. She would be making her home with her husband and thereafter only coming back for cherished visits.

With all said and tears dried, they headed out to their car for the drive to the New Hope Christian Fellowship where their friend and daughter would become Mrs. Franklin Newbury.

The church was already filled with well-wishers supporting the young couple, as they start out their life together as husband and wife. They met the remainder of the wedding party void of the groom and his attendants who were in the pastor's chamber waiting for the service to begin. The bride's attendants, flower girl and ring boy, along with Ina, waited outside the closed sanctuary doors for the prearranged time in which they were to enter.

They listened as the pastor addressed the congregation with some opening remarks and as gentle piano music filled the church, the groom and the groomsmen made their way to the appropriate positions as done in the rehearsal last night. The bridesmaids walked up the aisle and then a nervous 'maid of honour' slowly entered the sanctuary with over 200 pairs of eyes watching her every move. She was glad for the long dress to cover her shaking legs, and the bouquet to calm her trembling fingers. As she continued towards the front, she tried to avoid the eyes of Daniel who was sitting closely behind the immediate family, but she could feel his unswerving gaze upon her.

The bridal march sounded and Ina, being accompanied by her father, walked slowly up the aisle to meet Franklin.

With the photographs taken, they entered the reception hall with everyone applauding their entrance. They finished their meal and opened a huge mound of gifts and then the music started. The newly wedded couple began the traditional first dance and the next included the attendants, which caused Gwendalyn some discomfort as she was jostled around the dance floor with an ear-to-ear smiling Jonathon.

She remembered being rescued from his arms by Daniel at Ina's birthday, and to some degree, wished it could happen again just to be free of his mechanical dance style. She was relieved when it was all over.

Now, with the program ended, she was free to mingle with the other guests and visit with Ina's relatives and friends.

She was sitting with Dr. and Mrs. Evans having an enjoyable conversation when someone tapped her on the shoulder and she recognized the familiar voice of Daniel before ever seeing his face, asking her to dance.

"Oh sure, you can dance with her," came Dr. Evans reply before Gwendalyn could get her tongue-tied voice to respond, "we were just finishing up here anyhow and I think I'd like to dance with my lovely wife as well."

Gwendalyn felt obligated to dance with Daniel as it seemed Dr. and Mrs. Evans were standing to follow them out onto the dance floor. She was both relieved and discomforted to know that the next dance was a waltz. Relieved because she didn't care to, or even knew how to move around the dance floor as she had seen many other's doing this evening to the lively music, and discomforted to know she would be physically closer to Daniel than she ever expected herself to be again. She wanted these intimate moments to be shared with Anthony alone.

Daniel slid his left hand around her slender waist as she placed her hand upon his shoulder and then they both joined right hands.

"I don't think a day has gone by that I haven't thought of you," he whispered, reliving his memories of her. "I was wondering if you received the sketches I sent, and if you liked them."

"Yes, I did and I thought they were beautifully done. I am sorry for not responding to your letters but I must tell you..."

"No need to explain, Gwendalyn. I know our meeting was all of a sudden and probably too much to handle."

"Yes, I guess it was, but I really must say..."

"Don't concern yourself, I sent those sketches as reminders of our meeting and to let you know that I was thinking of you."

"Yes, but..."

"Let's enjoy the music and have this dance as friends and not talk any more."

Him saying 'friends' settled her for the moment and she began to relax and indeed she was beginning to enjoy this dance. Her head simultaneously lay against his shoulder and she allowed herself to fully absorb this moment. As the music began to fade they slowed and stopped in the middle of the dance floor and were spellbound looking into each other's eyes. Daniel bent his head and was about to kiss her when she all of a sudden realized what was about to happen and stepped back abruptly.

"It's the dream," she whispered, turning to make her way off the dance floor and heading for the punch bowl for a cool drink to regain her composure. Daniel had followed her and was now handing her a glass of punch.

"What was it you said back there?" he asked. "Was it something about a dream?"

"It was nothing," she said. "I just needed a drink."

"Gwendalyn, I think something was happening out there between us. Couldn't you feel it?"

"No, eh, I'm just tired. I wonder if the Evanses will be going home soon."

"I have acquired a car since you were last here. Maybe I could drive you home."

"Eh, no thank you. I think I'd better drive with Dr. and Mrs.

Evans."

With that, she turned away from Daniel and quickly found her way to them. They said they would be leaving as soon as they said their good-byes to Ina and Franklin, who were heading out right away. They each gave Ina and Franklin a hug and sent them off while a group of young people showered them with even more confetti.

"Are you feeling well?" Mrs. Evans asked Gwendalyn. "You seem flushed."

"Oh, I'm fine. It's a little hot in there and I am a little tired."

"Edward, I think we should be on our way home. Gwendalyn and I are exhausted."

"Yes, of course, my dear. I'll go and get the car while you two get your wraps."

Once at home, Vera brought tea into the parlor as the three conversed with each other about how well everything had gone. The realization that Ina wouldn't be joining them this evening set in and she was missed terribly, but all were happy for her.

They went off to bed shortly thereafter and next thing Gwendalyn knew she was awakened with the brightness of the sun streaming in her window. She got out of bed and then out onto the balcony without getting dressed. She closed her eyes and breathed in the fresh morning air feeling invigorated with each new breath.

She opened her eyes and was startled to see Daniel standing outside his car. He seemed to be looking down at something though she couldn't see just what. She quickly ran back inside her mind racing with questions.

Did he see me in my pyjamas? How long was he there? Was he there when I first came out and caught his attention? What was he doing here so early this morning?

She looked at the clock and was surprised that it read 11:15 AM. "It's not early at all and I've slept the morning away."

She got dressed and tidied her room and headed downstairs to find Dr. and Mrs. Evans already in the dining room enjoying a wonderful brunch.

"Come join us, my dear," Mrs. Evans spoke up upon seeing her come into the room. "We didn't know what time you would be awakening so we went ahead and got started."

"I'm sorry I slept so late, but this does look delicious. By the way, have you seen Daniel this morning?"

"No, we haven't," replied Dr. Evans. "Why would you ask that?"

"Well, I thought I saw him out front standing beside his car."

"I must go have a look," Dr. Evans said.

Voices were heard re-entering the house and soon Dr. Evans and Daniel joined the ladies.

"You were right, Gwendalyn. Daniel was outside and was just about to knock on the door when I opened it. I've invited him to join us for brunch. Vera will be bringing an extra place setting."

"Well, good morning, Daniel!" Mrs. Evans exclaimed cheerfully. "How good of you to join us for brunch. You're just in time. Gwendalyn came downstairs just before you got here. And to what do we owe the pleasure of your company this fine morning?"

"Good morning, Mrs. Evans, Gwendalyn. Actually, I came to see Gwendalyn and I've already had that pleasure this morning."

Gwendalyn immediately turned red and a look of disbelief washed across her face. She lowered her head as if to say a silent prayer for breakfast giving her an excuse not to look up into questioning faces.

"I was thinking about asking her to go out for a drive with me this morning but it appears it'll be afternoon before we would get started, if she were willing."

"That's a wonderful idea," Dr. Evans jumped in. "I mean if it's OK with Gwendalyn, and as long as you have her back in plenty of time for me to take her to the ferry."

Feeling as if she were put in a tight spot again, she felt she could do nothing else but give an affirmative answer.

They discussed some options of where to go that might be the most scenic and Daniel asked Gwendalyn if there was anything in particular that she was wanting to see before going home to Newfoundland.

She suggested going to a town near Sable Island to see the 'Widow Walks', or perhaps a trip to the Annapolis Valley and maybe to the nearby 'Port Royal Habitation'. Each trip would be too long a distance to travel before leaving for the ferry so they decided that they would take in the sights of Halifax, as Gwendalyn still hadn't seen a lot of them.

They left for their drive around 12:30 PM with Daniel reassuring Dr.

Evans that he would have Gwendalyn back by 2:30 PM. She could then pack and rest before having to set out again at 4:30 PM to be at North Sydney to board the ferry in plenty time before casting off.

For nearly two hours, the two drove together throughout the city of Halifax exclaiming over the different sites, especially the old Town Clock that was erected in 1803. At one time they sat at the harbour's edge and viewed Halifax's twin city, Dartmouth. The two cities seemed to challenge each other across the narrows of the Halifax harbour.

On their way back Gwendalyn had told Daniel that she had a really good time and that she was glad he had come over to take her out. After he parked the car he reached over and took her hand in his and raised it to his lips saying he was the one who was delighted that she had agreed to his suggestion of going out together, even if it was just for a drive.

He was looking intently at her and was about to say something when Vera came running out of the house calling her name. Gwendalyn quickly looked through the opened window to see the plump lady breathlessly run up to the car announcing that Ina was on the telephone and wanted to speak with her.

"I have to go, Daniel. Thank you again for the great outing."

With that she was gone and he was left alone with his unvoiced thoughts watching her run quickly into the house followed by Vera.

Ina had called to say good-bye and that they were just leaving for a short honeymoon at Franklin's family's cabin at Lake Ainsley on Cape Breton Island. She sounded so cheerful and happy that Gwendalyn felt a twinge of jealously surge through her but shook it off and expressed her happiness for her friend.

Dr. and Mrs. Evans set out at 4:30 PM with Gwendalyn to ensure they would arrive in good time before the ferry's departure.

"I'm glad to see that you and Daniel are becoming such good friends," Dr. Evans said. "He's such an honest hard worker and he seems quite interested in you."

"Yes, it seems we are becoming friends but I guess I'm just still getting to know him."

"I can vouch for his character," he continued. "He's very responsible and reliable."

Gwendalyn wondered about this topic of conversation and where it was leading. At one time she thought she heard him say that he had hoped that Daniel and Ina would have married, but he had lowered his voice so she couldn't be sure.

They stopped for dinner along the way and arrived at North Sydney just in time for Gwendalyn to buy her ticket and prepare to board. She hugged her dear friends knowing that with Ina married and in her own home, there probably wouldn't be as many trips to visit them.

She ascended the gangplank looking back to see that they were watching her, making sure she got safely on board. They were such loving people and she thanked God for bringing them into her life.

With the excitement of the wedding over and knowing she was heading back for normal life, she could relax and before too long she was asleep on a bit of floor space next to her seat.

When she awoke, she was happy to see a stir in the group around who were gathering their belongings saying that they were near shore. She got up and packed away her blanket and went to freshen up before meeting Anthony when they docked.

Sure enough, Anthony was there, waving to her as she came down to meet him. He was embarrassed by his own appearance and had told her that he had come yesterday evening and had slept in the truck. She reassured him saying that he looked 'just fine' to her.

They had been driving a little while when Gwendalyn's tummy began making gurgling and growling sounds and although she tried to hide it by talking, Anthony figured it out.

"I'm sorry, Gwenny. I never thought to ask if you had breakfast on the ferry. We'll stop at the next town for a bite to eat. I have a couple of oranges in the bag there. Why don't you peel 'em and we'll have a snack together."

They stopped at a nearby town and enjoyed a hearty breakfast.

As they talked, Gwendalyn was aware of just how much she was falling in love with him. He was always so considerate and kind. He seemed so stable and confident and knew just what he wanted out of life and how to make it happen. She sat dreamily, contemplating on what strong characteristics he had. His facial and bodily features would deem him more than attractive in the eyes of many.

She was thrust from her reverie by the sound of his voice saying that they should 'get back on the road'.

As they continued on the drive, Gwendalyn nonchalantly inched her way over to be nearer to him and when she was where she wanted to be, he slipped his arm around her shoulder, at which she smiled contentedly.

The next thing she knew she was awakening to realize she had been sleeping with her head turned in to his chest and felt him caressing her upper arm with his left hand. She felt deceitful continuing in this comforting position, but she wanted it to last a few moments longer. Anthony was now calling to awaken her and she brought herself up to sit correctly offering an apology for sleeping on him and now she had to act as though she were just waking up.

"No need for apologies," he said. "I enjoyed every moment of these past two hours. We're only about ten minutes from home."

"Two hours!" she exclaimed. "And ten minutes! Wow, that didn't take long. Time flies when you're having fun."

"Or sleeping," he reminded her.

"Yeah, that too," she laughed.

She thanked him and leaned over to give him a hug telling him how much she appreciated him taking the time off from fishing to escort her to the ferry and back. He held her hand and kissed her cheek before she got out of the truck saying that he wouldn't have wanted it any other way. Spending time with her was far better than being out in boat.

She noticed a new car parked outside their house but didn't pay any real attention to it, as different people had often parked there with Dad not owning a vehicle. Once in the house, she sat with her mother on the couch telling every minute detail of how Ina's wedding had gone, from her dress and the flower girl right down to her bouquet. Again she purposefully left out any mention of Daniel, as she didn't want anything concerning him to come up in conversations when Anthony was around.

CHAPTER 21
LOSS & GAIN

"We have some news for you, too," Calvin said grinning. "A couple of weeks ago Dad was asked to buy some tickets on a special prize. He only had enough money to buy one so he did. He didn't tell us because you know what Mom would say about that. Well, he won!"

"Won what?" she questioned excitedly.

"The car outside. Didn't you see it? Dad always said they were too expensive and now he's won one. He even let me drive it already. Come on, I'll show you."

Calvin fairly yanked her to her feet and pulled her out the door followed by Mom and Dad.

Dad took his family for their first ever, evening drive. Gwendalyn was thrilled and kept exclaiming over their good fortune.

* * *

With the good news, came the bad. The news of poor old Mr. Bridger's passing was the talk of Serenity Cove and even though it was a Friday, all of the fishermen, out of respect for him, laid aside their nets and traps until the day after the funeral service.

Anthony had known of his failing health, as it was how he had acquired his boat and motor and much of his fishing gear. He had faithfully gone daily over to the Bridger's to help in any way he could with chores, even after tiring days of fishing. He had spent many hours over the last winter at their home chopping and hauling firewood. Mrs. Bridger was always a kindly woman who baked cookies and had him in for visits when the choring was done. She had confiding in him on how Mr. Bridger's health was steadily decreasing. And now he was gone.

Anthony had gone to pay his respects personally to Mrs. Bridger bringing her comfort. He told her he would continue to come over as usual to help her in any way he could. She thanked him for his kindness. He was relieved, though, that her son had gotten word of his father's passing and had come immediately to console his mother and grieve together.

To match everyone's spirits, the day of the funeral was cloudy and threatening to rain. It seemed to continue in that way for the rest of the week but they had only two actual rainy days.

The following week cleared and life at the cove was back on course. The fishermen were busy fishing, cleaning, salting, and drying, while the women-folk cooked, cleaned, gardened, and helped with the on-shore work of the fishery, and on it went.

* * *

June 30 came quickly and Gwendalyn forgot all about her birthday with the capelin coming in and everyone around the shoreline excitedly catching the too numerous to count small silvery fish. Even the tiniest tots, all of maybe two to three years, were trying to grab the flicking fish that were tossed onto the rocks. Eventually they would grasp one only to have it slip from their chubby little fingers. It was an exciting week when the capelin came in, so it was like a celebration all around the shore.

* * *

She was surprised to see Anthony sitting at the table when she came down the stairs and was glad that she had freshened up and combed her hair. She had rested a little just before dinner, being a little tired out after gathering capelin all morning.

She looked at the table with pleasure, seeing that her mother had made several of her favorite dishes. They all sat around and when Dad prayed a blessing on her, 'this being her special day,' she remembered that today was her seventeenth birthday. After the amens, she opened her eyes saying that she had forgotten all about it. She looked around the table knowing that the people she loved, and was dear to her, had not let her day go unnoticed in spite of all the commotion over the capelin.

She got up and removed all the main meal dishes and left over food from the table and brought hot tea, cream and sugar, mugs and spoons. She was then told by Calvin to sit down, saying that he would get dessert.

He came in from the porch carrying a birthday cake all aglow with candles while everyone joined in singing 'Happy Birthday'. She cut each one a piece of Mom's homemade chocolate cake and they all sat around joking and laughing, sipping hot tea, and enjoying birthday cake.

Anthony spoke up and asked if he could take a walk with Gwendalyn but before she said anything she looked to her mother for permission and with her nodding in agreement, she got up from the table saying that she would be back to do the dishes.

They walked out the door and Anthony led her to the same forested area they had gone on that one moonlit Christmas Eve. He helped her, once again, through the thick bush and into the clearing. They walked a while talking about the capelin coming in today and anything else that was happening around the cove.

Anthony took hold of her slender hand and turned her to face him.

"Gwenny, I have something I need to talk to you about, to ask you. We've known each other all our lives and we are really good friends, real close, I mean, right?"

"Of course we are, you know that."

"For quite a long time now I've been thinking of the day when I could talk with you, I mean ask you if..."

He began rubbing his hands and shuffling his feet, which Gwendalyn knew, was caused by nervousness. At first she had no idea what was on his mind but now, by the way he was fidgeting, she had a suspicion of what he was trying to say.

"Well, Gwenny, I told you before how I felt about you, that I loved you and I do love you now, more than ever, if that's possible. I've thought long and hard and prayed earnestly about this and, well, I wanted to ask you if you would do me the honour of becoming my, eh, my wife."

He breathed out a deep sigh of relief knowing that he had gotten it out without messing up and now her silence concerned him and he wondered if this is what she wanted. He thought she wanted this as much as he did.

"You don't have to answer right away," he said, fidgeting again. "You could think..."

She opened her eyes and placed her fingers upon his lips.

"Sh-h-h," she said. "I've been wondering if or when you would say those words to me and now upon hearing them I was absorbing the moment, giving it its proper place in my heart. Anthony, I have loved you for a long time now and you mean more to me than you could ever know. I am so happy that you have asked me to become your wife. And, yes, I will marry you but I must tell you that it is I who am honoured that you would want me."

At that Anthony burst out a loud 'Woo-hoo' and picked Gwendalyn up swinging her around as he had done on her sixteenth birthday.

He steadied her back on her feet and his gaze fell upon her lovely face. She met his gaze and he reached for her and pulled her into his strong arms for a tender embrace. His eyes continued to penetrate hers and she lifted her lips to his and they engaged in a long and meaningful kiss. Gwendalyn felt the tingling sensations surge through her body, but this time it felt right and true being with the man she loved and was now going to marry.

"My darling," he whispered, as he again caressed her lips with his. "I've longed to do this many times over the past year but restrained myself out of respect for you."

"Oh, Anthony, thank you for telling me that. So many times I've wanted you to kiss me and wondered if you didn't enjoy our kiss in the moonlight. I was afraid that maybe it was a disappointment for you."

"My dear sweet Gwenny, if you only knew how hard it was for me to hold back. I have relived that one night over and over in my mind, holding on to it and waiting for the day to make it fresh again. I love you, my darling," he said, and again kissed her deeply.

"I almost forgot," he said, reaching into his pocket and pulled out a tiny white box. He opened it and turned it around for her to see.

"Oh my, it's beautiful," she exclaimed. "Anthony, I never expected a ring."

He lifted it out, placed it on her left hand ring finger, and brought her hand to his lips.

She threw her arms around his neck and whispered words of endearment in his ear.

He returned the sentiments and then began to speak.

"I'd like it if you would walk with me to the north shore. There is something else I would like to show you over there."

"I'd love to, but I promised Mom that I would do the dishes. How about we stop in on our way over. You could visit while I clean up."

"OK," he smiled, "and I might even give you a hand."

When they walked in the house the kitchen was totally clean and all dishes were washed and put away. It appeared that Mom and Dad were getting ready to join Calvin down on the beach to catch more capelin.

"Oh Mom, I didn't mean to be gone so long. I was really going to wash the dishes. Anthony said he wanted to show me something on the north shore but I told him I had to stop in before going over there. But Mom, look!" she said, putting her hand up close to her mother so she could see the ring. "Anthony and I are engaged to be married and he gave me this ring."

"Oh, Gwendalyn, it's beautiful," she cried. "Anthony, you didn't say anything about this."

"I guess that was a surprise for you all," he said smiling.

"You mean you knew that Anthony was going to ask me to marry him?" she questioned, looking at Anthony.

"Well, I had to ask your parents, especially your dad, before I could ask you."

"It was the right thing to do," said her father, "and if your young man has something he wants to show you, you best be going with him," he continued, giving Anthony a wink.

They left again holding hands and discussing when would be a good date to set for the wedding. They agreed that after Gwendalyn's 18th birthday would be the best.

They rounded the final turn and made their way out to the point of the north shore.

Upon approaching the recently-built house Gwendalyn noticed it faced the south overlooking the bay to the homes on the other side. The east side looked out over the ocean, and the west view was of other homes around the cove. It looked somewhat similar to the Evans home in Nova Scotia except that this one was smaller. Even the balcony and porch continued in a U-shape around the west, south, and east side. She was awed by its sight but looked away and started walking on toward the point. She determined that no matter how wonderful she thought it looked, she would be happy for Mary and David, or whomever it belonged to.

Anthony came up beside her and turned her back toward the house. "What do you think?" he asked.

"I think it's a beautiful house," she said. "Are you finally going to let out your secret of who's building it and for whom?"

"Yes, I think I might, but how about we go inside and have a look?"

"Do you think it's right for us to go in? Did you get permission or something? And didn't you say you had something to show me out on the point?"

"Yes, Gwendalyn, I do have something to show you, and you're looking at it."

"I don't understand," she said, confusion showing on her face.

"This house is ours, Gwenny, it'll be your new home."

"It can't be true," she gasped, looking at Anthony.

"It is true, my darling. Over the last year we've been working at it as much as we could, and even harder, trying to keep it a secret from you. I wanted to wait until we were married to let you know, but too many people around the cove knew about it. I knew it wouldn't be a secret much longer so I chose the day of our engagement to reveal this long-kept secret."

"Oh, Anthony, this is all too wonderful."

"Well, how about we go in and I'll give you the grand tour?"

He opened the door and made a motion for her to enter first. "After you, my lady," he said.

She stood in the entranceway and was awed by how much bigger it looked on the inside. The scent of fresh-cut lumber awakened her senses even further as she took in the scene before her.

"There is a big closet over here on the left and if you'll follow me I show you your kitchen and dining room. I know we eat in the kitchens in our parents' homes but I wondered if it would be better to have them separated a little."

They walked a short distance to the right and went through the entrance to the kitchen. Right away Gwendalyn saw something across the room that grabbed her attention. She walked up to it and ran her trembling fingers over the most beautiful old-fashion wood cook stove she had ever seen.

"It was my grandma's," he said quietly. "My grandpa bought it twelve years ago when the fire box in the old one finally burned through. She loved the new one, but it was only a year later that Grandpa died and then Grandma died three years after. It's only had four years use and since then the house was sold. Before that, Dad, Carl, and I moved it into storage because Dad really wanted one of us to have it in one of our homes. When Carl and Stephanie moved so far away, Dad asked me if I would like it. I immediately said yes knowing your appreciation for these stoves, even though the electric ones seem easier to use."

"I'm so glad it's here. I will treasure it always."

"Over here is the dining room and I thought that having the kitchen and dining room opened to each other with cupboards and counters separating it a little would be easier for serving and clean up, as well as heating. If you want though, we could make it two separate rooms."

"I think I like it this way. It makes the whole area look more spacious."

Anthony led her out through the dining area's carefully designed archway and to the right, to a small room.

"This will be the bathroom and you will have the comforts of an indoor flushing toilet, a sink, and a large bathing tub that you can stretch out and soak in. There will be hot and cold running water in the sink and tub and also in the kitchen sink. I'm hoping that it'll be finished and working well by the time we're married and ready to move in."

"Over here is the room for washing clothes. There's this new electric wringer-washing machine that washes the clothes and then you put the clothes between two rollers that brings the clothes through, squeezing the water out. I'll try to have one of those for you before we're married. There'll also be a large sink here to get the water from and hand-washing other clothes. That door leads outside where I'll have some clothes lines set up."

"Anthony, I can't believe all this. I know this is possible from what I saw in the Evans home, but how can you afford all these modern things?"

"Don't worry, Gwenny. For three years I've been saving the share of the profits dad's been giving me. I did buy Mr. Bridger's boat and motor, but he practically gave it to me because of the deal I made with him about doing work around his place. This is the second year for me to be working on my own and all the money I earn goes into the house. Dad's been helping me out with his savings, no matter how many times I said no. He says that I'll be around to help him out when he needs it. So while I'm out fishing, he goes ahead to town and picks up the things your dad says we'll be needing next."

"Did you say my dad?"

"Yes, he's been in on this little secret for months now and helping out a lot with the building and planning. It sure helps having a real carpenter around."

"I can't believe I never knew anything about this before now," she said, looking around in wonderment.

"Come, I want to show you the rest of the house."

He led her from the laundry room to the living room saying that they would have a fireplace, comfy sofas and chairs, as well as shelves lining the far wall for books. Next they went upstairs and Anthony explained to her that the whole upstairs was dedicated to bedrooms.

"This will be our bedroom and as you can see it looks out over the ocean and across the bay to where your parents home is. The other three bedrooms will be for our children. The smaller one next to ours you can use as a sewing room or anything you want until we need it for a bedroom."

Speaking about such an intimate aspect of their relationship caused Gwendalyn much embarrassment and she lowered her head to hide her flushed face.

"I know it's not finished and it may not be even after we're married but I'll do my best to make so. It will be liveable and I know it won't be long till..."

"Oh, Anthony, you have already given me everything. This house is beautiful and I will always cherish you as my husband. You mean everything to me and I will be happy working beside you to complete our home together. I love you for you, not what you can give me or how our house will eventually be."

"Gwenny, you are the dearest girl I have ever known and you have made me the happiest man in the whole world."

He gathered her in his arms once again and lowered his head as she lifted hers as their lips met. At length Gwendalyn laid the side of her face against his shoulder and she could hear and feel the rapid beating of his heart. This brought her pleasure knowing that he was stirred in this way because of her. She longed for the day when she could give herself totally to him. There they stood, enjoying the comfort of each other's arms, allowing time to slip away as they strengthened the bond between them.

They were interrupted from their sweet embrace with the sound of knocking on the front door below. Anthony led the way and opened the door to find his parents, as well as hers, along with Calvin standing outside bearing goodies and ginger ale.

"We've come to help you celebrate," Mrs. Bowman said cheerfully.

They filled glasses with the bubbly drink and proceeded to toast the newly engaged couple. Smiles, laughter, and cheers were joyously shared in the small group.

Gwendalyn took the ladies on a tour of the house sharing every detail Anthony had first shared with her. When they got back, the men were discussing what was to be done next, with her father steering them in a higher priority direction.

Gwendalyn expressed her thanks to everyone in the group for all the work each one had done. She went up to her father and hugged him lovingly, stating with tearful joy, how much she appreciated him helping in the building of her soon-to-be home.

* * *

In her room, later that night, Gwendalyn fingered a second envelope she had received in the mail. The first was from Ina, sending her birthday greetings. Even though just recently married, her dearest friend wouldn't let her birthday go by without writing a letter and sending her warmest wishes. If Gwendalyn's parents had a telephone, Ina would've phoned her and they would have talked for a long time conversing about everything new that happened in the past three weeks since the wedding. And now, Gwendalyn had even more exciting news to share with her closest friend. She'd have to write soon, maybe even before she went to sleep tonight.

But now, the envelope she held in her hands, daring her to open it, stirred unwelcome feelings once again in her heart. The all-too familiar name on the return address let her know what contents she felt sure it would hold. Because of it, her mind wandered back to the wedding and the dance they had enjoyed. She chastened herself for the remembrance and decided she would just open it, look briefly, and stow it away with the others she had accumulated over the past year or so.

Daniel had again outdone himself with this simple sketch. It was of her again. She was portrayed beautifully walking down the aisle carrying a bouquet of flowers. She looked at length at the picture, awed by it's life-like qualities and then contemplated the natural skill by which it had been drawn.

She turned it over with some apprehension to read the expected note.

"My dearest Gwendalyn,
Your appearance, that day, gave new meaning to the word beautiful. I treasured our dance and felt as if something had happened between us, something strengthening our friendship or moving us on to something more. Did you feel it too and does it hold special remembrances for you? I can only hope that it does. Yours always, Daniel."

Gwendalyn tried to deny it, and tried ever so hard to have it mean nothing, nothing at all, but the feelings were still there. She couldn't help it. She couldn't make them leave her. It was real. Something did happen.

As she placed the drawing and its message inside the hidden box, she determined in her heart and mind to push it far from her.

She could not and would not allow her feelings or thoughts to go anywhere near him. She was engaged to be married. She loved Anthony. Even if something, something that would soon be insignificant, had caused her some desire to be with another, she would set her mind and will to forget it and go on with the security and love she had found in her fiancé.

She would write Ina immediately and ask her to talk to Daniel, telling him about her relationship with Anthony and their recent engagement. She couldn't bear to write Daniel personally for she knew she would have to put a lot of thought into a letter, and she was afraid of where her thoughts might take her.

With that in mind, she accomplished the task and then put her heart and mind to rest knowing she wouldn't see any more of these sketches that always caused such heart-felt and mindful intimate intrusions upon her. Daniel was just a friend now, had to be just a friend, nothing more.

CHAPTER 22
PREPARATIONS

The rest of the summer and fall sped by with planning the wedding and sewing curtains and stuffing cushions. Her mother always guided her to colors reasoning this or that why the color would be a good choice.

Anthony was working very hard in the fishery to bring in as much funds as possible to have their home ready to live in by July 14, 1952. That was the date of their wedding and Gwendalyn was surprised how quickly that date was coming upon them.

During the winter she had many times gone to the house to help Anthony and the others with whatever she could, but mostly by bringing hot and cold drinks and baked goods, for refreshments.

There were times when just the two of them would sit on the floor in front of the roaring fireplace enjoying a simple meal Gwendalyn had brought from her home. She was pleased to serve hot tea from boiling water that had just been boiled on the old cook stove that was now very operational. She would imagine herself preparing savory mouth-watering meals for her husband over this magnificent reliable treasure. It was amazing that on such cold wintry days, this wood-stove, along with the fireplace, would send warmth through the entire house. They had decided to have the living room open to the rest of the house to allow the welcoming heat to distribute itself throughout.

They would make the living room somewhat private by using shelving as a divider from the foyer for books, trinkets, and houseplants. Gwendalyn loved to see the green plants growing in her mother's home, and through the cold months, blooms of vibrant color would be bursting forth, defying nature.

Gwendalyn was more than happy to help in the designing and situating of her kitchen cupboards, and then was delighted in seeing her ideas become a reality. She felt so blessed to have such a home and watch her dreams come true.

Anthony had gone away for the months of April, May, and the first two weeks of June with Gwendalyn's father working on the construction of several new homes and businesses in the city of Corner Brook. He had taken every possible opportunity to add to his finances to secure his future with Gwendalyn.

She had received, to her surprise, two more sketches from Daniel, one at Christmas and one at Easter. She wondered why he would be continuing to send her sketches but reasoned that it must be out of friendship only. And so, it was intimate memories of Anthony that filled her heart.

She had missed him terribly but busied herself as best she could with helping her mother in the home, and Calvin with repairs on the nets. She was glad for the time she spent gardening, now working with the newly warmed soil.

It was during one of those times that her mind went to the garden she would one day have herself. From those ideas, she decided to check out the possibilities of a garden beside her new home. She had brought her prong and shovel and finding an area that she thought suitable, she began working the soil, removing roots and rocks to make it a productive vegetable garden.

On one of those outings, Mr. Bowman came upon her preparing the soil and admiringly told her that this was where he and Anthony had first thought would make a good garden. He then took one of the tools and began helping with the hard but fulfilling work.

Before long it was ready for planting and Gwendalyn prayed God's blessings on her garden as she dropped each seed into place.

Each day she would visit this quiet place willing the vegetables to grow and if the soil looked too dry or hot she would water it lovingly. Her inner sense of joy and even pride in what she had accomplished was all she needed in return for all the hard work she had done. She often gave thanks to the Lord for all His blessings and especially for Mr. Bowman who had, every day, when seeing her heading to her garden, would show up to work beside her.

Even though the task was completed, he would again be there to talk with her on his way to the house to work on some project inside the house.

It was three weeks later, on one of those days, while she was watering the now appearing seedlings, that she heard the familiar footsteps approach from behind her.

"Here you are, my darling Gwenny." Anthony's voice broke through the beautiful peaceful scene and upon hearing his voice she dropped her watering can and rushed into his arms.

"My father thought you'd be here. He has told me you have been spending a lot of your time over here working on a secret project," he said, holding her. "And now I see, and I am overwhelmed even more by your limitless qualities of being a productive, loving, and caring woman. I was reading in the Bible through the book of Proverbs and at the end was where I found you. It went like this: *'Who can find a virtuous woman? for her price is far above rubies'*. That's you, my darling. You are worth far more than rubies. There's much more I can relate to you from that passage and I will read it all to you one day soon."

She looked into his eyes and saw that they were red and brimming from unshed tears.

"I love you so much, Anthony Bowman. What ever did I do to make you love me so?"

"Just being you is, and always will be, reason enough for me to love you. I have said a couple of times now that you have made me the most happiest man in the entire world, but the day you say 'I do' will indeed surpass the rest."

* * *

"I have a surprise for you," Anthony had said once again as he had in the years past after enjoying a birthday dinner with her family. This time Anthony's parents came over to help celebrate their daughter-in-law-to-be's 18th birthday.

She looked toward her mother for permission and with the acknowledging nod, she arose from the table to take yet another walk with Anthony.

They walked the distance around the cove toward their new home. Anthony had banned her from coming to the house since he returned from Corner Brook, although she couldn't keep away from her ever-growing garden. Every two to three days she would be there picking out any weeds that poked through. She could hear the hammering and other building noises coming from inside the house and was tempted many times to go in but kept her distance. Now, today, she was to be shown whatever secrets the house now held.

Anthony held her hand as they stepped inside and then asked her to close her eyes as rounded the corner to the left toward the living room.

"OK, you can look now," he announced.

"Oh, Anthony. Where on earth did you ever get such beautiful furniture?" she asked in astonishment.

"It was my Grandma's. We had it stored in the attic in our house. Dad was more than willing that we have it and so this is a birthday present for you as well as a wedding present for us."

"I can't believe it! The colors in this furniture will match the curtains I've been working on for the windows. Even the cushions will be perfect. Actually, it was Mom who convinced me to use these colors. Did she know about this?"

With the nodding of Anthony's head, she realized why Mom had been so adamant with her suggestions and only agreeing on certain colors.

"There is another piece of furniture you must see. It's here in the dining room. This was Mom's. Dad wanted Grandma's dining room set moved in long before her house went up for sale, and so Mom's set was moved to the attic and now it's here."

"Anthony, I don't know what to say. I feel so blessed but at the same time wonder why all this should be mine, ours, I mean."

"I do know what you mean, Gwenny, but it was you who told me years ago about the verses in the Bible that said that if you trust in the Lord and do good, and if you delight yourself in the Lord, then He would give you the desires of your heart. It was you who taught me to trust in the Lord and He has certainly given me the desires of my heart. And from what I have seen, you have lived a life dedicated to the Lord and so He has blessed you, and us."

Gwendalyn, overcome by emotion, spoke softly, as if to herself.

"Psalm 37. I've read it over and over again entrusting my life to God, but I never dreamed it would lead to all this. God is so loving and kind but I still feel so undeserving."

"Thank Him for His blessings, Gwenny, and if I say so myself, you're the most deserving person I know of."

She wrapped her arms around him and Anthony held her gently, soothing her, as she cried tears of thankfulness on his shoulder.

He then took her by the hand and led her to the bathroom where he showed her the flushing toilet, tub and sink and then motioned for her to turn the tap. Gwendalyn squealed with delight as warm to hot water flowed from the faucet. The large sink in the laundry room had a scrubbing board and Anthony apologized for not having the new washing machine he'd hoped for before their wedding. He explained that he wouldn't be able to buy it for another couple of months as the finances came in. He also apologized for the empty space between cupboards where the new electric range was to be.

She took his face in her warm hands and kissed him gently on both his cheeks and then placed her lips on his expressing her love and appreciation for him.

"My dear sweet Anthony, you have already given so much more than any woman could ever hope to have. Fall and winter will be here again soon, and I don't think I would even use an electric range if I had one."

He held her hand and squeezed it with appreciation and then again led her upstairs. The three smaller bedrooms were yet unfinished but the main bedroom, theirs, was pretty much finished and set up beautifully with a new bedroom suite. Carefully situated around the room was a dresser with a mirror, a chest of drawers, and a new large decorative bed frame supporting a box spring and mattress still in it's protective plastic covering. The built-in closet still needed doors and the floors needed rugs but it looked wonderful and homey to Gwendalyn.

She was glad that over the past five years, since turning thirteen, she had started a hope chest and it was now overfilled with the many domestic furnishings she could put to use in this, her new home. She imagined the two carefully stitched quilts and the cheerfully colored, knitted afghan she had finished not too long ago, now dressing this comfortable bed.

"With the wedding being only two weeks away, do you think I could start bringing my things over and get them situated?" she asked Anthony.

Anthony was only too pleased to have Gwendalyn take such an interest in their home and already wanting to decorate it.

She, along with her mother, made several trips around the cove in the next two weeks and spent many joyous hours hanging curtains and arranging necessities for each room.

Anthony had been kept very busy, daily bringing in an abundant catch and working steadily with the in-shore cleaning, salting and drying. Much of the time his father worked beside him sharing words of wisdom and encouragement for the new change in his life that was about to take place.

A week and a half had passed since her eighteenth birthday and there was no sign of any sketches from Daniel and although its absence relieved her, she did feel a slight wave of melancholy wash over her. She felt as though a part of her life, that had helped her grow and mature in things of an intimate nature, had definitely ended. She had said good-bye to Daniel for good after this reality had finally been received.

She excitedly planned with her mother and other ladies around the cove the final arrangements for the outdoor reception preparations. They had hoped and prayed for a beautiful sunny day but if the weather didn't co-operate, the pastor had given permission for the reception to be held in the church basement.

CHAPTER 23
THE WEDDING

Gwendalyn awoke early on the morning of July 14, 1952, or she thought it was early. Her room still remained darkened and no sunshine brightened her room this morning. She looked at the clock and was amazed to see that it was 9:15 AM. She threw off the covers and went to the window and was disappointed by the view outside. The skies were indeed grey and threatening to pour out its accumulated condensed water vapour.

She flicked on her light and that brightened her room somewhat. She was determined not to let dismal weather hamper her cheerful spirits. This was to be the best and most memorable day of her entire life and nothing could change or suppress the inner joy that she could hardly contain herself. This afternoon, at 2:00 PM, she would become Mrs. Anthony Bowman, and that thought brought her a greater happiness than she had ever known.

There was a skip in her step as she entered her mother's kitchen. Mom and Dad were sitting at the table finishing their breakfast and a plate with just a few crumbs and an empty mug was all that remained in her brother's place.

Upon her arrival Mom started to get up to prepare her daughter a hearty breakfast but Gwendalyn laid her hand on her mother's shoulder saying she would be happy to do it. It wasn't much to prepare as Mom had pan-fries and bacon already prepared and moved to the side of the cook stove to keep them warm.

She quickly had two eggs fried easy over to perfection, and feeling quite hungry, piled the remainder of the bacon and potatoes onto her plate. As she joined her parents at the table, Mom cut a thick slice of fresh homemade bread from a loaf she had baked just yesterday. To finish her meal she enjoyed yet another slice of bread thickly spread with her favorite bake apple jam. Mom and Dad both commented on, and were delighted with her appetite this morning, in spite of the nervous excitement she displayed.

* * *

Now arrayed in her simple but elegant white wedding gown she looked at herself in the longer mirror in her mother's bedroom. The front sides of her long shining hair adorned thin braids with thin white ribbon throughout it and gathered at the back and then hung loosely down her back. Her veil still sat on the dresser waiting to be pinned into place. She held her beautiful bouquet of domestic flowers cut fresh from her mother's and neighbour's gardens earlier today. Her neighbour, Mrs. Williams, always had a knack for arranging flowers and she was thrilled that Gwendalyn had asked her to prepare the bouquets for her and her bridesmaids.

Her closest friends from the cove were waiting downstairs dressed in their violet bridesmaid dresses admiring their bouquets.

Dad entered the room as Gwendalyn sat on the bed while Mom continued to place bobby pins where needed to secure the veil.

"I don't think I've ever seen you looking more beautiful than you do today, my beauty," he said as he sat beside her.

Mom sat on the other side and all three looked into the mirror as the two proud parents sat admiring their youngest daughter.

"We wanted to tell you how happy and blessed we felt all these years watching you grow and mature," Mom began. "You've always been respectable and responsible and you've treated your father and me with the utmost respect. How I've loved seeing you grow into the woman you are today. You've always made the right choices and today we are especially pleased with your choice of a husband."

"All these years I've called you my beauty. But you are indeed an indescribable charm full of grace and your beauty goes far beyond the outer appearance. Much more important, though, is that of your inner beauty that continually shines through, even in your old fishing gear. I want to tell you how much joy you have brought me over the years. All those fishing trips together meant so much to me and I can still see the excitement on your face when we hauled in that 30-pound salmon. I'm so very happy that God, in His master plan, saw fit to grant this old man such a daughter. I sure hope you'll find time to go out in boat with me again."

"You're not old, Dad," she chastened lovingly, "and you can be sure that our fishing trips are not over. Anthony wouldn't mind sharing me, at times, with the first man in my life."

She wrapped her arms around each of her parents as they continued to share last minute sentiments.

Once again they dried the eyes that had spilled tears several times during their warm conversation. At long last they made their way down the stairs to meet the patient bridesmaids and headed off to the church.

Gwendalyn was more than pleased that the grey clouds had drifted away to produce a beautiful sunny afternoon. It's warmth and cheerfulness caused her to give thanks again and again to her heavenly Father for this, His gift to her. They would indeed be having their reception outside as she had so hoped for.

The church was filled with family and friends but Gwendalyn really missed her best friend, Ina. Ina was due any day to have her first child and couldn't make the trip. Gwendalyn planned to go see her soon after the baby made his or her appearance.

They stood in the entryway as her bridesmaids straightened her dress and fixed her veil. She could hear the murmur of the many soft voices beyond the doors but as they were opened everything quieted as the spectators watched the bridesmaids make their entrance. Next they saw Anthony's niece and nephew, Rosemary, the flower girl, and Clyde, the ring boy, make their entrance. Rosemary confidently tossed flower petals as they made their way slowly down the aisle with Clyde nervously clutching her arm looking about ready to cry.

With the music changing to the bridal march, Gwendalyn, looking more radiant than ever before, gracefully made her way up the aisle holding the crook of her father's arm, smiling a sure and confident smile and looking into the eyes of her soon-to-be husband.

The pastor's voice boomed, "Who gives this woman to be married to this man?"

"I do," Gwendalyn's father replied, but before letting her go he partially lifted her veil and gently kissed her on the cheek.

"I guess I have to let go and share you for good, my dear. Just remember, you'll always be my 'beauty'," he whispered in her ear.

She purposefully wrapped her arms tightly around her father. "I'll always love you. You've been everything a girl could ever need or want in a father."

He then took her hand and placed it within Anthony's who nodded and whispered for his ears only, "Thank you."

Anthony continued his gaze on this irresistibly attractive young woman before him and some time had slipped by and he had missed some of the pastor's opening remarks. He now heard him say that he would read from 1 Corinthians 13, the love chapter. Anthony had read this chapter before but today it was more meaningful and held great responsibility. He felt he could love Gwendalyn this way but he knew he would need to seek God and be reminded of this scripture often to fully love her the way God intended.

"Anthony Wilson Bowman, do you take this woman, Gwendalyn, to be your lawfully married wife?"

"I do."

"Gwendalyn Mary Gillard, do you take this man, Anthony, to be your lawfully married husband?"

"I do."

With Anthony blinking away threatening tears and Gwendalyn dabbing at her eyes with her handkerchief, they both repeated the meaningful vows after the pastor. Vows that spoke of love, trust, honesty, and to grow with each other through joys and griefs and committing themselves to each other, and to the Lord, for the rest of their lives.

Anthony had secured the ring that once was a symbol of an engagement, but now being worn as the bride of a wonderful man. This union, blessed by God, and encouraged by all in attendance, as well as those from afar, was now sealed with a gentle kiss.

The pastor raised his voice so all could hear, and made the announcement that Anthony, at this time, had something special to share with his new bride.

Facing Gwendalyn, looking into her eyes, and then with his voice clear and strong, he began reading Proverbs 31: 10-31.

"Who can find a virtuous woman? For her price is far above rubies. The heart of her husband doth safely trust in her, so that he shall have no need of spoil."

Gwendalyn stared unbelieving into the face of her husband, her eyes glistening with tears. Just how much she loved this man, she was still discovering and she knew that the years they would have together would be wonderful.

"...She riseth also while it is yet night, and giveth meat to her family... She stretcheth out her hand to the poor; yea, she reacheth forth her hands to the needy."

By this time tears were streaming down Gwendalyn's cheeks and she was indeed thankful that her mother insisted she carry a handkerchief.

"...Her husband is known at the gates, when he sitteth among the elders of the land... She maketh fine linen, and selleth it... Strength and honour are her clothing; and she shall rejoice in time to come... She openeth her mouth with wisdom; and in her tongue is the law of kindness... She looketh well to the ways of her household, and eateth not the bread of idleness... Her children arise up, and call her blessed; her husband also, and he praiseth her... Many daughters have done virtuously, but thou excellest them all..."

As Anthony closed the Bible, Gwendalyn wrapped her arms around him and cried gently on his shoulder. He held her lovingly, whispering words of endearment for her alone. She wasn't even aware, at this point, of the crowd watching this beautiful, intimate scene. All she knew was that she loved this man before her and there was an earnestness to show him how much this had meant to her.

After the signing of the registry, the pastor's voice boomed once again. "Ladies and gentlemen, may I introduce to you, Mr. and Mrs. Anthony Bowman."

The crowd of loved-ones stood and cheered the newly-wedded couple, ...but there was one uninvited guest that slipped out as quietly and unnoticeably, as he had come in, his heart heavy.

* * *

The outdoor reception in the churchyard was glorious. Laughter and conversation filled the air and sunshine added to the already warm hearts. Several times throughout the reception, the tinkling of tea cups and glasses could be heard above the chatter summoning Anthony and Gwendalyn to stop what they were doing for the traditional kiss. Each time it happened, Gwendalyn couldn't keep her face from growing flush. These moments, she felt were private, but she conceded in spite of her embarrassment, which delighted the crowd who whistled and cheered the spectacle.

The gifts that were received were practical and ranged from linens to cutlery. Gwendalyn was emotionally stirred upon seeing her father and Calvin carrying to her, a beautiful, hand-carved trunk that she could place at the foot of her bed. Lifting the lid and looking closely, she read the inscription: Anthony and Gwendalyn Bowman, July 14, 1952.

By 7:00 PM, the crowd had dwindled and the tables had been cleared so the men could take them with their matching chairs to their proper destinations. Many of the families in the immediate area of the church were more than happy to share their belongings for this festive day.

Anthony's father and brother filled their truck with the abundance of gifts and delivered them to the couple's new home. Once they returned, Gwendalyn and Anthony thanked everyone for all their effort, said their farewells, climbed into the truck, and made their way home together.

They walked to the front entrance and Anthony swiftly picked Gwendalyn up in his arms. He awkwardly opened the door and carried 'his bride' over the threshold. He shut the door with his foot and continued to make his way up the stairs to their bedchamber. The curtains were drawn and glowing candles around the room met them. He alighted her to her feet as they took in the carefully arranged romantic interlude. Ornamenting the mirrored dresser was a vase of fresh flowers, a tray of fresh fruit and a plate of baked goodies wrapped for freshness. A bottle of ginger ale sitting in a bowl of partially melted ice chips, and two long stemmed elegant glasses were placed on the chest of drawers.

"I think our mothers are responsible for all this," Anthony stated, breaking the silence, "and Dad and Carl must have lit the candles when they dropped off the gifts."

"It's totally wonderful," Gwendalyn managed, finding her voice.

"Yes it is, my darling, but it is you who are truly wonderful. Have I thanked you, today, for becoming my wife?" he asked as he presented her a brimming glass of the chilled refreshment.

They each took a sip and before Gwendalyn could answer, Anthony gently kissed her moistened, soft lips.

They sat on the edge of the bed enjoying the drink and munching the delicious fruit, as they really hadn't eaten much during the reception. Their conversation was light and they shared with each other the highlights of their wedding day.

"Anthony, I was so surprised when you read that passage from the Bible and I will always remember those words and how they made me feel. You are truly a wonderful man and I will cherish you forever."

Anthony stood and placed the now empty glasses on the dresser and returned to hold her hands and helped her to her feet to meet him.

"I know we're both new to this, eh, married life, but are you OK with..."

"I've thought of this night many, many times and grew nervous, but I love you, Anthony, and that's all that matters."

He gently gathered her into his embrace and tenderly held her, whispering his love for her and softly kissing her cheek. She brought her lips to meet his and their lengthened, meaningful kiss caused any questioning to fade into the past.

CHAPTER 24
MARRIED LIFE

Gwendalyn fell into a routine of getting up early, before dawn, to prepare a hearty morning meal for her and Anthony. They would then head down to the wharf together and would be on their way to the salmon nets before daybreak was upon them. Anthony was well pleased with Gwendalyn's skill in the boat and although she was an expert with the paddles of the dory, the out-board motor took some getting used to. He taught her well and now she handled it with ease and as confusing as it was to operate this modern contraption, she soon wondered why Dad hadn't allowed Mom to buy him an out-board motor when she wanted to a few years back.

"I just don't want you wasting your money on a needless piece of equipment. My back and arms are strong. Why would I need one of those machines?"

She remembered his words as if they had been said just yesterday. He still didn't have one but today she was glad that Anthony had acquired 'one of those machines'. It made the work a lot easier and it was faster getting to the nets and back home again in time for mealtimes.

Gwendalyn loved working beside her husband. She enjoyed their conversations in the boat of planning for future goals, and especially when he made mention of their first child. He was hoping for a girl, just like his beautiful wife, while she wanted their first-born to be a strong and handsome son, like his father.

She was glad that she could be a true helpmate for him in all the knowledge and experience she had gained while working with her father. She often thought of her father while out at sea, and was true to her word in that she made time to go out in the evenings with Dad, ever so often.

The evenings that were the most enjoyable, were the ones she and Anthony would sit or lay in front of the fireplace reading to each other or talking about events passed or things to come. Many intimate hours

177

were passed in this, their now favorite room of the house. Many of the afternoons and some of the evenings she would spend with her mother berry-picking up in the hills or over beyond the church yard where the raspberries were plentiful, large and juicy. Before long she had sixteen jars of tasty raspberry jam.

Shortly after the raspberries were finished, blueberries were ripe and ready for picking. For a week straight she bent over blue covered low bushes gathering the plump berries. This time a dozen jars of homemade blueberry jam lined the cupboard and on Sunday, she and Anthony carried a couple of fresh blueberry pies to his parents' home to share in a Sunday dinner.

They had already been in on the bog and managed to gather together enough bake-apples, a small yellowish-orange berry, resembling a raspberry, and had stored away with the other jams four jars of this special treat. Now, with fall making its presence surely known, she and her mother headed once again into the bush to pick yet another of the Provider's creations. Low bush cranberries or partridge berries, however people called them, but to the people in the cove they were known as 'patchy' berries. The jams, pies, and tarts that were made from these, and served with thick cream, were a treat beyond compare.

* * *

Gwendalyn had received news a while ago about the birth of Ina's baby girl and had longed for the opportunity to go see her best friend and congratulate her in person. There was so much catching up to be done between the two of them, and she wanted to relate to her all the special memories that had come with her wedding day.

She spoke with Anthony about taking a short trip to Nova Scotia and he reluctantly agreed to the trip, as he would miss her terribly.

This time they borrowed Gwendalyn's father's car and Anthony watched as she boarded the ferry that would take her away from him for the next five days.

The trip across was uneventful and Gwendalyn was happy to see Dr. and Mrs. Evans waiting to pick her up. They congratulated her on her marriage and apologized for not being able to come. Gwendalyn thanked them for the thoughtful wedding gift they had sent.

Mrs. Evans could hardly be silenced, which was totally out of character for her, for she went on about her little granddaughter. She must have spoken of every gurgle and burp and how cute her little fingers and toes were. She just knew little Jacqueline was the spitting image of her mother.

It was early afternoon when they arrived at their home but Gwendalyn felt that she would rest and then visit with Ina in the evening. She would be staying with the Evans but spending much of her time visiting with Ina.

The baby was indeed a gem and Gwendalyn fell in love with her from the moment she saw her. A bright and strong baby girl and she did look a lot like Ina but resemblances of Franklin were evident.

Gwendalyn handed a carefully wrapped package to Ina saying it was a gift she had made for the baby. Ina was delighted to see the beautiful articles of clothing that so much work had gone into. Gwendalyn had knitted a bright pink baby outfit consisting of a sweater with a matching cap and booties. She also knitted a woollen blanket for the baby's bed and lovingly sewn a warm quilt with delicately embroidered pictures crafted into several of the squares. Ina was overjoyed at the thoughtfulness of her dear friend and continued to express her thanks over and over again.

Ina shared with her the whole story of giving birth, from the unbearable pain to the joy of holding little Jacqueline after she first entered the world.

Gwendalyn told her that she was longing to be pregnant and have her own little bundle of joy. She gave her a detailed account of her wedding including how she had cried when Anthony read Proverbs 31.

For the next three days Gwendalyn spent most of her time with Ina. They talked a lot but she really enjoyed the hours when she was totally responsible for caring for the precious little one. Ina still was very tired at times and Gwendalyn was more than happy to send her off to bed while she took care of Jacqueline.

One day while she was sitting reading in the parlor in the Evans home, Dr. Evans came in and presented her with a letter. Surprised, she took it and opened it immediately. She was astounded by what she pulled out. It was another sketch from Daniel. This time it was of her and Anthony standing in front of the church getting married.

"How can this be?" she questioned incredulously. She flipped over the sketch and sure enough, there was a letter from Daniel.

"It took me a long time to decide if I would give you this sketch and write this letter. Ina told me of your wedding day and I had to come and witness it. I couldn't believe it unless I saw it for myself. I felt I couldn't reveal myself, so I remained hidden until the service was over and then I left. I know now what had been taking your time and why you never wrote to me. He looked as if he truly loves you and it seems you love him as well. You could have told me, but I can only guess that you expected that Ina would have given me the news long before the wedding date. I guess she was caught up with her own wedding and then with pregnancy and baby and neglected to tell me. I wish you had written me yourself. It would have saved me this heartache. I still can only think the best of you and probably always will. Take care of yourself and I wish you every happiness. I don't think I'll ever forget you even if you do belong to another. I won't be writing again. Have a happy life, Daniel."

Gwendalyn couldn't believe what she had just read and the sketch unnerved her. Daniel had been at her wedding. She realized for an instant just how much he did care for her and felt saddened by the state in which he might be. She wished with all her heart that she had written him and told him everything about Anthony right from the start; from the time she received the first sketch. Her heart went out to him but she had no idea how to fix things up or help his heart to mend. She decided she would see him while she was here. She would talk with him and apologize for all these mix-ups. She felt she owed him that much.

She phoned Elsa's Boarding house and when she heard his voice, she almost lost hers. She was very nervous and right now she didn't know what to say, or if meeting with him was a good idea, or if he would even want to meet with her. She mustered up her courage and finally spoke.

"Hi Daniel," she said. "This is Gwendalyn. I received your sketch, eh, letter and I'd like to talk with you about it, if you wouldn't mind."

180

"I don't know, eh, I didn't think I'd hear from you, now that you're married."

"I know, and I'm sorry I didn't write after the first sketch you sent, but I was still unsure of things at that time. Things just developed over time and up until Anthony asked me to marry him, I still didn't know what direction I was going in. I really cared for you, and do still care."

"I see."

"I had asked Ina to talk with you about this over a year ago and now I've found out that she didn't have any conversations with you at all until just before my wedding. I'm really not trying to make excuses for what happened and not writing myself, I just want to say that I am truly sorry for hurting you and I'm sorry for not letting you know of my intentions sooner."

"It's OK, Gwendalyn. I don't blame you. I just allowed myself to get too emotionally involved."

"Well, take care of yourself, Daniel. I will always consider you a good friend."

"You too, Gwendalyn. Good bye."

"Good bye, Daniel."

She breathed a heavy sigh after replacing the phone in its hanger. Her heart was still a little heavy from the thought of causing Daniel pain. She really did care for him, perhaps even more than a friend at one time. But now things had definitely changed and her heart totally belonged to Anthony. She prayed that God would heal any wounds Daniel may still have and prayed for his salvation. Afterwards she felt released having left him in God's care.

Gwendalyn went to Ina's bright and early the next morning as this would be her last day with her. She shared with her the conversation she had had with Daniel the night before and it was Ina who now apologized for not talking with Daniel sooner.

All too soon, it was time to leave again and Gwendalyn, teary-eyed, said her good-byes.

* * *

She was both thrilled and relieved upon seeing Anthony waiting for her to disembark.

"I've missed you more than you will ever know," she said wrapping her arms around him. "I'm so glad to be home with you again."

"You sound as if you didn't have that good a time," he said walking beside her and holding his arm around her waist.

"Oh, I did have a good time and Ina's baby is the cutest baby I've ever seen. It's just that I missed you more than I thought I would."

"Well, I missed you, too, and I'm glad to have you back."

* * *

Gwendalyn was thrilled with the abundance of produce she was getting from her garden. Most of the garden peas they had eaten fresh off the vine and sometimes had some steamed with an occasional evening meal, but there was still enough to can ten jars for the winter's use. The onions were drying daily in the sun and would soon need to be stored away. She would leave the cabbages in the ground as long as possible as they could take the cold and maybe a little snow. The turnips had grown well and now were sweetened by the frost. They were so enjoyable that she was sorry she hadn't planted any more than half a row. She and Anthony worked together pulling carrots and digging potatoes. By the time they were done they estimated over 200 pounds of potatoes and around 70 pounds of carrots. Anthony's father helped them, with the use of his truck, to carry the vegetables to his root cellar, as Anthony hadn't had time to prepare one as yet.

Fall was also a time for canning meats and fish of different kinds. Gwendalyn already had 30 jars of salmon and 24 jars of seal meat stored in the pantry. Dad and Calvin had gotten a moose and now, once again, she was busy in the kitchen canning many quart jars of delicious moose meat. She knew the taste of the savory meat once warmed in a pan of sautéed onions, and so her hard work was enjoyable when looking forward to the many meals she would prepare using these canned goods.

* * *

Winter was now upon them and the ice-packed cove hindered any fishing till next spring. Gwendalyn appreciated the winter for the gift

182

of time it gave her with her husband. Although, they would still be busy, at times, with mending nets and of course working on finishing the house, they could always work together. She loved the long, intimate evenings in front of the fire sharing conversations of a relaxed nature.

May came all too quickly and the ice in the cove was breaking up again. Gwendalyn could see the children out on the ice floes 'copying', hopping from floe to floe as men, and perhaps their own fathers would be doing, while out on a seal hunt. She loved this game and the sudden urge took over her and soon she was out enjoying her childhood game with the other children from around the cove. It was while she was at this that Anthony came looking for her and she was a little embarrassed for her childish antics. Her embarrassment turned to outright laughter and joy as Anthony skipped across a number of floes to join her and then carefully made their way back to shore together.

The ice was soon gone and fishing was a part of the daily life. Gwendalyn spent many hours out in boat, cleaning the fish down at the 'stage', or placing salted cod fillets on the flake. She was careful to turn them over at midday and keeping a close watch on the weather in case of a sudden rain shower. By the end of May she had her garden planted and was willing the plants to grow.

June slipped into July and it was cause for celebration on July 14 as Anthony and Gwendalyn entered their first year anniversary. Each of their parents wanted to have them over for dinner so they resolved on inviting Anthony's parents to the Gillards for dinner and then they all took a walk to the Bowmans for tea and dessert.

CHAPTER 25
TRAGEDY

The next day Gwendalyn was feeling low and concerned as she realized that a whole year had come and gone and still no sign of a baby. Anthony had found her crying while drying the lunch dishes and comforted her after finding out the source of her tears. He consoled her saying that this first year of marriage had been so wonderful growing together in love and that he was glad for their precious time of being alone together. He told her that he felt sure that their little blessing from God would make his or her presence known in due time.

She felt much better after voicing her fears and sensing Anthony's confidence on the subject. She was even more happy when he told her he wouldn't be going out in boat any more today so he could spend a relaxing evening at home with her.

As they sat in front of the fireplace, Anthony started singing a love song to her and got up and pulled her into his arms and they both danced to his music. When he had finished, they stood gazing into each other's eyes and then their lips met in a passionate encounter.

The next morning Anthony slipped quietly out of bed as to not disturb his sleeping wife and after picking up his clothes; he gently kissed her ivory cheek and tiptoed from the room. He had decided that this morning he would allow Gwendalyn a full night's sleep and would see her around noon.

She was surprised to awake and see the sun streaming in their bedroom. She looked to Anthony's place beside her on the bed and realized lovingly that he had gone off on his own this morning to let her sleep in. Well, she would just prepare him a special lunch for his thoughtfulness.

Sure enough, she saw him come in the cove around 11:00 AM with his boat weighted with numerous salmon and cod from this morning's catch. She moved the meal of fried potatoes with onion, sliced ham in an orange sauce, and diced carrots to the cooler end of the stove and prepared to rush down to the wharf to help her husband with the

185

cleaning before lunch. The fresh patchy berry, apple pies would have cooled enough for dessert by the time they were done cleaning the fish. She was more than thankful for the gallon of milk she had gotten from the neighbours, who kept cows, yesterday afternoon. The cream had now risen to the top and she would scoop it off to go with the delicious pies.

She was dressed in her old clothes and down at the stage by the time Anthony had the boat secured to the side. Once he had climbed the attached ladder to meet her, she swiftly threw her arms around him and kissed him soundly.

"What was that for?" he asked, holding her tightly.

"Just for being you, my darling," she answered. "Now let's get the cleaning done, fast. I have a special lunch made for the two of us to enjoy."

The cleaning did seem to go rather quickly and they were at the house, cleaned up, and Gwendalyn had lunch ready on the table by 12:15 PM.

"This is a meal fit for a king," he complimented while taking her in his arms once again, kissing her gently. He then pulled out her chair and seated her before seating himself.

"Heavenly Father, I do so thank You for Your abundance of provisions and blessings. I thank You for the blessing of my dear wife, Gwenny. I pray that You would bless her, for always being such a wonderful helpmate and joy to me. You have blessed me and my life is complete and full of contentment. Thank you, again, Father, and especially for this wonderful food on our table. In the name of Jesus Christ, Your Son, Amen."

As he finished, he lifted her hand, still clasped in his, to his lips and kissed it.

They fully enjoyed their meal together with Anthony going on about how wonderful the meal was and the patchy berry pie with cream was the best he'd ever had. They brought their tea from the table and sat in the living room where they relaxed sitting close beside each other.

"Did you want to come out in boat for this afternoon's trip?" he asked, as he so often did after lunch.

"I was thinking about finishing up a few things here and then going over to visit with Mom this afternoon."

"Very well," he said as he gathered his necessities and then kissed her again. "See you at supper."

She watched him through the window and when he was about to pull out from the wharf she went outside to see him off. He saw her and waved and she waved back as he headed out to the open sea.

She went in and finished the dishes and some cleaning she wanted to get done and then headed to her mothers. They were having a great visit while working on another quilt with Gwendalyn telling Mom how wonderful a husband Anthony was and how he always treated her so special. They were about to make tea when Calvin burst into the house saying that rain was coming and that they'd need to get the fish off the flakes.

They were out the door in a hurry and were surprised to see how dark the clouds were. The wind had picked up incredibly and it seemed they were in for a storm. Gwendalyn ran to their flake and was quickly gathering the cod into the shed. She could hear out-board motors coming in from the ocean and she was thankful Anthony would be home early. She had just gotten the last of the fish in the shed when the rain started coming down in torrents. The dark clouds were now blackened and the blustery winds now came in violent gusts. She tried to see if Anthony's boat was brought up on shore as he normally did when the waters were rough but because of the wind and the rain she was unable to see anything. She thought about staying in the shed till the storm blew over, for it seemed that this was one of those storms that went away almost as quickly as it came. She waited for a while and decided to venture out into the storm to head home, as it didn't appear to be letting up.

She fought her way through and by the time she got to the house, her long hair was whipped from its braid and tangled around her face and she was soaked through. Anthony wasn't in the house yet and she figured he went to his parents' home, as they were closer to the wharf they were now using until theirs was built.

She was thankful for the running hot water and the long tub for now she was chilled and a hot bath would warm her through. She lingered in the tub allowing the warmth to penetrate her whole body while the winds continued on their destructive path. She was glad she had done the wash yesterday because she was sure there would be no clothes left

187

on any line today.

She was surprised to see that the storm had not passed by the time she finished her bath. She decided a hot cup of tea would warm her spirits. She stoked the stove and moved the kettle to its hottest section to get it steaming quickly.

With tea in hand she went in to the living room where she had already started a fire in the fireplace and enjoyed its warmth as she sipped her tea. With her tea finished she laid back, staring into the orange and yellow flames and drifted into a light sleep.

Something startled her awake. "Thunder," she thought and got up to look outside. The storm was now subsiding and evening was approaching. She changed out of her robe and decided to go to the Bowmans to see if Anthony were there.

There was just a breeze blowing now and the rain had almost completely diminished. She knocked on the Bowmans' door and let herself in. Her parents-in-law smiled to see her and invited her in.

"I was just wondering if Anthony was here."

She looked around while still speaking and realized he wasn't there.

"He went out in boat early this afternoon and hasn't been home yet. He's probably at my parents because I told him I was going to be visiting with Mom this afternoon. I'll check there."

"OK, dear," they said, exchanging concerned expressions as Gwendalyn closed the door and continued up the road towards her parents' home.

"Hi Mom, Dad. Did Anthony come here during the storm?"

"No, we haven't seen him at all. He's not home?"

With the shaking of her head they quickly added, "He's probably with his parents," added Dad.

"No, I just came from there. I'm going down to the wharf to see if he's there," she stated, trying not to let fear overwhelm her.

"Just hang on," Dad said. "I'll come with you."

He grabbed his coat and walked with her to the wharf but to Gwendalyn's dismay, his boat was neither tied up at the wharf nor hauled onto the beach.

"Dad, something's happened. I just know it," she said bursting into a flow of tears.

"Now, hold on a minute. I've been out in storms like this and when

I've seen it coming I made for the shore to take shelter till it passed," he said comforting her.

"But Dad, he would have started in when it was calming down and should be here by now."

"Settle down now. It is getting dark. Maybe he figured he'd just stay put until morning. Don't get all worked up without knowing what's going on."

Gwendalyn's dad said all the right things for his daughter's comfort but inside he was growing more and more concerned.

"You come up to the house and spend the night with us. When you see his boat come in the morning, you can just run down and meet him. It's a lot closer than your place."

He put his arm around her and led her up the path and into the house.

"He's not there?" Mom questioned.

"Dad thinks he might have taken shelter for the night and come in at day break, but Mom what if something happened?"

"Let's not talk about 'what ifs' right now. Your father is probably right and the best thing you can do is have something to eat and stay here with us. I don't suppose you've had supper."

With the shaking of her head, Mom went directly to work and warmed Gwendalyn a plate of leftovers from supper and sat in down in front of her.

"I don't feel very hungry right now, Mom," she said, her eyes red from crying and threatening to spill again.

"Never mind hungry. You have to eat or you'll be sick."

"OK Mom," she conceded and managed to eat most everything on the plate.

Mom then brought her a cup of tea and they all enjoyed some of Mom's homemade chocolate cake and tea.

* * *

Gwendalyn snuggled herself in the mound of quilts and blankets that were once her normal comfort. Tonight, though, she was unable to fall asleep. She prayed until she could pray no more for the safety of her husband, and when she felt she could cry no more tears, she drifted off

189

in a disturbed sleep.

The next morning she awoke to sunshine streaming in her window and blinding her eyes. It was as if nothing was wrong in the world. She looked at the clock and it read 9:35 AM. She couldn't believe she had slept so late. She quickly threw off the covers and dressed faster than she ever had before. Anthony would be wondering where she was.

In the kitchen she was met with long faces that immediately switched to smiles as she entered the room.

"I'm going to run and check and then head off home," she said grabbing her coat and hurrying into her shoes.

"No dear," her dad said softly. "You should stay here with us now."

"But Dad, I have to check! Anthony might be home now!"

"I've already checked and he's not home yet."

"What do you mean, he's not home yet? He's got to be home! We've had daylight for a couple of hours now. Anthony's got to be home."

"I'm sorry, my beauty. His boat hasn't come in yet. You know, he might have decided to check his salmon nets before coming in and so that would make him late."

"Come sweetheart," Mom said, taking her daughter by the shoulders and guiding her to the table. "We'll have some breakfast and wait a while longer. He's bound to show up any time now. Calvin will keep watch for him and tell you when he gets in."

Mom spread out a breakfast feast before her and the others and sat down beside her. Gwendalyn ate very little and picked occasionally at her food. At the sound of a motor, she quickly jumped up and tried as fast as she could with now trembling hands to get her shoes on.

"It's Harry's boat just going out," Calvin announced, looking at Gwendalyn who looked up and again burst into tears.

"I just can't take this waiting. I'll go down to all the wharves and ask if anyone has seen him out on their run this morning."

"That's a good idea," Dad agreed, "but you'll have to wait till 10:30 or 11:00 o'clock before anyone gets back in."

She left her shoes where they were and went to the chesterfield and sunk into a corner. Anthony's parents knocked on the door and came in and at once Gwendalyn rose up and went to meet them.

"Have you seen him," she asked.

They shook their heads and Mrs. Bowman took hold of Gwendalyn and gave her a hug of comfort.

She sauntered back to the living room and found her place back in the corner of the chesterfield.

Mom served the Bowman's tea and they talked as if any time Anthony would be coming in the cove. Everyone was trying to be as positive a possible, although as time slowly ticked by, hopes were fading.

By the time most of the boats were due to come in they had split into three groups, the Bowmans; Calvin and Mom; Gwendalyn and Dad; to wait at the different wharves to ask anyone who came in if they had seen Anthony.

They met back at the Gillard's house just after lunch with no words of encouragement.

Calvin spoke up to try and bring some hope. "If Anthony was close to Herring Harbour when the storm hit, maybe he went in there till it was over and just got held up this morning."

They appreciated what Calvin was trying to do but they all were now trying to come to grips with the fact that Anthony may be lost forever.

Four days had passed and still no sign of Anthony or his boat. Dad had spoken to Gwendalyn about maybe making some funeral arrangements but she wouldn't hear of it.

"I can't Dad," she cried, "that would be admitting that he's... that he's gone."

Her cries of grief were heard all over the house, and she couldn't be comforted by anyone.

On Wednesday, seven days after the storm, Dave Hanks, came in the cove towing Anthony's boat behind him. Gwendalyn, along with her family and Anthony's family, as well as many people of the cove came down to the wharf to see what had happened.

"I was crossing over by the point going towards Herring Harbour when a bit of this boat caught my eye. It was almost completely swamped and was beating up against the shore. I bailed it out and pulled it home. I looked everywhere but there was no sign of Anthony anywhere. It seemed that the wind and the waves must have just blown and pushed it over there from wherever, eh, eh, Anthony was lost."

"No! Don't say it, Dave! It can't be true!" Gwendalyn cried and screamed and was overwrought with grief as she climbed down into her husband's boat. There she sat crying and wouldn't be comforted by anyone.

Gwendalyn had finally accepted the fact that Anthony was gone and so the funeral service was held three days later. She was stricken with grief, pain, and sorrow over her loss. Towards the end of the service, Dad picked her up and she lay limp in his arms as he carried her home.

Two weeks had passed and she was still unable to go to her own home. She was sick with a lot vomiting and slept a lot during the day, probably because of the inability to sleep at night. Mom, Dad, and Calvin had gone to her house for her personal belongings and whatever else she needed.

Many visitors had come by expressing their condolences and sharing encouraging and comforting words from the scriptures. She turned away every time someone mentioned any scripture or God, and she hadn't picked up her own Bible since that dark day. It seemed that everything that was said to bring her comfort was not comforting at all.

Gwendalyn was numb. She didn't talk to anyone. People, to her, floated in and out of the room she was in. She saw them come up to hug her but she didn't feel the hugs. She listened to their words up until they talked of God and His love and comfort. These words caused her pain and she couldn't listen to them. God had not saved her husband. He let her down. Didn't He know how much she loved him? He could have saved him but He chose not to. She couldn't open up to Him anymore. He had let her down in the worst way possible. Yes, it would have been better if He had taken her very life.

Another week had gone by and her mother and father sat beside her sharing their love and expressing their understanding of her sorrow.

"I don't know... if I'll... ever be able... to get... over this," she said between hiccups.

Her mother held her tenderly encouraged by her now speaking, and saddened at the same time because of her words.

"Of course, you will. Your father and I are here for you. We'll help you get through this."

"Thank you, Mom. I love you and Dad."

CHAPTER 26
FROM GRIEF TO JOY

Slowly Gwendalyn started coming around and within another week she was coping as though things were almost normal. Only almost because she no longer mentioned God and her joy was no longer evident. She still slept often throughout the day and was bothered ever so often with vomiting.

Mom continued to make appetizing food and almost had to force Gwendalyn to eat. Gradually her eating habits picked up and so did her health and mental well-being. She began smiling and even laughing every once in a while although she would still get defensive whenever anyone would talk about God or His goodness.

She decided that it was time to go back to her home and face each room with its memories. She would never forget all the wonderful times she had had with Anthony. Memories were all she had left, and she would be holding on tightly to the only remaining part of him.

Her mother went with her, walking in silence, the long trek around the cove to her house. At the front step she paused as flashes of her wedding day came flooding over her. Anthony had carried her across this threshold just over a year ago. She resisted the urge to run from the home, not wanting to re-enter without her husband.

Mom opened the door slowly and Gwendalyn managed to step in allowing her eyes to roam and take in the familiar sights. She guided Gwendalyn to the kitchen, and crossed over to the dining area where Gwendalyn sank into a chair. Mom began commenting on what a great cook stove Gwendalyn had while building a fire to prepare tea. She had brought the necessary items knowing that there wasn't much here and had planned to sit and talk over tea before making the emotionally difficult tour of the rest of the home. Once the kettle was filled with fresh water and placed on the stove she sat beside her daughter. Gwendalyn's eyes were again stinging as she told Mom about the last meal she had had with Anthony and about the last evening they had shared together.

"Did I tell you that he didn't even go fishing that night? It seems that somehow he must have known what was about to happen and wanted to have more time with me. It was the most perfect evening, and the next morning he didn't even wake me to go out in boat. That's why I felt good about preparing a special meal for him. Our last meal..."

She was in tears again and Mom did all she could to bring her comfort. Mom knew she needed this time to cry and share whatever moments and memories to help in the healing process.

They heard the door open and Dad's voice announcing that it was he who had come in. He joined them as they walked into the living room.

"This was our favorite room. We spent so many wonderful evenings here. Anthony would read to me as we lay here on the rug and sometimes I would massage his aching back after he had worked a long day. How will I ever be able to live a normal life after this? Will it ever get any better?" she asked them as her burning eyes continued the endless streams.

"Come, my dear. I want to tell you a story," Dad said as he motioned her to the couch. "As you know, your mother was not my first wife. After Harriet, my first wife, died, I thought life was over for me. I was angry and even became bitter. I grieved for months and no one or nothing made sense. Finally I met someone who helped me get back on my feet. She was like an angel sent from heaven. I told her about my loss and she shared with me words of comfort and encouragement from the scriptures. It was then that I knew that God had sent her to be my life-long love and companion. I know you're feeling angry towards God for not keeping Anthony safe and for taking him home so soon. But that's where he is, my beauty, he's home. I know that he would want you to go on and take care of yourself and most importantly to keep on loving and serving God so that one day you will meet again in heaven."

"I know you're right, Dad, and I know what I'm feeling is wrong, but I can't move past this just yet. I am angry with God and I've lost my trust in Him. I thought God would take care of Anthony and me. I trusted Him to do that and now I feel so let down. I served and loved Him all my life and He let me down."

"Don't harden your heart towards God, my dear. He's the One who can get you through this. Turn back to Him and things will get better." Gwendalyn looked away, not wanting to continue the conversation in the way it was leading. Dad moved to the fireplace and began building a fire. Gwendalyn got up from the couch, and with Mom following, proceeded up the stairs to her bedroom. Again a fresh wave of tears washed down her cheeks as she continued to share intimate memories with Mom.

By the time they re-entered the living-room, the fire looked inviting and cheerful. Calvin had come over and Dad announced that they were going to play the board game he had set up on the floor. Gwendalyn looked at him in surprise, but he just told her to come sit and join in. He knew she needed to get her mind off her grief and start living again. They were half way through and she was actually laughing, which surprised both herself and the others, and they continued playing late into the night.

Mom tucked her into bed before leaving and Gwendalyn told her that she was glad for the evening they had just had. After Mom left, she was alone with her thoughts and once more she cried herself to sleep missing Anthony.

She had slept in the next morning till 10:30 AM for which she was thankful. Lately she was sleeping more during the day than at night. She hoped, maybe, she could start getting back to normal. She went downstairs to find Calvin asleep on the couch. Mom and Dad had decided it would be best to have someone close by if she needed them. He must have been keeping the fire in all night, as the house was warm and cosy. She added some wood to the hot coals, which awakened Calvin.

"Good morning, Gwen," he said, sleepily. "How are you feeling this morning?"

"A little better, I think," she responded. "It was good seeing you there when I walked in. I'll go make us some breakfast so you can have some privacy to get dressed."

"Looks like you're getting your appetite back," Calvin said as he sat enjoying the meal his sister had prepared. He was feeling relieved that she was finally starting to come around. "I hated seeing you so miserable."

"I guess I have to make myself go on, even if I don't feel like it," she returned.

Calvin left for home around noon and Gwendalyn went through the whole house cleaning, and looking for something to clean. She felt that if she kept busy it would give her less time for thinking. She decided that she would wash some clothes so she picked up the few items she had taken off last night and went to the other side of the bed to get a glass off the night stand and was startled to find some of Anthony's soiled clothing. Just a shirt and some socks.

She knelt down and fingered his shirt and then picked it up to smell it. It was almost like having Anthony with her once again. She kept breathing in his scent and holding the shirt close to her bosom. She couldn't wash away this last remnant of him. She took off her own blouse and put on his shirt. It was big on her and the sleeves hung below her hands. She tightened it around her and curled up on her bed as too many memories came flooding back. She was crying again and soon sleep had taken her into its hold.

It was in this position that Mom had found her when she had come to check on her late in the afternoon. She stood watching the now peaceful figure before her on the bed with reddened eyes from continual bouts of crying. Mom sat beside her and she awoke to her mother's loving touch gently smoothing her hair from her face.

"Hi Mom. I found this on the floor on the other side of the bed. It still has his smell. I want to wear it. It makes me feel like he's around me somehow."

Mom just nodded and hugged her as she came up in a sitting position. Mom asked her to come over for supper to which she agreed. She rolled up the shirtsleeves and took a jacket for the walk back home after supper.

Calvin walked back with her carrying a care-package Mom had put together and again slept on her couch in case she needed company, or anything else, for that matter.

* * *

Two months had passed since Anthony's fatal accident and Gwendalyn decided she would like to take a trip to see Ina. Maybe a change of scenery where there was not so many reminders of Anthony would be good for her.

She telephoned the Evans household to ask if it would be OK and to plan a day when she could come.

She was on her way to the ferry on Thursday morning and Dr. Evans would again be waiting for her when she arrived.

Ina was happy to see her but they both cried in each other's arms over Gwendalyn's loss.

There was hardly time for those sentiments as Jacqueline crawled up to them, pulled herself to a standing position and began squealing for attention. They both laughed as Ina picked up her daughter, who immediately started giggling. Gwendalyn began tickling her toes and enjoying the child's carefree abundance of joy. She was soon taken into Jacqueline's world and her own thoughts were pushed into the background. She helped with diaper changing, and fed the child the mush her mother prepared.

It was Gwendalyn's finger that the little 14-month old girl clung to as they walked around the house and played with different toys.

Gwendalyn and Ina talked only of recent news as they tiptoed around the subject that would indeed cause pain. Ina told her of Jonathon's interest in one of his school chums and how Franklin's father had changed the name of their business to Newbury and Sons Hardware. She also mentioned how Daniel had taken up an interest in Carmen and how they were spending a lot of time together.

Gwendalyn was happy for him, but remembered the last conversation she had had with Daniel. Deep down, she still cared for Daniel and hoped for him and Carmen, happiness always.

Saturday afternoon, while Jacqueline was taking her nap, the two young women really began talking.

"How are you doing, really, Gwen?" Ina asked sincerely.

"I don't know. I didn't think anything could ever be so painful. I miss him terribly. I don't understand how this could happen. I don't know why God hadn't protected him. That's the other thing. I've slipped away from God. I don't know if I can ever trust Him again."

"You know, Gwen, God's the only true source of comfort for your deep sorrow. Maybe that's why you're having such a hard time coping. If you would just reach out to Him, everything will be a lot better. I think you lost more than one love the day Anthony died. You abandoned your first love, Jesus, and I believe that has a lot to do with your suffering. Gwen, you've known, loved, and served God all your life. He's been your source of strength and inspiration and now you've allowed Him to die in your life, as well. You know how greatly you loved and cared for Anthony, well, Jesus loves you far more than you could ever love him. God loves you, Gwen, and He's waiting for you to come to Him so He can help you through your grief. Open up to Him. He hasn't let you down. You've let yourself down by pushing Him away."

They continued their conversation until the baby woke up again and by this time Gwendalyn was feeling too low to appreciate the little one's cheerfulness. She told Ina that she would walk back to her parents' home instead of phoning for Alfred. She said she needed some time to think, and the walk would do her good.

Her walking alone made her feel how very much alone she felt. No one to talk to. There was a time when she would purposefully take solitaire walks just to talk with her very best of friends, Jesus. Today, though, her whole being was once again thrown into a state of confusion. How could she turn back to the One who could have prevented such a tragedy and all this grief?

An approaching car coming up beside her interrupted her thoughts. It slowed down and stopped. The driver was Daniel and he asked her if she wanted a ride. Daniel had known of her loss three weeks after it had happened from conversations with Dr. Evans. Mrs. Gillard had written Ina, telling her what had happened and how hard Gwendalyn was taking it, and asking for her and her parents' prayers.

"No thank you. I'd rather walk," she told him.

"If you wouldn't mind, I have something for you," he said handing her an envelope. "I am truly sorry for your loss, and you have my deepest sympathy."

"Thank you for the card, Daniel," she said.

"Take care of yourself," he said, and drove slowly away from the curb.

She carried the unopened envelope to her room and put it on the dresser. She lay down on her bed feeling quite weary and fell into a deep sleep. Some time later, a soft knocking on the door awakened her.

"Come in," she said sleepily.

"How are you doing, my dear?" Mrs. Evans asked, coming into her room.

"OK, I guess," she said. "I just feel so tired all the time."

"Yes, and I've noticed that you were vomiting yesterday."

"It started after I realized that Anthony was gone and it mostly happens when I'm feeling really down. But I guess I've been feeling down a lot in the last couple of months."

"Has it been a long time since you last saw a doctor?"

"I guess it has been a while but I haven't had any need to."

"I was thinking about asking Edward if he thinks you should maybe go into his office for a check up. I could set something up with him on Monday if you agree."

"I'm sure it's just part of my grieving and I've vomited only once since being here. Maybe this trip was good for me but if Dr. Evans thinks I should see him, I'll be willing."

"Good, I think it's a good idea. Now, how about you come down for some supper? Vera has prepared a fine meal."

"Sounds great," she said. "I am feeling quite hungry."

* * *

After enjoying a delicious supper, Gwendalyn and Mr. and Mrs. Evans relaxed in the parlor and then got involved in playing a board game. It was nearly 10:00 PM when Gwendalyn was trying to suppress the continual oncoming yawns.

"I think we should all turn in early," Dr. Evans announced. "Church starts at 10:30 in the morning and we will need to be up early enough to have some breakfast before leaving."

Gwendalyn wasn't sure if she really wanted to go to church. She'd missed several services since Anthony's death. She knew it would be impolite not to go so she just nodded her head and said goodnight.

She went to turn out the lamp and saw the card from Daniel sitting on the dresser. She opened it to find a card, which read: *"May God Be With You...'call upon me in the day of trouble: I will deliver thee'...PSALM 50: 15."* And on the inside: *"May faith in our Lord*

light your way and comfort you. With Deepest Sympathy, Daniel."
She didn't know if she wanted to open up the familiar paper with the pencil drawing but went ahead and was alarmed by what she saw. This picture seemed to reach deep into her soul, stirring her spirit. It was a sketch of the anchor they had seen on the docks, that morning so long ago. That was the day that Daniel had snapped suddenly at the mention of Jesus. Gwendalyn had explained a powerful meaning of what great value Jesus has in our life being the anchor that keeps up from drifting into sin. He didn't want any part of it at that time, but now this picture, and the religious sympathy card, seemed to enlighten her that maybe a change had taken place in his heart.
She turned the paper over and began to read the full-page letter.

"Dearest Gwendalyn,
That day on the docks brought back memories that caused a lot of suffering to resurface. I couldn't bring myself to tell you about it then, but now I feel I can.
I had great faith in God in my younger years and that faith was tested through the loss of my little sister. She had become ill, flu-like, and too-suddenly she was taken from us. I couldn't understand why God could allow such a little girl so full of love and joy to be taken from life when so much of life was still ahead of her. I grew bitter and angry towards God and I didn't find any more use for Him. (It did cause me to work hard to become a doctor so I may be able to help out people who are sick and maybe save them from a premature death.)
I began going to church with the Evanses after several conversations with Dr. Evans at the office. Three Sundays following I could feel the Holy Spirit of God tugging at my heart trying to bring me back to Him. On that fourth Sunday I couldn't hold on any longer to that misery of living apart from God and I cried out to Him. At first I told Him how much I hurt and the pain I was feeling concerning my sister's passing in nothing less than angry words. With all that expressed, I asked His forgiveness and He then softened my heart and I was able to cry out all that pain and hurt, and receive His healing.
I feel so free now and my life has true meaning once again.

It was hard living under that dark shadow all these years, but I am thankful to God that He has forgiven me, set me free, and now has given me true joy once again.

Don't blame God for your loss, as I did. It can only bring more sorrow and years of pain and anguish. Keep your eyes upon Him, your heart close to His, and soon your grief will be easier to bear.

Take care, dearest Gwendalyn. Your friend, Daniel. "

She closed the sketch back into the card aware of the compassion she now had for Daniel. He had suffered a great loss and had grieved much the same way as she had. She was comforted somewhat by his words, knowing that someone else knew what she was going through and was understanding of her feelings toward God.

"Sure, he found his way back to God, but I don't know if I'll ever be able to find mine," she said aloud.

She climbed heavily into bed and shed many tears before being able to fall asleep.

* * *

The beginning of the song service was cheerful but Gwendalyn wasn't able to enter in. After the announcements were made, they entered into a time of worship and no matter how hard she tried to not be influenced by the words, the presence of the Holy Spirit stirred her spirit.

She didn't know how long she was lost in thought but something in what the pastor was now saying brought her from her reverie.

"Sometimes hardships come our way so that our faith in God might be strengthened. If everything was always going along smoothly, how could our faith be tested to see if it were true? Times of trials come our way to help us search our own hearts to find out how much we are truly grounded in Christ. It is in those times that we need to choose Jesus and His love to see us through, and by doing that, we develop a much closer walk with Him.

Is there anything in your life that may have caused a separation from Jesus? You may not remember what had happened, if it happened so long ago, but you know in your spirit that you are not as close to Him as you once were, or now want to be.

Let's bow our hearts before God and take a moment to ask Him to reveal anything that may have done so, and then let us draw close to Him, and allow the Holy Spirit to minister reconciliation between ourselves and God."

As things remained quiet and the soft music began to play, tears began to well up in Gwendalyn's eyes. This time it was different from the pain that caused bursts of crying after Anthony's death. This time streams of repentance flowed from deep within her inmost being. She kept sharing with Jesus how sorry she was for turning her back on Him and not trusting His ways. She asked His forgiveness and also, in the midst of heart-breaking sobs, told Him she forgave Him as well. She knew these words were strange, but it was something she felt she needed to say to release all the bitterness and anger she had allowed herself to build up within her towards Him. She knew He was the Almighty and that all His ways were righteous. She also realized that everything He did was for her benefit, even if she didn't understand it right now. Tears of healing continued to flow and she felt the confusion, bitterness, and anger, all melt away.

She felt His love begin to grow strong within her once again and all of a sudden she was crying out, "Lord, I love You! I love You! Thank you for never leaving me nor forsaking me even though I rejected You. Forgive me, Father. Thank You for loving me back to You. I love You, Jesus!"

Her voice quieted to a whisper and she continued to express her love towards her Heavenly Father.

When she finished she was surprised that the church was empty except for the pastor and his wife, along with her dear friends, who were gathered around her, dabbing at their red eyes, and praising God for His deliverance and His healing power.

She hugged and held each one at length as trickles of tears of relief and joy continued down her face.

She stood aside drying her eyes and blowing her nose when a movement down the aisle beside the sanctuary doors caught her attention. There Daniel stood with head his lowered and she could see that he too was wiping away tears.

CHAPTER 27
GOD'S GIFT

Monday morning dawned brightly adding to Gwendalyn's now more cheerful spirits. She awoke feeling the best she had felt since Anthony's passing. The inner joy that had been suppressed by grief for so long was now beginning to grow within, once again. Today, for the first time in a long time, she felt like smiling.

She met Mrs. Evans in the dining room for a light but healthy breakfast as the hour was now approaching 10:00 AM. Dr. Evans had left for the office earlier that morning and would be expecting her at 11:15 for the pre-arranged medical visit at the clinic.

Alfred was out front waiting in the car by 10:50 AM, but Gwendalyn was nervous about this visit with the doctor, that she had for years called her friend, and had at a many times been a father-like figure to her. Mrs. Evans talked with her, helping her to be at ease, and by the time she was ready to leave, she felt so much better about meeting with the 'doctor'.

While she was waiting to be called in, Daniel came and sat beside her.

"How are you doing this morning, Gwendalyn?"

"Much better today, thanks. I'm just here because Mrs. Evans wanted me to come in for a check up."

"That's a good idea after what you've been through."

"I really appreciated your card and the letter with the drawing. I remembered our walk down to the docks and I am so happy you've found your peace with God and now have a relationship with Him again. I was really bitter and angry with God as well after Anthony died, so your letter really comforted me. How did you know that I was feeling that way?"

"To be honest with you, I didn't. I just knew the pain it caused me when my sister died. I've come to grips with that now and believe it had to be for a reason, maybe for my decision in becoming a doctor, or maybe even being a small part of helping you through your grief. No,

I didn't know you were suffering with the same pain I had suffered from, but I guess it was God who inspired me to write those words to you. I'm glad they helped. Gwendalyn, I..."

"Gwendalyn Bowman," the nurse/receptionist announced. "The doctor will see you now. Follow me."

"I guess I have to go and by the way, I'm happy for you and Carmen," she said as she arose to follow the nurse.

Daniel just nodded his head and then looked up in surprise upon hearing those words and watched as she disappeared behind the now closing door. He then went in the direction of the other treatment room where a patient of his was waiting. He decided he would have a talk with her before she went back home.

"So, Gwendalyn, tell me what's been going on with your health lately," Dr. Evans began.

"Well, soon after Anthony first went missing and then knowing he was gone..." She lowered her head and her eyes began misting again.

"I understand. Just take your time," he comforted.

"Um, eh, I began vomiting and was more tired than usual but I guess that's understandable considering that I wasn't sleeping much at night. Now the vomiting has almost stopped and I'm starting to sleep better at night, although I still find myself tired during the day. Other than that, I guess I'm fine."

"You say that this started soon after Anthony's death."

"Yes."

"Well, it's probable that it was just from the grieving but let's have a look and see if there's any other reason that might be causing it."

"What are you thinking it could be?"

"Let's just have a look before we make any assumptions, all right?" he asked, as he offered her a gown and left the room.

She undressed and put on the gown and soon after Dr. Evans re-entered the room.

After a thorough check-up and some tests were done, Dr. Evans left the room a second time while she got dressed saying that he would be back in a few minutes to discuss his findings.

"I'm fit as a fiddle, right?" she questioned as he came in to talk with her.

"Yes, you are healthy," he returned, to which she smiled

reassuringly, "but I do have some news for you. You said that your menstrual periods in the last two months were very irregular and you've had slight bleeding. You also said that your breasts have been tender for quite a while."

"Yes, but the last time there was any sign of bleeding was almost a month ago."

"Gwendalyn, I must tell you that I believe you are pregnant. Two months pregnant, if my opinion of the examination is correct."

"Two months pregnant! That means that this child was conceived just before Anthony... This is too good to be true! Are you sure?"

"Yes, I am relatively sure. I could have Dr. Sorrenson examine you as well to be sure."

"No, thank you. I think I'll trust your opinion. Yesterday was a glorious day and now today I've been blessed with the knowledge that I am carrying Anthony's child. Thank you so much, Dr. Evans. I don't think I've ever been so happy in a long, long time. Thank you."

Gwendalyn left the office filled with a joy she never thought possible to have ever again. During the car ride back to the Evans home she was thanking God with an overjoyed heart. She once again repented for her ill feelings she had had towards God and now thanked him for this precious gift He had given her.

"Oh, thank you, my Father that You have left me this part of Anthony. I will always cherish this little child as a gift from You and raise him or her to serve and love You all the days of my life. I love you, dear Jesus. Thank you, again."

* * *

Around 4:00 PM that afternoon Gwendalyn was packed and on her way to the ferry with Dr. Evans driving, after sharing her wonderful news with Ina and Mrs. Evans. Dr. Evans continued to tell her that she needed to allow her body all the rest it needed for the safety of the child. He told her he was concerned about the bleeding and told her to stay off her feet until she felt much stronger and knew for sure that the bleeding was stopped completely.

"There is a slight possibility of a miscarriage," he had told her, "so you really need to be careful."

"Not to worry, Dr. Evans," she told him. "When I tell my mother all about this, she will insist that I stay with her so she could take care of me. And I guarantee that between my mom and dad fussing over me, this baby will arrive safely."

"Don't do too much walking around the ship. Here's some money to buy yourself a berth. Sleep as much as you can and stay off your feet."

"Thank you, Dr. Evans, you are so kind and I just wanted to say that I love you and your family so much."

"You have been like a second daughter to me and I love you, too. Take good care of yourself and your little one. There is a doctor nearby that you can consult with and get regular check ups?"

"Yes, there is one about 30 miles away and now that Dad has a car, he'll be taking me to see him regularly."

"I'm glad," he said giving her a final hug. "Take care and good bye."

"Thank you, Dr. Evans. I'll let you know either by letters or phone calls how things go. You take care, as well. Good bye," she said as she boarded the grand ship.

Back at the Evans home a disappointed young man exited the house upon hearing that Gwendalyn had made a phone call to one of her parents neighbours, who had a telephone, to get a message to her father that she would be arriving in Port aux Basque the next morning.

* * *

Dad was there to meet her at the ship and he was excited to see that her countenance had changed into the lovely, cheerful, young lady she had once been. They hugged each other and Gwendalyn told him how glad she was to see him.

"I see that this trip was good for you, even though you decided to cut it short," he said smiling and taking her by the arm to walk her to the car.

"More than you know," she said, with her eyes gleaming.

"You look like you have a secret that you can hardly wait to tell."

"You're right, Dad. I had set in my mind not to tell you until we were with Mom but I don't think I can hold it in until then. First of all

I want to say that I've found my way back to God and now that I have, I really wonder how I could have turned my back on Him in the first place."

"I'm glad you've found Him again but I do understand why you drifted from Him for a time. I knew you'd come back but I was beginning to be concerned about when."

He helped her into the car and went around to the driver's side, let himself in, and began the long drive home.

"I have some more news, Dad," she spoke again. "I had a visit with Dr. Evans at his clinic. Mrs. Evans talked me into it after she saw that I was throwing up and sleeping a lot."

"I'm glad you did, and what did the doctor say," he said studying her face periodically and looking concerned.

"I'm fine," she reassured him, "and I have wonderful news. Daddy, I'm going to have a baby, Anthony's baby."

He looked at her in surprise and shock, and after seeing her glowing face shining with delight, a big smile spread across his face.

"I'm so happy for you. I'm going to be 'Pop' to another grandchild, and this one yours. Oh, my beauty, this is great news! Your mother will be so happy, especially with you almost back to your normal self."

"God has given me something more to live for besides Himself and I am so thankful. This little one is a part of Anthony I'll have with me forever."

With the news shared, and a delicious lunch that Mom had packed was devoured, she fell asleep and the next thing she knew she was being gently awakened by her father saying that they were home.

Upon entering the house the delicious smells of a pork roast dinner greeted them and Gwendalyn's mouth began watering knowing she would soon be enjoying her favorite meal.

During the meal she shared with Mom and Calvin the news of her short stay away and Mom rejoiced with her daughter over the blessed news. They decided that they would invite Anthony's parents for dinner the next day to celebrate.

Mr. and Mrs. Bowman cried with joy over hearing the joyous tidings and immediately began fussing over Gwendalyn asking her if there was anything she needed, or if she was taking care of herself.

Mom shared with them the concerns of the doctor stating that she would be staying at home, despite Gwendalyn's objections, where she could be properly cared for until she was able and strong enough to care for her home.

"Her father will make sure things are well taken care of at her house until she's able to go back home."

"Good idea, and I am more than willing to help out with that as well. We want to make sure Anthony's wife and child are in the best of health when the time comes for him or her to be born," Mr. Bowman agreed.

* * *

Gwendalyn spent the next two months under the careful eye of her mother and by now she was feeling like it was time to go home. Any signs of an ill nature never showed up the whole time she was there and they all were thankful to God for the safety and protection He was continually giving to this young mother and child.

She had knit four woollen outfits for the new baby in different sizes, as baby would grow, as well as several knitted blankets. She and her mother had sewn three and half dozen cloth diapers, which they both agreed that it might be overdoing it. They also made light blankets for warm days and five quilts for cooler days. They enjoyed these days of preparing the necessary items for the little one. They knew these necessities could be purchased, but they thoroughly enjoyed designing them.

Anthony's brother's wife had sent along all the baby clothing she would no longer be needing as they decided that their growing family had reached its limit of five children. The youngest one, now two and a half, had recently grown out of many of the clothes and so they were given to Gwendalyn.

* * *

Gwendalyn finally moved back into her own home after many debates with her parents and they consented under the condition that Calvin would be spending any time he wasn't out in boat with her, and sleeping at her house.

There wasn't a day that went by that Gwendalyn didn't think of Anthony and she missed him terribly the day she felt the first movements of the baby within her, knowing it would have brought them both such joy to share it.

Christmas came and went and she spent many hours in a weeping state remembering their first kiss on that moonlit Christmas Eve as well as many other intimate memories of him associated with this festive season. Her parents and Anthony's did everything they could to brighten her spirits and many times she laughed heartily with them especially with Calvin around sharing his humour and jokes, for which she was very thankful.

Her pregnancy was progressing naturally without any complications. By the end of February, with only about a month and a half remaining till the due date in the middle of April, Gwendalyn was feeling quite heavy and cumbersome. The baby was kicking and moving around regularly.

She got a call from Dr. Evans saying that he was thinking on coming out to check on her about the last weekend of March. She had told him that there was no need saying that she was feeling great and that she had gone to see a doctor in the nearby town three times since being home. He insisted, telling her that she was his patient first. She knew that in spite of his medical terms, he was coming just to make sure for himself that she was OK, and she smiled to herself for his concern. She told her parents of his intended trip and they were pleased over his care of their daughter and said that they would be preparing her old room for him to stay in.

* * *

The evening of March 19 most of the ladies around the cove got together at Anthony's parents' house to throw a baby shower for Gwendalyn. It was a time of joy and laughter as the ladies visited and played the different games. There were so many gifts for 'baby' and Gwendalyn expressed her thankfulness over and over again.

The following Friday, while Gwendalyn was outside walking around the yard, Calvin came out to meet her.

"Hey Gwen, Dr. Evans just phoned and said that he wouldn't be able to make it to check up on you because of some emergency with one of his patients."

"That's fine, Calvin, I'm feeling just fine anywise."

"He says he's sending his associate, Dr. Sorrenson in his place and he should be here on Saturday around suppertime."

"Daniel," she said, her voice barely audible and then went into deep thought.

CHAPTER 28
THE CRISIS

After supper while Dad and Calvin were talking in front of the fireplace, Gwendalyn asked her mother to come upstairs. Once in her room, she took out a box partially filled with several letters and cards and one by one, starting from the first she had received, she showed them to her mother.

Her mother went through them gazing upon the different sketches and reading the letters and notes wearing expressions of amazement to shock as she realized that her daughter had received these before and during her courtship with Anthony.

"Who is this Daniel and where did you meet him?" she asked somewhat confused.

"He's the Dr. Daniel Sorrenson I mentioned to you after one of those trips I made to Nova Scotia. He's the Dr. Sorrenson that's coming here to check up on me in the place of Dr. Evans."

"I don't understand."

Gwendalyn went on to explain the whole story from the time they first met when she fell off the planter, to the scene on the porch, to everything she had experienced with him. She also told her mother about how she was beginning to feel toward him before Anthony made his intentions known. She told her that she continued to receive letters and sketches up until just after their wedding, when he found out for himself that there was to be nothing between them ever again. She also told her mother that she had asked Ina to let him know about what was going on but she hadn't talk to him, and that she wished she had written him herself.

"When I went to visit Ina, a couple of months after the wedding to see her baby, I phoned him and apologized to him for not clearing things up earlier myself and asked his forgiveness. He said it was OK and that he didn't blame me."

"He sounds like a very respectable young man who has had deep feelings for you for a very long time," her mother piped up. "And what

211

is it you're feeling now?"

"I don't know, Mom," she answered, "and I really don't want to feel anything at all. Anthony is my love and it's like I'm being disloyal to him if I allow myself to begin to feel something for someone else. And anyhow, Daniel's involved with another girl over in Nova Scotia whose name is Carmen."

"My dear, Anthony was a wonderful man who loved you, I believe, more than he loved himself. He would want you to be happy and not mourn him for the rest of your life. You're so young and you have so much of life ahead of you. If love comes your way again, don't be afraid to reach out and take hold of it."

"It's just too soon, Mom, and anyhow, if Daniel was at one time interested in me, he isn't any more. I just wanted to share all this with you because I have kept it a secret for far too long and needed to tell someone about it."

"Is that all this is all about, and why would you say he's not interested in you any more?"

"I really don't know what all this is about, but I do know he isn't interested in me because he's found another, the girl Carmen."

"I see. Well, I'm glad you shared all this with me and always know that I am here whenever you need to talk. Come, let's go down stairs and join your father and Calvin."

They spent the rest of the evening playing games until Gwendalyn began yawning and they bid each other goodnight. She saw her parents out and made sure Calvin was comfortable on the couch before climbing the stairs to ready herself for bed.

* * *

In the middle of the night Gwendalyn awoke feeling strangely and then began having pains in her abdomen. She decided she would get up and walk around thinking it may be pent up gas that was causing the pain.

She went downstairs to the kitchen and placed more wood in the stove and set the kettle to boil. She was glad that Calvin was staying over, as she hadn't needed to stoke the fire in the middle of the night or start a fire in the morning. He would get up during the night and keep the fires going so that when she came down the stairs in the

212

morning she would be greeted with welcoming warmth coming from the living room as well as the kitchen.

"Ow-ooo-ooo!" she screamed in pain which brought Calvin running into the kitchen.

"What is it, Gwen?" he asked, with fear showing in his face.

"You better run and get Mom," she managed, her face tight with pain.

He was dressed and out the door within two minutes and ten minutes later she heard car doors slam and then Mom, Dad, and Calvin came bursting in. They found her in the living room sitting and wringing her hands in concern.

"What's going on, sweetheart?" Mom asked as she came to sit beside her.

"I was having pain in bed so I got up to walk it off and then when I was in the kitchen trying to make tea when a terrible pain shot through my stomach all of a sudden."

"How are you feeling now?"

"Well, the pain goes away and then comes back."

"How long was it since your last pain?"

"I had a real bad one when Calvin went to get you and another one just before you got here."

"You try and relax and I'll make us some tea. Elijah, you and Calvin keep her as comfortable as possible."

Mom was out of the room no more than five minutes when another pain gripped Gwendalyn.

"Mom!" Calvin yelled. "Come in here quick!"

Mom was there in an instant consoling and comforting her daughter.

"Just breathe deeply, sweetheart. That's it. In through your nose and out through your mouth. I found that it helped me when I was ready to have my babies."

The pain subsided and Gwendalyn breathed out a sigh of relief.

"Mom, I'm not ready to have this baby yet. It's too early. I'm not supposed to give birth until the middle of April. That's still three weeks away."

"Babies come when they want to and I'm thinking this one wants to make an early entrance. Calvin, you go finish getting the tea ready and Elijah, you get a pan of cold water and a wash cloth."

Ten minutes later came another pain, and Mom continued to breathe through the pains with her daughter.

"Elijah, I think you'd better go and get the doctor because by the time you get back the baby might be ready to come."

He finished his tea and headed out the door with haste and much concern for his daughter.

Two hours later he was back without the doctor.

"The doctor was called out to Herring Harbour on an emergency last night and his wife doesn't know when he'll be back. She said she'd send him right over as soon as he gets back."

"Herring Harbour is not that far so there's nothing to worry about. He can still be here in plenty of time to help birth this baby. The pains are still ten minutes apart so we've got some time yet."

Lunchtime came and went and still the doctor hadn't showed up. Gwendalyn's pain had gotten increasingly worse and closer together.

By 4:30 PM Gwendalyn was travailing with pain and anguish. Mom continued to wipe the perspiration from her brow and face as she laboured with little relief. The pains were now three minutes apart and the doctor still hadn't come. Calvin had gone for the Bowmans several hours ago and they had gathered in Gwendalyn's home hearing her cries of pain, and praying for safe delivery of the child.

Mr. Bowman, upon the instruction from Dad, had now gone to the Gillard's home to await Dr. Sorrenson who was due to arrive any time.

He arrived shortly after 5:00 PM and was rushed over to Gwendalyn's immediately. After assessing the situation he gave instructions to which Mrs. Gillard and Mrs. Bowman left the room to make the preparations ready of all the things he needed to help with the arrival of the little one.

Once they had left the room he took the cloth and soaked it in the cool pan of water, squeezing out the excess, and gently wiped her still perspiring forehead.

"It'll be OK, Gwendalyn. I brought everything needed with me in case such a turn of events happened. Just hold on. I know you're in pain. You and your baby will make it," he comforted.

Another hour had passed and still no baby. Daniel was concerned as well as both mothers who were sitting on either side of Gwendalyn comforting her as best they could.

Daniel examined her once again and announced that he could feel the head.

"Gwendalyn, on your next contraction, I want you to push."

The next pain came and the coaching began.

"Bear down and push," Mom said, placing her hand behind her head and the other holding her hand.

"Good girl, Gwendalyn," Daniel soothed. "You're doing great. I can see the top of the head. Here comes another contraction, now push! Push! The head is coming. Gently push. OK, stop pushing. Stop pushing." Daniel cleaned out the baby's nose and mouth and once again encouraged her pushing. Once the baby was delivered, he cut and clamped the cord and then lifted a tiny boy onto his mother's stomach.

"Well done, Gwendalyn, you have a fine son. He's small but he looks very healthy."

Grandma Gillard wrapped the baby in a warm soft towel and placed him in his mother's arms. Gwendalyn smiled and said, "Anthony, you have a son, and you, my darling boy, will be called Anthony."

"Ow-ooo-ooo," Gwendalyn screamed again as pain gripped her again. Daniel motioned for one of the ladies to take the baby and Mrs. Bowman gathered the little one into her arms.

"Something's happening," groaned Gwendalyn. "I feel like I have to push again."

"It's just the placenta, you may have to push again to birth it as well," Daniel informed her. "That's it, a little more, there. Good girl. You're finished now, just relax. We'll take care of you."

Daniel and Mom began cleaning up when Gwendalyn's body tensed once again in pain.

"What's wrong, sweetheart?" Mom asked.

"What's happening, Gwendalyn? Daniel interjected.

"I don't know but I'm having more pain and I feel like I have to push again."

Daniel examined her again and shock washed across his face.

"There's another baby but it's completely breech. It's lying across the birthing canal and it won't be able to be born unless I turn it or we operate. Being twins the baby is small so it may not be too difficult to turn. Hold on Gwendalyn."

Her face winced in pain and she cried out.

"Hold on, darling," he crooned, "I'm almost done. Thank God. The bottom is closer than I thought. There! Now on your next contraction I want you to push. The baby is going to come bottom first and we want to get him out quickly. Here comes the contraction. Now push!"

Gwendalyn determined that she was going to do everything possible to save her second baby, and as hard as her strength could muster she pushed, drew in another breath, and pushed again.

"Great job, Gwendalyn. Your baby is here," he said as he continued to clean out the air passages. The baby was limp and still didn't breathe on its own. Daniel's eyes misted as he noticed the second baby was a little girl. He began administering to her artificial respiration.

"I don't hear anything. Is he OK?" Gwendalyn asked but no one answered.

Daniel continued giving the baby artificial respiration determined not to give up. All of a sudden the baby drew in a quick breath and started crying softly. After he was sure of her health, he wrapped her in another soft towel and handed her to her mother.

"You have a beautiful baby girl," he said.

"A girl! Oh Mom, I have a girl, too. I'll call her Anna. Anna and Anthony," she said and broke into tears.

"Anna," Daniel whispered as he turned around to allow a rush of tears flow down his cheeks, "dearest little Anna."

After he regained control over his emotions he turned around and took care of anything that needed further medical attention. He then proceeded down the stairs where he ran into the other doctor making his way upstairs.

"You must be Dr. Sorrenson," the older doctor greeted him. "Sounds like you've done a marvellous job. Twins too. I'll continue up the stairs to check on our patient," he said as he patted him on the back and congratulated him.

Downstairs, Daniel could hear the cheers and praises to God for the safe delivery of the two babies and the health of their mother. He made his way to the bathroom to clean up and then outside for some fresh air and to talk privately with his God for His help in this trying ordeal.

Gwendalyn looked over into the beautifully carved crib that her father had made for her little one and now realized that Dad would now have a job of designing another crib. Her dear little ones lay on opposite ends of the crib, both facing their mother, sleeping comfortably and soundly.

She now lay comfortable in her freshly made bed and was thanking God for His goodness and going over in her mind what had just happened.

"What had Daniel said to her just before little Anna came into the world. Did he actually call her 'darling' or was it her imagination?"

She had no time to think further on it, as she couldn't keep from drifting into an exhausted sleep.

CHAPTER 29
A NEW COURSE OF LIFE

Gwendalyn awoke to a crying baby and opened her eyes to see Mom bringing little Anna to her to nurse.

"This little girl may have had a hard entrance into the world but she's got strength and a will to live. She's hungry now."

Gwendalyn held her 'Anna' close to her thanking God for keeping her safe. Soon the baby had finished and Mom had placed her back in the crib with her brother who was now beginning to stir and needing his feeding. On this went every couple of hours or so and their tired mother slept while they slept. All her food was brought to her bedroom and she got out of bed only for trips to the bathroom.

She sleepily opened her eyes to find Daniel sitting close beside her.

"Hi there sleeping beauty," he said. "I've come to tell you that I'm almost ready to leave."

"So soon," she said wearily.

"It's Sunday afternoon, my dear," he said brushing loose strands of hair from her face. "I have to catch the evening ferry across."

"What about the babies, do they need any special care?" she asked.

"I've instructed your mother how to care for them and left some necessary items she may need. Your babies are very healthy and little Anna seems to be a real fighter. Your physician from the nearby town brought a weigh scales with him and weighed them. Anthony is a big boy weighing 5 lb. 2 oz., and little Anna weighs 4 lb. 6 oz. You did a great bringing your children into the world. You should be very proud and pleased."

"I am, Daniel. Thank you for coming. If you weren't here little Anna may not have made it. Please come and visit us again soon and... eh... bring Carmen with you... You'll both be welcome. I'm sorry, I'm just so ti..." she said between yawns and fell into a deep sleep.

Daniel stood over her watching her sleep

"There's so much you need to know, my darling. Sleep now," he said, as he bent down and kissed her lightly on the forehead.

Before leaving, Daniel found Gwendalyn's mom in the kitchen. "Could you make sure she has lots of food that's high in iron? Being pregnant with twins and then the blood loss has caused her to become very anaemic. She's going to be very tired for the next few months until her iron count gets built up."

"Not to worry, doctor. I'm planning to live here and do all the cooking and anything else until she's strong and up on her feet. Elijah and Calvin are moving our bed into the room next door to Gwendalyn so we'll be here to help her day and night. Even the Bowmans have been here since she first started labouring and I believe they're going to be doing everything they possibly can to help. Mrs. Bowman has busied herself in here making tea and meals for all concerned."

"I can see she's in good hands. I guess I'll be leaving now."

"Thank you, doctor, for everything. I don't even want to imagine what may have happened if you hadn't showed up when you did. Thank you so much for coming. Here's some food I've prepared for you to take on your trip. Take care of yourself. You're welcome here whenever you desire to come."

"Thank you, Mrs. Gillard, I may just take you up on that. Good-bye."

"Please do, and good-bye."

* * *

A month had passed and the babies were growing steadily. Gwendalyn remained in a weakened condition but was gradually making some progress with her health.

Mom continued to bring her meals upstairs and help her with feeding times for the infants.

It was during one such time that Mom engaged her in a conversation concerning Daniel.

"Daniel was wonderful during the birth of your children."

"Yes, he was great, wasn't he?"

"He was so caring and supportive. Gwendalyn, he seemed to go beyond what the every day doctor would do. He did what someone who really cared for or maybe even loved his patient."

"Mom, how can you say that? He did care for me in that way at one time but now he has Carmen. I'm not ready for another relationship even if he was feeling anything for me, which I doubt."

"Well, I watched him during your labour and birth and what I saw, and heard, definitely goes beyond a doctor/patient relationship."

"What do you mean, heard?" she asked, her curiosity building.

"I heard him call you 'darling' and his manner with you was that out of love, and more than just care."

"I'm sure it must have been a slip on his part. How could he love me when he has Carmen? I've met her and she a very pretty and respectable girl," she finished, and began yawning uncontrollable.

"Perhaps you're right. You go to sleep now and regain your strength."

"Thanks Mom," she said watching her mother leave the room.

Although she was tired she couldn't help thinking over again about what had happened that March 26th. She did hear him call her darling and his manner was indeed very caring. It may have been considered actions of love. She also vaguely remembered drifting off to sleep hearing him call her his 'sleeping beauty' and felt the gentle touch of his lips upon her forehead.

"It was probably just a dream," she thought, but in her heart she had come to grow more than fond of Daniel and the birthing experience with him bonded her even closer to him. She still had the pangs of missing Anthony come upon her but she was beginning to feel also that he would want to have a God-fearing, respectable man to be a father-figure to his children, and to take care of her.

She knew the decent man her husband was and the thought of his unselfish nature and caring ways threw her into a state of melancholy and she fell asleep crying.

* * *

Over the next four months Gwendalyn grew stronger each day and now the babies were straightening out their bodies, lifting their heads and wiggling around as if swimming. This was a joy to see them grow strong as compared to having their legs tucked up to their tummy and resting their heads to one side.

Although Anna was a little smaller than her brother Anthony, she was strong and often did things a step ahead of her brother.

Gwendalyn was now helping her mother with cooking, and washing the continual dirty diapers. They both were glad they had sewn the number of diapers they did because with two little bottoms to keep dry, the job was constant. They were very pleased with the results the washing machine gave and it made for speedy cleaning. Dad had set up two lines running through the open area of the downstairs to hang diapers and other clothing to dry on the rainy spring days.

Now that July was here, there were few wet days and the clothing could be hung outside to dry. There were the occasional days when rainstorms blew in and both mother and daughter were glad to have the lines hanging in the house.

It was on such a day, when the rain had lasted for three days straight, that someone had come for a visit. Heads had to duck to make it into another room of the house because of the lines being filled with 'wash'.

"Is it Mrs. Bowman?" Gwendalyn called from the other side of the lines.

"It's me," came the familiar voice of Daniel as he parted two tightly hung diapers and came through to face her.

"Daniel! How good it is to see you!" she exclaimed.

Daniel stood gazing at this beauty before him. Her hair was braided and hung down her back while little unruly wisps of hair, that she now tried to put into place, added to her attractiveness. She was all aglow, partially from being busy with her little ones, and of course, her natural beauty gracing her face. The dress she wore today had a slimming effect on the nearly back to her pre-pregnancy figure. She looked so vibrant and full of life. Daniel couldn't help remembering the day he first met her when he helped her up off the snow after she fell from the planter.

"She is beautiful," he mused thoughtfully.

"Did you bring Carmen?" Gwendalyn asked as she looked around him to see if she were with him.

"No, I didn't bring her. There is something I would like to talk with you about..." he began but was interrupted by her sudden burst of excitement.

"Come, Daniel," she said grabbing his arm and fairly dragging him. "I want you to see the little miracles you helped bring into the world."

They both peered into the crib to see the two bundles of joy sleeping peacefully close to each other.

"Dad built another crib, this one. We use the one upstairs for nighttime sleeping. We tried to have them sleep separately in their own cribs but they want to be together and they definitely sleep better together. I don't know how I'll separate them when they get too big for both of them to sleep in this crib."

"This is little Anna?" Daniel asked as he held her little hand in his large one. "I never told you but 'Anna' was the name of my little sister who died when she was still so young. It caused me such joy, and sadness, when I heard you call this little one by her name."

"I'm sorry, Daniel. I had no idea."

"Please don't apologize. I love the fact that she is Anna."

"Your own little sister may have been taken from you, but it was you who saved this little Anna from an untimely death and I will always be indebted to you. You are my very special friend."

"Do you really mean that?"

"Of course I do," she said, matter-of-factly, and squeezed his arm that she was holding, closer to herself.

Daniel's spirits soared at this first open display of affection she shared toward him. How much he loved her and had loved her for so long and now there was the possibility that she may return the cherished feeling.

* * *

Later that evening, after enjoying another of Mom's home cooked meals, the five of them, along with the Bowmans, were sitting in the living room, visiting and taking turns holding Anthony and Anna. The conversation was light, and laughter floated throughout the house.

Mr. and Mrs. Bowman announced that it was getting late and that they should be getting home.

"I'll walk with you," Calvin said. "Are you ready to come along, Dr. Sorrenson, eh, Daniel?" he corrected after being let know that Daniel would like to be addressed by his first name as it sounded like being in the clinic and business-like every time someone called him doctor.

Daniel smiled as Calvin corrected himself.

"I think I'd like to visit here a little longer. I'll be able to find my way when we're done. Good night."

After the three had left, Gwendalyn and Mom took the twins upstairs where they were nursed and tucked into bed for the next six hours. She was glad that they were sleeping longer at night. Anna was always the first to awake, be changed and nursed, and then followed by Anthony twenty minutes to half an hour later. Gwendalyn was also glad for this schedule. It was Mom who helped this process to become a schedule by soothing Anthony, still in his bed, while Anna was being fed and then it was his turn.

The ladies joined Dad and Daniel back in the living room but it was Dad who said that he should be getting to bed himself knowing that dawn broke early and he was going out in boat with Calvin again tomorrow, as was the routine all summer long. Mom joined him in saying 'good night' and they went upstairs to bed.

"I've told them that they've given me a great start with the twins and that I'm feeling so much better, but Mom insists on staying another month till they're six months old. She keeps cooking me liver and turnip greens almost more often than I can stand it. And the raisin pie you said you enjoyed so much tonight, it has been a regular dessert."

"I think that's partially my doing," he smiled. "I told your mother that it would probably take six months before your strength is back totally and that you would need lots of food high in iron. I'm glad she took me seriously."

"She took you seriously all right and high iron food is mainly all I've been eating since you left. I'm glad now, though, because I do feel healthier and stronger and I only take a nap every second day or so now. In the beginning I was so tired, I could hardly get out of bed."

"Your mom and dad are great parents and I'm sure you're thankful for them."

"Oh, I am, but I wanted to ask you how you are doing. You've heard everything about all of us, what about you? How have you been doing, and how's Carmen?"

"I'm fine and I guess Carmen is too, but I haven't really talked with her since you left to go home back in September."

"I don't understand, Daniel. I thought you and she were becoming a couple."

"Gwendalyn, you've known how much I've cared for you and although you were married, I still cared for you. I tried to go on with my life by developing a relationship with Carmen. I knew I was being unfair to her when my heart was still attached to another. After the dreadful loss of your husband and the thought that maybe one day you might reconsider me, I told her I couldn't continue in the relationship with her. We were courting only a month and all that time I still didn't have intimate feelings for her. It was truly unfair to her and I knew I had to end it. She was heart-broken for a time, but not too long ago I happened to see her with another young man.

"Ina brought her daughter in for a check up about two weeks ago and let me know that Carmen and her young man were engaged to be married."

Gwendalyn sat quietly as he told her everything.

"Gwendalyn," he said, turning to face her and taking her hand in his, "I know it still may be too soon, but do you think you could ever consider me a possible suitor?"

She looked away and her eyes began to mist again and then threatening to spill over. He turned her face to meet his and as he did the tears flowed down her cheeks.

"I don't know, Daniel. I loved Anthony and no one could ever replace him. I don't think I could ever love anyone like I loved him. I know my children need a father and I feel you would make a good father but I don't know if I can do this."

Daniel wrapped his arms around her trying to console her but she pushed him away.

"I can't do this," she said and left the room crying and hurried up the stairs.

Daniel slipped quietly from the house and walked slowly around the cove. He thought a lot about what had just happened and realized that she was still mourning her husband's death. He decided she still needed time and that the healing process wasn't quite finished. If it were time she needed, then he would be patient.

* * *

225

The next day Calvin came over in time for breakfast around 9:00 o'clock and Mom and Gwendalyn both were surprised to see him.

"I thought you were going out in boat with you father this morning," Mom said.

"I was, but Daniel met us on the wharf and asked if he could come along. Dad said that I should stay and make sure that both our houses had plenty of firewood."

Gwendalyn had told Mom all about what had happened last night, and the look between them, and the silent communication, told them that both knew the purpose of this twosome trip.

It was at 11:30 AM that Gwendalyn saw and announced the arrival of the two paddling their way up to the wharf and then watched as they unloaded the morning's catch. Calvin was already there helping unload and then the three disappeared into the cleaning shack to finish the job.

They all showed up, clean and ready for a noon meal, after stopping at Dad's to make themselves presentable.

They sat at the table with Daniel looking a little green and when Dad had asked the blessing on the food, they all began dishing up a scrumptious meal of roast chicken with all the trimmings and gravy. Daniel's appetite returned with the first bite of the roast chicken and he ate a hearty meal.

Calvin was the first to comment on Daniel's first outing in the small dory.

"By the way Daniel was talking while we were cleaning the fish, he must have threw up everything he ate all week," he said laughing.

"Now, hold on a minute. I think the sea is something that a person has to get used to. It wasn't so hard on the ferry but these small boats will need lots of practice, or never go out in them ever again."

With that comment they all laughed again with Daniel joining in the cheerfulness, even if it was at his expense.

Dad and Calvin made the second trip out in boat today without the good doctor. Daniel spent the afternoon walking about the cove and talking with whomever he met on route. He met Mr. Bowman down by the shore and was invited to his house for a cup of tea. He stayed at their house visiting for two hours and upon seeing Dad and Calvin making their approach, he thanked them and excused himself making his way to the wharf as the boat was secured.

Gwendalyn once again watched from the window as the three repeated an earlier scene. She still wasn't sure what to make of this and her heart continued to be troubled.

During the night Calvin and Daniel were startled awake with a banging on the door. They both came downstairs to find a distraught man who immediately pleaded with Daniel to come and check out his young son who had been burning up with fever and now was becoming delirious.

Daniel finished putting on his shirt and grabbed his black bag that he never went anywhere without. When they arrived, they found that young boy was indeed quite ill.

"What has happened for this boy to get so sick?" he demanded.

"We don't know. Yesterday he was complaining with pain in his right side. He was somewhat fevered all day and now, tonight, he's crazy in pain and there's no way we were able to control the fever."

Daniel felt the boy's side. He knew immediately what was wrong, as he had encountered this a few times in the past two years.

"Where is the nearest hospital?" he asked.

"It's about two and a half hours away but Dr. Martin is in the next town about a half an hour away."

"The boy has acute appendicitis and needs surgery right away. He may not make it if we try to get him to the hospital. Calvin can you take your father's car and drive out to get Dr. Martin. I'm going to have to start this without him but he may be here to help part way through."

"Sure thing, doc," Calvin said as he ran out the door.

"Where's the best light in the house?"

"The kitchen light is the brightest."

"Make the kitchen table comfortable to lay him on and make everything in it clean and sterile. Boil some water to keep the instruments sterile. If there are any other lights or lamps that can be taken to the kitchen, do it now."

He laid out his sterile instruments explaining the importance that no one cough or sneeze or even breathe on them and everyone moved away from the table.

With everything ready, Daniel looked at the clock. A knock brought everyone's attention to the door and the boy's father opened it as Mrs.

227

Gillard hurried in.

After Daniel had explained the situation to her, she had washed and scrubbed her hands and was now ready for Daniel to instruct her in whatever he needed help with.

"Twenty minutes before Dr. Martin gets here. Maybe I should wait."

"Don't wait, doctor, if you think the boy may die," his father said, his worry noticeable in his voice.

He contemplated the situation and thought about what had happened in Gwendalyn's case. Dr. Martin had showed up too late to help her, as his other emergency took longer than he ever anticipated. What if he's now out on another emergency and may not show up until it's too late again.

He decided he would have to start without him and hoped that Dr. Martin would show up soon. He administered the proper medication and soon the child was sleeping soundly. He'd never done this kind of thing on his own before. He had only assisted in these types of surgery and was still in training. He started trembling and then closed his eyes and prayed for God's guidance and his peace to take control of the situation.

He now steadied himself and made the incision. Mrs. Gillard was careful with each instruction she was given and was encouraged with Daniel's constant reassurance. He was now lifting the inflamed and infected appendix from the boy's body.

He cleaned out the wound and began stitching the opening. The door burst open and Dr. Martin and Calvin entered the room. The doctor assessed the situation and looked at the diseased appendix.

"Looks like your actions may have saved the boy's life," he said. "Continue on, you're doing a good job."

Once everything was completed and the boy was comfortably sleeping in his own bed, Daniel spoke with the boy's mother saying that he should be fine now. He went on to say that if he began fevering again, to give him a medication he would leave with them, three times a day in case of any infection that may develop from the surgery itself.

Dr. Martin stood agreeing with Daniel's advice and the medication he'd given to the mother. He reassured both Daniel and the mother that he would be checking in on the boy regularly until he was well again.

The father kept shaking Daniel's hand thanking him over and over again for saving the life of his son.

Calvin and Daniel went back to their beds to get some well-deserved sleep as Mom headed back to her's.

They missed church the next morning and met at Gwendalyn's for a brunch at 11:30 AM. Gwendalyn had prepared a feast of fried ham, poached eggs, pancakes, hash browned potatoes, and toast with homemade jam. She served orange juice along with hot tea to drink with the meal.

CHAPTER 30
A NEW LOVE

Gwendalyn and Daniel had several times throughout the meal caught themselves watching each other, both having thoughts and feelings they didn't know how to express.

After a restful afternoon in the living room playing with the babies, Daniel spoke up saying that he would have to get ready to leave. Mom prepared a homemade lunch for him to take along and Gwendalyn agreed to walk him around the cove to see him off.

"I could hardly believe what happened last night. You were wonderful, the way you saved that boy's life."

"God was my helper and with your mother's assistance, everything turned out just fine. I checked on the boy on my way over this morning and he seemed to be doing great."

"I think we need a full-time doctor here with the cove growing into a town this size."

"I've been thinking the same thing," Daniel said glancing in her direction.

She looked away and changed the subject.

* * *

Daniel had collected his belongings from her parents' house and was now inside his automobile saying his final farewells.

"Would it be OK if I wrote you?" he asked.

"Of course. I've told you, you are my special friend, and I'll be glad to write you as well."

He took her hand in his and his voice became husky.

"Gwendalyn, you know how much I care for you. Won't you please consider what we talked about Friday night?"

"Daniel, you mean a great deal to me, maybe more than you know, but I just can't bring myself to have intimate feelings for another man, not yet."

"I understand, dearest Gwendalyn, and I'll not push you. Take all the time you need and take real good care of yourself."

He squeezed her hand and she reciprocated it. She watched as he drove away, her mind swimming with confusion. A part of her wanted to run after him and tell him 'yes, I'm ready now', while the other part told her she was being disloyal to Anthony. She walked back home feeling low in spirit.

* * *

The twins turned nine months old and their eyes danced with excitement as they stood in their crib watching the sparkling lights and shining bulbs of the Christmas tree. Gwendalyn had broken the tradition by decorating the tree today, almost two weeks before Christmas day.

Over the past four months Daniel had written three times, sending sketches. The first sketch was of Gwendalyn, the way he had seen her as he made his way through the line of diapers on his last visit. He expressed to her, through words of endearment, how much he cared for her and hoped that she, too, would grow to feel the same for him.

The second sketch was of the twins upon the first moment he saw them laying close beside each other in a peaceful sleep.

The final sketch was beautiful to look at. Gwendalyn sat on the couch nursing little Anna. She was embarrassed and wondered when he had seen her there. She had always been discreet when nursing and so smiled that even though she didn't know of him watching her, he didn't reveal himself to embarrass her publicly. She loved the picture in spite of its circumstances.

This time she could hardly wait to have some quiet time to write him again. She had written twice but never anything of an intimate nature. Mom and Dad had moved back home three months ago leaving her with plenty of quiet time to think things through.

Two weeks ago, Mr. and Mrs. Bowman had come over for a visit bringing with them the Christmas tree. They thought that they would leave it outside until closer to Christmas but Gwendalyn had insisted on bringing it in right away. It seemed to brighten her mood. After the tree was standing and had plenty of water to keep it from drying out, they sat with Gwendalyn in the living room enjoying a hot cup of tea and some goodies Mrs. Bowman had baked and brought along.

They got into a discussion involving memories of Anthony. Gwendalyn shared with them how much she loved their son and that she was still missing him.

Mrs. Bowman talked about the fact that the children shouldn't always be without a father. She made mention of Daniel and asked Gwendalyn if she had ever considered him a possibility.

"He seems to be a very responsible and respectable young man and he seems to care very much for you. He had a visit with us when he was here back in August and he told us of his intentions regarding you. He really is a nice young man," she had said.

"I can't believe you're saying those things," Gwendalyn said. "For quite a long time now I've been suppressing different feelings and hanging onto memories of Anthony because I thought that if I allowed myself to feel for another I would be abandoning Anthony and what he meant to me, being disloyal."

Her tears had flowed and she cried desperately letting out hurt and confusion that had held her for so long. Both Mr. and Mrs. Bowman consoled her saying it was all right for her get on with her life. They told her they knew she loved their son and that she wouldn't be disloyal to Anthony by making a better life for her and the children. Anthony, as well as they, would want to see her happy and raising his children in a secure home with a loving father.

She spent a lot of time in prayer after they left seeking her Father's will in this major decision for her life.

The relief she felt afterwards was inexpressible. She felt like a crushing weight had been lifted from her shoulders. For the first time since Anthony died, she was beginning to feel free to live and love again.

*   *   *

The twins were tucked in bed for the night and wouldn't be awakening until about 6:00 o'clock the next morning.

She sat in the living room admiring the tree and enjoying the warmth of the fireplace. She took her pen and some paper and began to write a letter to Daniel. She didn't give a lot of explanation or details because she felt she would rather talk with him face to face when sharing these sensitive issues. She wanted his reaction to be personal and to create memories she could build with him. She wrote about the twins, her parents and Calvin, and the happenings around the cove. The last thing on the letter was an invitation for him to come calling, if he still desired to do so, saying that she was at long last ready to try starting again and that she was willing for him to come.

* * *

Christmas Eve had come and Gwendalyn was excited about the celebration that was soon to take place at her house. After supper at about 7:30, Mom, Dad, Calvin, Stacey with her husband and son, the Bowmans, with son, Carl, and daughter, Stephanie, along with their spouses and children, would be showing up for a special Christmas Eve party. Everyone was to bring all the goodies so all she had to do was to have a punch and hot tea ready when they got there. Calvin was to be dropping off Mom's punch bowl earlier so she could have the punch ready by the time they all showed up.

She was in the living room playing peek-a-boo with her little playmates when she heard a knock at the door.

"Come on in, Calvin," she said, and heard him enter "You can put the punch bowl on the counter in the kitchen, and since when do you knock before coming in here?"

She heard him deposit the punch bowl in the kitchen and continued to play with her babies as they laughed and squealed with delight.

A flash of bright light startled both her and the children and she turned around suddenly.

"Sorry, I didn't mean to frighten you. I just wanted to capture this moment on film."

"Daniel!"

"Hi Gwendalyn. I thought I might surprise you."

"It's definitely a surprise, a wonderful surprise," she said smiling. "What was that flash of light just now."

"This is a camera. It takes pictures but you need this flash to produce enough light to make the picture clear and bright enough to

234

see. I'll send you the picture when I get the film developed."

"Daniel, I've heard about those. This is so exciting. This means I'll have a picture of my babies to show them when they grow up."

"Yes, and many more besides. I plan to take a lot of pictures while I'm here. But let me see this big boy. Anthony, you've grown so much."

He lifted Anthony far above his head and began jiggling him to which he responded with bursts of laughter.

He put him back in a sitting position in his crib and proceeded to lift Anna out. She immediately started to cry and held her arms out to her mother. Gwendalyn came over and rescued the frightened little girl.

"I think she needs to get used to you before you hold her."

Baby Anna settled in her mother's lap and Daniel once again gathered Anthony from the crib. He sat beside Gwendalyn and began to talk softly to Anna, who was now smiling slightly, knowing she was protected in her mother's safe arms.

Anthony played with Daniel's buttons on his shirt and soon Anna was venturing over to discover what had taken Anthony's attention. Before long, Daniel was holding both babies while Gwendalyn, after careful instruction, snapped a picture of the three of them together.

They put the babies back in the crib and Daniel followed Gwendalyn to the kitchen where she prepared a sandwich and a cup of tea for them both.

"We're having a Christmas Eve party here at 7:30 and there'll be a lot of people showing up," she told him. "That's why I didn't make much for supper with all the baking and treats we'll be enjoying tonight."

"This is great," he told her, "but I'll be looking forward to sampling some of the baking as well."

After they finished their light supper, Gwendalyn put the dishes in the sink and began to make preparations for the punch. Daniel took her by the hand and turned her around.

"I really want to talk with you more than anything else. I've so longed to be with you and..."

"Daniel, I..."

"Come with me, we need to talk," he said leading her out of the kitchen and into the living room.

"Daniel, I don't know how to begin," she said as they sat on the couch. "It's been so hard. There were times when I so wanted to reach out to you. To lean on you for support."

"Why didn't you?"

"Well, I just couldn't allow myself to let go of Anthony and if I did let go of him, I felt as if I were giving up everything we had together, and that it didn't mean as much any more. It's still hard."

"I understand, Gwendalyn, really I do. That's why I decided to give you all the time you needed to heal of all this."

"I wanted to be over this sooner. Just wait here. I have something I want to show you."

She left the room and hurried upstairs and came back holding a small box. She placed it on her lap and opened the lid exposing all the sketches he had sent her over the years. She took them out one by one and placed them in his lap until the most recent one he had sent her was sitting on top of the pile.

"What does this mean?" he questioned her.

"I cared for you since the day I met you but I made a choice to love Anthony because I had known him all my life and then I learned to love him deeply after our courtship started. I'm sorry Daniel if this bothers you, but I feel that I have to tell you everything so that I can leave it all behind and be able to go on with you."

"I understand. Please go on."

"Anthony was my first love, since childhood, and he meant everything to me, but I have saved all these because I cared for you. Over the past couple of years, as we were getting to know each other and becoming friends, I've learned to care for you even more. After finding out about your little sister I felt so much compassion for you and wanted to comfort you because I now understood your grief, after losing Anthony."

Gwendalyn started to cry and Daniel tried to comfort her.

"No Daniel, I need to say it all. It was you who helped me to understand my feelings of anger and bitterness towards God because of grief. And then, again, it was you who helped me with the birth of these beautiful babies and you saved little Anna's life. I know there are strong possibilities for you and I, but I'm still trying to see my way past losing Anthony. Daniel, I'm so sorry for taking so long and I do, now, want a relationship with you, but it's still so hard."

She was crying out of control now as he stroked her arm and tried to console her.

"Please help me, Daniel. I need you to help me through this if you can, and are still willing. I don't understand how you could continue to wait for me. What do I have to offer but still many sorrows, and here I am a widow still in love with her dead husband. Oh, Daniel."

She bent over her lap allowing the tears to run freely and Daniel gently gathered her into his arms to comfort her.

"I understand, dearest. I couldn't get involved with another even after you were married because I hadn't gotten over you. If there were ever any chance for us, I would wait for forever to be with you. I love you, Gwendalyn, and I want to be here to help you through all this. I want to comfort you through your sorrows. I feel God has given me a second chance with you. I'll never be Anthony, but I'll be Daniel, a man who fell in love with you the day we met and has loved you ever since. Won't you let me love you and care for you?"

"I still don't understand how you could, but, yes, yes, I'll give us that chance. I'll let you love me and I will do my best to love you, as you deserve. Perhaps it'll come more naturally with time."

"I know it will, my darling."

"It won't be long," she said returning his embrace. "After sharing with you everything that's been locked away in my heart, I suddenly feel free. Thank you, Daniel."

By this time the twins were getting tired of playing with each other and growing fussy.

"Oh my, it's 6:30. I've missed their supper. They usually eat between 5:30 and 6:00. Can you try and entertain them while I prepare their food?"

Daniel began playing peek-a-boo as he had seen Gwendalyn doing earlier and although Anna was still unsure of him, she became a little more comfortable watching her brother. Soon, she was giggling as well.

"All ready," Gwendalyn announced as she entered the room. "Can you bring Anthony?" she asked Daniel, as she lifted Anna from the crib.

Once she had secured them both in the high chairs Dad had made for them, she handed Daniel a bowl and spoon and gave him a 'would you?' look.

"I'm going to have to learn this sooner or later," he said preparing to feed Anthony.

By the time they were finished both Anthony and Daniel needed a changing. Gwendalyn picked up her cloth and tried to wipe off Daniel's shirt but the smears ended up almost as bad as the splatters of food.

"It's OK," he said laughing and taking her hand in his. "I'll just go out to the car and get a fresh one."

She washed both children's faces and wiped off as much food as she could from Anthony's clothing. She picked him out of his chair and sat him on the table saying, "don't move." She then quickly lifted Anna from her chair, placed her on her hip, gathered Anthony to the other, and headed upstairs to change both children.

Coming back down she smiled as she saw Daniel in his fresh shirt stoking the fire in the fireplace. He stood to meet her and asked if he could help.

Thankfully, she handed him Anthony, sat down, threw a blanket over her shoulder giving privacy to Anna as she nursed.

With Anna now sleeping, she carefully placed her in the crib and stretched her arms to Anthony who was more than willing to come. She repeated the scene and soon both babies were sleeping comfortably while the adults looked on. Daniel brought his arm around Gwendalyn's shoulder enjoying the moment.

"I need to make the punch and get everything ready for tea," she whispered, moving away toward the kitchen. "You just have a seat and enjoy the fire."

As Daniel sat, he took his heart-felt requests to God in prayer and finished by saying, "may it by Your will, Father, that I become a part of this family. May I be the husband to Gwendalyn, and father to these beautiful children, that You would be pleased with. Guide me and help me to know Your will, and Lord, help me to be patient and understanding of Gwendalyn. In Your name, Jesus, I pray, Amen."

Gwendalyn had finished in the kitchen and had gone upstairs to change for this evening's celebration. She came down, her hair done so that the front sections were tied at the back with a ribbon while the rest hung loosely around her shoulders. She was wearing the teal green dress that Ina and her mother had given her.

Daniel stared at her not saying a word, but just drinking in her beauty.

"Don't move," he said reaching for his camera. She stood paused on the stairway while he took a picture.

"I couldn't believe I could still fit in this. It's a little more snug now than when I first wore it but I just feel so happy tonight and wanted to wear something special."

"You look beautiful. Come. Sit with me before the others get here."

Daniel held her hand and surprised her as he kissed her cheek.

"I know we still have a ways to go but I believe this is the greatest day of my life. I've longed to hear, for so long, that it was your desire to be with me. You've made me very happy, Gwendalyn."

"I don't think you should get ahead of yourself," she said humorously. "You still have to ask my dad if you can come courting."

They laughed and continued talking in the living room until sounds at the door told them that the guests were arriving.

Everyone was dressed up in some of his or her best clothes and as they came in, cheer and laughter added to the excitement of the evening. Gwendalyn had made introductions for those who hadn't met Daniel and visa-versa. They munched on snacks and baked goods while they played charades and other such games being careful to include the children who could understand the game.

By 9:30 PM things were beginning to quiet down with little groups forming as they caught up on the latest news.

Dad made an announcement that now was the time for the Christmas story so everyone turned his or her attention to him as he opened the Bible and began to read.

The story had relaxed the smaller children who were beginning to yawn and telling their parents they were tired. Stacey, Carl, and Stephanie left with their spouses and children, calling out "Merry Christmas" as they went.

The older couples, along with Calvin, stayed enjoying another cup of tea and treats and conversing with each other.

The twins, who had awakened upon everyone's arrival, had just been taken upstairs, readied for bed, and then tucked in for the night.

Soon 'good-nights' were shared at the door and the remaining few walked together around the cove saying good-bye to the Bowmans as they turned off onto their path leading to the house.

Gwendalyn was glad that both Grandmas had helped with the cleanup as now she was feeling very tired. She climbed the stairs, talked to and thanked her Father, and then sank into her bed exhausted, but happy.

* * *

The next morning, after feeding the twins their breakfast and readying them for the day, she flicked on the radio and the constant Christmas carols pushed away the loneliness she was feeling on this Christmas morn. She would be going over to her parents' home a little later this morning.

She sat on the floor in front of the Christmas tree singing to her children as she handed them each a brightly-colored package. They began to play with it and then Anthony decided it might be something good to chew on.

"No, no," she said as she heard a knock on the door.

"Come in," she called and proceeded to take the piece of soggy paper from his mouth. "This is what you do," she said as she began to help each of them open their gift."

The sudden flash of light told her who had come in and she looked up smiling.

"Good morning, Daniel. Come join us," she welcomed him.

"Looks like you three are having fun," he said sitting on the floor beside them.

He helped Anthony unwrap his present while Gwendalyn helped Anna with hers. They each pulled out a stuffed teddy bear. Anna's teddy was white with a pink ribbon and she immediately buried her face in the soft fur making contented sounds. Anthony's teddy was light brown with a blue ribbon and he grabbed the ear and began chewing on it. Gwendalyn and Daniel laughed at the antics displayed before them. Daniel got up quickly and snapped another picture.

After the children were in their crib playing with the teddy bears,

Daniel brought a small package out of his pocket and gave it to Gwendalyn.

"Merry Christmas," he said as she opened it.

"Oh, Daniel," she said, taking a small golden charm with the words "I Love You" molded in gold. "How did you know I had a bracelet for these?"

"Just perception," he said. "I saw it when you were in the clinic, and when you were giving birth, and then again the last time I came here."

"Anthony gave me this bracelet," she said quietly, "but I will add this beautiful charm to it."

"It is you who are a beautiful charm," he said. "I talked with your father last night and asked him if I could begin courting you and he has granted us his blessing. Come here, my darling," he said pulling her to her feet.

They stood facing each other gazing into each other's eyes. "Can I kiss you?" he asked, and got his answer with the nodding of her head.

He bent his head as she tilted her face up toward him. Her soft lips met his and they kissed gently.

A sudden cry from the crib interrupted them and they both rushed over to see what had happened. Anna had fallen back and bumped her head against the crib's frame. Gwendalyn picked her up and soothed her and as she quieted and snuggled close, her mother looked at Daniel smiling.

The children were again changed, nursed, and bundled for the walk across the cove to join the others for a traditional Christmas dinner. Daniel and Gwendalyn carried the twins enjoying each other's company and the fresh air.

They came back in Daniel's car, as they had now been sent on their way with left over turkey and all the fixings to be reheated for supper or tomorrow's lunch. Several gifts were also piled on the back seat with the food.

Later in the evening, after the Bowmans had left, Daniel and Gwendalyn again sat alone together after tucking "A & A," as Daniel had called them, into bed for the night.

"I was thinking, Gwendalyn. This town is growing and in need of a doctor. If things work out between us, I think I'd like to start up a practice here, if you're in agreement."

"What do you mean 'if I'm in agreement'?"

"Well, I'm not sure where you'd want to live. Maybe in Nova Scotia to be near Ina?"

"Oh Daniel, my parents and the Bowmans would be devastated if I even mentioned that I wanted to move away. I think they may have those fears already with you being from Nova Scotia, and like you said, this town is in need of a doctor. I'd hate to have to leave this house."

"It's settled then, we'll live here and I'll be the town's new doctor."

All of a sudden, deep inside, somewhere she never thought possible, an imposing and intrusive thought made its way into her heart and mind.

Had Anthony really died in the storm? What if he made it to shore or someone rescued him? He may have hurt his head and couldn't remember his life here. Could she really go on with Daniel if there were a possibility that he could still be alive?

No, this troublesome thought brought her too much pain. It couldn't be true; she mustn't think so.

Daniel's last words, and the ill-fated thoughts, caused her to momentarily withdraw.

"Daniel, this is sounding too fast right now. I need time to think, to adjust."

"I'm sorry. I didn't mean to sound presumptuous. I was just thinking and perhaps I'm getting ahead of my thoughts. I'm sorry."

"It's OK, but I think I need us right where we are right now, in the present."

"I understand."

* * *

Sunday afternoon had come too quickly and Daniel was saying his farewells.

Yesterday, they had had a wonderful day together. They went for walks and talked a lot. Daniel had taken her to the city nearest Serenity Cove to go out for dinner while her parents had spent the evening at Gwendalyn's, taking care of the twins.

She watched him drive around the cove, stop at her parents' house for his belongings, and then continue on his way.

Daniel wrote Gwendalyn often sending her many sketches of her and the twins, as well as some of the actual pictures he had taken when he was there at Christmas.

The twins had their first birthday to which Daniel had sent gifts to help in celebrating their special day. He also wrote to say that he would be visiting at Easter.

After sharing letters and talking on the telephone, Gwendalyn found that she was truly falling in love with Daniel. She liked the new feelings that were growing inside her towards him. She had finally taken off her engagement/wedding ring Anthony had given her and placed it on her right hand.

Tomorrow Daniel would be arriving and she could hardly wait to see him. The evening seemed to drag by and she awaited the time when she could tuck the children in bed for the night and go to sleep herself.

The next day she prepared a couple of blueberry pies, Daniel's favorite, and a rhubarb pie as well. Fresh homemade cookies she had baked yesterday overfilled the cookie jar on the counter. She now had a roast of beef with a pastry now browning in the oven and the vegetables were almost cooked. She decided to run upstairs to change into one of her best casual dresses.

She looked across the cove to see the familiar car drive past Mom and Dad's on its way to her house. She smoothed down her dress pressing out imaginary wrinkles. She noticed the ring on her right hand and considered taking if off altogether. She couldn't, just yet.

She heard the car pull up and continued to wait just inside the door. She couldn't wait any longer, and so without thought, she threw open the door and ran to meet him, throwing her arms around his neck.

"That's a wonderful greeting," he said smiling, "but how about I unload my arms so I can return it."

They walked back inside and Daniel deposited his jacket and some small packages.

"Now then, how about we try that again?" he said humorously.

They stood inside the closed door holding each other in a meaningful embrace and Daniel lowered his head meeting her lips with his own. "I've prepared you a home-cooked meal to welcome you home, eh, I mean here," she said, pulling away slightly.

"Home sounds great, my darling."

"Yes, it does, doesn't it?"

Soon the table was set with all the trimmings and Daniel came in smiling saying that the twins still hadn't awakened. Daniel prayed for the food, the privilege of being here, and all of God's blessings.

They both appreciated the quiet meal with each other to talk and catch up on the news. Daniel had told her all about how much Jacqueline had grown and about the new arrival of Franklin and Ina's new son, Edward, named after Ina's father.

Gwendalyn told him about the three emergencies that had occurred in Serenity Cove and that one of them had resulted in death because of the doctor not making it in time.

Daniel felt saddened by the incident, as he was in the business of saving lives, or doing his best to save them.

He brought his attention back to the meal and complimented Gwendalyn over and over again on how good everything tasted.

She set out the tea and his eyes brightened as she brought him a man-sized piece of blueberry pie with fresh cream on top.

They were each finishing their tea in the living room in front of the fireplace when the children began stirring, then awakened from their nap, and wanting their supper.

Gwendalyn went to the kitchen to reheat the children's food and Daniel came in carrying both Anthony and Anna. Anna looked like she was on the verge of crying but Momma took her in her arms and then secured her in the high chair. Once Anthony was ready, Daniel began feeding him and he realized that today it was going a lot easier than it had a few months back.

They spent a quiet evening playing a board game and talking and had made plans to go out to the city for dinner if Mom and Dad agreed to care for the twins.

Mom and Dad were more than willing to watch their 'favorite grandkids', and so they decided to leave right after lunch as soon as Gwendalyn had fed and nursed the twins and put them down for a nap. Mom would feed them their supper and give them something to drink from a cup and then Gwendalyn would be back to tuck them in bed for the night.

* * *

Daniel had taken her to one of the finest restaurants in the city and they were enjoying a romantic candle light dinner. A violinist came to serenade them during dessert and when he had left Daniel reached over the table and took Gwendalyn's hand in his.

It was indeed an intimate scene with light from the flickering candle dancing on their faces.

"Gwendalyn, I believe you know how much I care for you, but what I want you to know is that I love you with every beat of my heart. From the day I met you, your beauty, and even more importantly your inner beauty showing up in your graceful mannerisms, wholesome personality, and even more your faith in God, has made you the most attractive woman I've ever met. You are a dream that I thought would never come true for me, but now you are here, and we have grown close."

He stepped out of his chair, came around the table, and again took her hand in his. He knelt on one knee to the floor and looked up into her misting eyes.

"All these months of being with you, and getting to know you, have been the most wonderful of all my life. You have given my life more meaning than I could ever have imagined possible. I believe the Hand of God has brought us together."

He reached into his jacket pocket and brought our a tiny box over-laid with soft velvet and opened it to reveal its contents to Gwendalyn.

"I will always love you and be devoted to you if you would do me the honour of becoming my wife. Will you marry me?"

By this time tears were trickling down over her soft ivory cheeks and her heart was overfilled with deep emotion and love for this man kneeling before her.

"Daniel, you have shown me in many ways how much you do care for me, and how much you truly love me. And even my children," she put in. "You are indeed a man with high morals and a sensitive loving heart. It is I who am honoured that you have considered me. Yes, I will marry you and love you forever."

He placed the exquisite diamond ring on her finger, stood, and pulled her into his embrace. Gwendalyn was so captured by the moment that she didn't realize all the occupants of the restaurant were watching them. She met his lips with her own and they kissed unending until the applause and cheers of everyone in the room brought them from their almost private moment.

Gwendalyn immediately felt her face grow flush and she, embarrassed, but at the same time delighted, took her seat, smiling lovingly at her recent fiancé.

* * *